SET MY HEART BONFIRE

BLUEBALL BAND OF BROTHERS #4

MARIKA RAY

SET MY HEART BONFIRE

First Edition: March 7, 2024
Cover Model: Aaron W.
Photographer: Katie Cadwallader Photography
Cover Artist: Jennifer Olson

Ebook ISBN: 978-1-950141-72-2
Original Paperback: 978-1-950141-74-6
Special Edition Paperback ISBN:

DEDICATION

Thanks to Joanne Cote-Felaccio and her father for the scene inspiration. ;)

He's a dashing millionaire who thinks everything in life is one big joke, probably because he bathes in piles of money each morning. He's also my new neighbor, and after a humiliating experience in the cemetery that is my backyard, he becomes my shadow, showing up everywhere just to annoy me.

I'm not a fan of happy people. They bother me with their constant grins and rainbows coming out of their ears, and Vander Booth is the king of smiles. Despite my efforts to scare him away with both my profession as an undertaker and my general need for frowning through most of my workday, he sticks around like a bad case of poison ivy.

He is gorgeous though. I'll give him that. And when I see the way he coordinates outfits with his grandma just to make her happy, I'll admit my biological clock starts ticking. Add in his fear of real human connections and suddenly I find myself cheering for the guy instead of plotting his death.

Though opposites can attract—and boy is my black lipstick attracted to his glow-in-the-dark smile—they don't stay together long-term. And they certainly can't co-exist when they're fighting constantly in a knock-down, drag-out competition for the same piece of land for their business venture. Or can they? *Cue ominous organ music...*

CHAPTER ONE

ander

I SLID right off the damn couch and nearly cracked my head on the solid wood coffee table. Linen shorts and plastic couch covers were not a good combination.

"Jesus, G-Mil," I groused, climbing back onto my feet and gingerly perching my ass on my grandmother's ancient couch. "Don't I send you enough money to afford a couch without plastic?"

She waddled into the room, tinier every single year, which only made anxiety climb in my throat. Grandma Milly was my best friend. The only human on earth who understood me and loved me as the flawed human I was. Hence the move to the tiny town of Blueball. Believe me, this town wasn't my first choice for early retirement, but if G-Mil was here, that's where I planned to be too. I'd floated the idea of moving her out to Scottsdale with me and she'd sent me articles about haboobs, scorpions, and off-the-charts heat indexes until I'd gotten the message. Grandma Milly was never leaving Blueball.

"If you saw how much tea Gertie spills every Thursday, you'd understand why I need the plastic." Grandma Milly placed a tray of cookies on the coffee table. They were the dark cookies shaped like a windmill that tested the strength of your teeth instead of the homemade kind she'd presented me with most of my life. The fact that she was resorting to store-bought made me feel like I'd shown up in just the nick of time. "Did you enjoy your nap, Vandy?"

Only G-Mil could get away with calling me Vandy. I nodded, snatching up a cookie and watching her get settled in her old recliner like a hawk. She moved slower now too. More careful, like she was testing the limits of her bones and soft tissue with each move she made. She hadn't mentioned any of that in our weekly calls the last few years, and I chastised myself mentally for not coming out to check on her in person like I had been until work got crazy.

"Like the dead," I replied, making a list of all the doctor appointments I wanted to take her to now that I was in town for good. I wondered if Blueball had a physical therapist I could hire to come to the house. Maybe I could get a nurse in here full-time to keep her moving. Or a chef so she ate all organic.

Grandma Milly frowned, the lines on her face stacking up. "Oh, at my advanced age we don't joke about death, dear."

My mouth dropped open, another layer of guilt slamming into me. "I'm sor—"

Grandma's face broke out into the smile that everyone said looked just like mine. "Gotcha, sucker!"

She cackled and hooted, looking downright gleeful while I gave her a disapproving look. But like always, her joy spread and I couldn't contain the smile on my own face. It was good to see her happy.

I reached over and held her gnarled hand in mine. "I've missed that laugh, G-Mil."

She patted my hand, quieting down. "And I've missed you,

Vandy. You send me so much money I just end up giving it away because that's not what I want. I want my boy."

Damn, the woman was probably more than halfway to senile, but she could always grab me by the heart. "Well, your boy is here to stay. I sold the company and my house. All my stuff is on a moving truck headed to Blueball. I appreciate you letting me stay here for a few nights."

Grandma's shoulders did a little shimmy. "I do love a good sleepover! We'll do face masks and I bought popcorn. You pick the movie and I'll choose the takeout."

I grinned, the fatigue of driving out here this morning fading away fast. "Sounds good to me. I just need to meet up with my realtor and get a tour of the place before escrow closes."

"You go do that, dear, and I'll catch up on my shows."

I shook my head. "Still watching that dating show?"

"Damn right I am. Never too old to watch a good love story unfold."

Standing, I let go of Grandma's hand and reached for the gift bag I'd stashed in my truck. "I got you a little something."

"Is it a puppy?"

I huffed out a laugh. "It's not a puppy."

Grandma's face fell. "Well, shit."

I lifted the cashmere out of the bag and wrapped it around her neck. The iconic check pattern in camel, black, and red looked silly over her floral blouse and slacks, but nothing was too good for my grandma. If she'd let me, I'd deck her in nothing but designer ballgowns and dripping jewels.

"Soft as a puppy," I assured her.

She rolled her eyes. "More expensive than a damn puppy, I'm guessing too." Her hands stroked the cashmere repeatedly, in opposition to her words. "This is highly unnecessary. In fact, it's frivolous. You really need to stop throwing around your money, Vandy. Save it! Invest it!"

"I do, I swear!" I did the sign of the Boy Scouts, though I'd never been one. "But I like to spoil you, G-Mil. You're my girl."

"I'm eighty! Hardly a girl." Her eyes flashed but the corners of her mouth gave her away, tipping up slightly. "You need a girl your own age. Speaking of, I know—"

"Oh, look at the time. I'm about to be late. I can't keep Audrey waiting. It would be incredibly rude to show up in town and be late to my first meeting with a citizen of Blueball," I announced, tapping the watch on my wrist that cost as much as most people's cars.

Grandma Milly frequently went on tangents about my dating life. Maybe the dating shows she watched gave her ideas about what could happen if I found the right woman. I'd tried a dozen times to disabuse her of the idea of happily ever after, but she stubbornly refused to listen to reason.

Being thirty-two, most of my acquaintances had already gotten married and started having kids. Not one of the women I'd dated over the years seemed like someone I wanted to spend forever with. In fact, that sounded terrible. Just like ice cream flavors, I needed variety. One couldn't just eat vanilla every night for the rest of their life. Even peanut butter moose tracks with sprinkles and a cherry on top got old after the fourth or fifth time in a row.

Grandma Milly pulled the scarf from her neck and whipped me with it. Thankfully, cashmere makes a bad whip. She pushed to the edge of the recliner and then doubled in half, pushing herself to standing in slow motion. I reached out a hand to help her, but she growled at me. When she finally got to her feet and stood straight up—well, as straight as her back could get—she looked up at me, complete clarity in her eyes.

"Promise me, Vandy. Promise you won't throw your money around here in Blueball."

I opened my mouth to protest such a ridiculous promise, but she wasn't done. Her finger pointed right in my face.

"If I have to be on a fixed income, so do you."

"But—but you *don't* have to be on a fixed income, G-Mil! I literally send you money every month so you don't have to worry about anything." Add going over her finances to the list of things to do now that I was in town.

Grandma tutted. "Having so much money isn't good for someone so young. Plus, you flash the cash and we'll be robbed!" She dramatically grabbed the pearls around her neck and I tilted my head, realizing I was being hustled by someone who barely cracked five feet tall.

"We're not going to be robbed. Blueball is a safe town. I looked into it, believe me." Grandma looked like she was gearing up for another stab at a ridiculous reason for not spending my money, so I put her out of her misery. I held her by the elbows and leaned down into her face. "I promise I won't flash my cash."

She smiled and then kissed my cheek, smelling like cookies and icy hot. "You're a good boy, Vandy. Now hold on just one more second. I made you a sweater!"

I really was going to be late if I didn't get going, but nothing and no one could pull me away from Grandma Milly when she had something to give me. She'd been sending me things in the mail every few months, like she was slowly gifting me all the family heirlooms before she died. Not that I had any plans for her to kick the bucket for at least another decade. I'd get every longevity doctor and biohacker in here to extend her life past one hundred. Cost was not an issue.

I followed Grandma into the kitchen where she pulled a pea-green sweater off the back of a barstool and presented it to me. Her eyes were sparkling and wide, her smile lighting her up and making her seem ten years younger.

"Ta-da!" She thrust the hideous sweater in my direction. It was a crocheted cardigan, buttons sewn down the front and a few patches sewn into the chest. Mr. Rogers would have worn this thing like a boss and you better believe I had every intention of doing the same.

I took it gently from her hands and admired the handiwork. She must have spent months knitting this labor of love. Warmth spread through my chest, and I almost teared up. I couldn't remember the last time someone had given me a gift from the heart.

"It's the best sweater I've ever seen, G-Mil." I swept her up into a careful hug, pulling her off her feet and spinning her until she swatted at me to put her down.

She clasped her hands beneath her chin while I put it on, oohing and aahing once I got my arms through. The sleeves were just right, skimming my wrists, and the width was perfect for my broad chest. I wasn't sure if the green went with my shorts, but I didn't think Blueball was the height of the fashion world anyway.

"So handsome, my boy," she whispered, tears in her eyes.

"I got the good-lookin' gene from you," I whispered back, throwing my arm around her shoulder and steering her back to her recliner. "Now don't get into trouble until I get back and can join you."

Grandma sat down and lifted her nose in the air. "I can't make any promises. Oh, and while you're out, find yourself a girl-friend, would you?"

I shook my head. She'd been telling me to find a girlfriend ever since I graduated high school, like somehow that would bring me success in life. I left her place, happier than I'd been in a long while. Scottsdale had gotten stale lately. All the same restaurants, colleagues, and women. New beginnings stirred my blood in a way I hadn't felt in years.

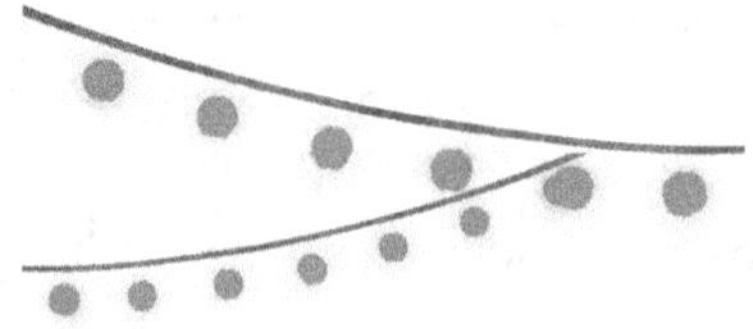

The Skinner house came into view after I punched in the gate code and climbed the long winding driveway. Tall trees lined the driveway, making a grand entrance. The pitch-black roof offset the stacked stone facade and creamy white keystones above each window. The place looked like a modern-day castle with a turret on one side and a sweeping front entry of no less than ten stairs leading to a wooden door that belonged on the front of an architectural magazine. I fucking loved it.

Audrey Hellman, the realtor I'd hired over the phone based off Grandma Milly's suggestion, stood by the stairs, patiently waiting for me. She had on a navy suit jacket, paired with gray slacks and the kind of heels that couldn't possibly be comfortable but made every man's thoughts plummet to the gutter. Seeing that I was five minutes late, I slid out of my truck and hustled over. I felt guilty when I was late to anything, a side effect of having parents who doled out punishment for being tardy. Sadly, I was late a lot growing up and I had yet to grow out of the guilt.

"Mr. Booth? So nice to finally meet you." Audrey shook my hand. I had to give it to her, she didn't look put off by my sweater in the slightest. She looked happy to see me. I imagined she was, given that the commission on this real estate transaction would be close to six figures. I wasn't naive enough to believe her enthusiasm at my appearance was for any other reason.

"Vander, please. And yes, it's lovely to finally be here in Blueball."

"Did you just get in today?" she asked, climbing the stairs while somehow still looking over her shoulder to keep eye contact. The woman was a goddamn professional.

"I did. Swung by Grandma Milly's place first. Thanks for meeting me for a walk-through."

She jostled the front door lock and the oversized door swung open. "Of course. You just bought the most stunning house in all of Blueball."

My first glimpse of the house left me speechless. From the rough-hewn stone floors to the aged zinc wagon wheel chandeliers to the floor-to-ceiling velvet draperies, nothing was basic in this house. I stepped inside and had the strangest feeling come over me. It wasn't a feeling of being haunted by the previous owners like one would think from the architecture style, but more like a sense of coming home. To have arrived in a place that was as mine as the scar on my left elbow from falling off my bike when I was eight. I'd never seen the place before, but it was home. All six thousand square feet of it.

"If you're looking for one of a kind, I can imagine that this view would do it for you," Audrey was saying, having walked over to the expansive front room that Grandma Milly would surely call a parlor. She gestured out the window with a quirk to her mouth.

I joined her to take in the view of the entire valley, seeing the edge of downtown Blueball on the far-left side. Treetops blocked most of the view, but what I could see made me feel like I was the resident king on the hill, surveying the peasants. My gaze dropped lower.

Make that the *deceased*.

"Is that...?" I trailed off.

Audrey lost the fight with her smile. "Yep. That's Blueball's cemetery. The building directly below is Blueball Endless Eternity, the funeral home that oversees the land."

I vaguely recalled Audrey telling me these same details before I sent over the offer on the house, but I hadn't registered the meaning until I was staring at a hundred tombstones glowing in the late afternoon sunlight.

"Thankfully I don't spook easy," I replied, turning from the window, eager to check out the rest of the house.

Audrey spent the better part of an hour with me crawling all over the three levels in the house before we closed the place back up. Once the funds officially transferred tomorrow, this place would be mine.

"Off to go celebrate?" Audrey asked after we shook hands.

I shrugged, giving off the easy smile I had down to a science. I could be sitting naked on a red ant hill and still give off that smile. "Got a hot movie date followed by face masks and ice cream."

Audrey chuckled. "Sounds heavenly. I'll have to see if my fiancé is up for the same."

"Pretty sure snuggling in front of a movie is fiancé mandatory behavior." Not that I'd know. Sounded about right though if Grandma's shows were anything to go by.

Audrey's face went soft and I could tell she was madly in love with whomever this fiancé was. "He's a very good snuggler. Though he doesn't have a super soft sweater like you. I might have to suggest it."

I smoothed my hands down the front of my yarn catastrophe. "Nothing says young and single like a cardigan."

Audrey laughed like I hoped she would. "I think you're going to fit in just fine around here, Vander."

I wasn't so sure about that, but I nodded anyway and headed for my truck. Fitting in had never been my style. I mostly blew through towns, events, and social gatherings like a stand-up comedian, dazzling everyone with my wit, but never connecting with anyone. Blueball, however, did not have enough places for me to move on to greener pastures socially, so I'd have to find a way to make actual friends.

Or I could just hang out with Grandma Milly until we were both six feet under one of those headstones.

CHAPTER TWO

*M*arlo

"MARLO! YOU NEED TO EAT!"

Dad's shout carried through the first floor where I was currently on my hands and knees collecting wrappers from under the wooden pews in the reception room. Someone at today's funeral had had a mighty hankering for peppermint candies.

And a lack of decorum regarding littering.

"Coming!"

Right on cue, my stomach growled so loudly it might have woken up Ralph Waldo (uncle to Auburn Hill's old chief of police, James Waldo) had he not been deaf as a doornail. And if he were alive. Currently, he was lying in the casket at the front of the room, his hands peacefully folded over his chest after receiving the entire town of Auburn Hill and part of Blueball earlier today. I'd done a particularly skilled job with his makeup, if I did say so myself. It was quite the artform to make the dead look living without also making them look like a Vegas showgirl.

"See you in a few, Ralph. I'm hoping Mom made meatloaf. If I recall correctly, that was also your favorite too, huh?"

Ralph did not answer.

Tucking the wrappers into the can at the back of the room and making a mental note to take the trash out to the curb later tonight after I buttoned up things with Ralph, I shut the lights off, washed my hands, and headed for the stairs that led to our family's private quarters.

Dad was waiting for me at the top of the stairs, looking like a million bucks in his polo and slacks. It felt like a personal triumph that Mom and I had talked him out of his suits a few months after his heart attack. I can't remember a single day of my youth where Dad wore something other than a three-piece suit. Pre-heart attack, that is. But he remained steadfast with his hair gel, coifing that thick black hair into the kind of style that would have made James Dean light up a cigarette in solidarity.

"You're working too hard, girlie," he rumbled, pulling me under his arm the second I cleared the top step and enveloping me in a cloud of his cologne. It was safe to say I was a daddy's girl, probably because I had the best one west of the Mississippi.

"No harder than you ever did." I lifted an eyebrow, daring him to deny that he'd given his whole life to the family business.

He made a noise in his throat, but kissed me on the top of my head. "You should be dating men and making babies, not running yourself to death handling the business."

I shrugged. "Death kind of *is* our business, Daddy."

He lifted his arm off my shoulders and gently pushed me toward the table where Mom had laid out a healthy dinner like she always did since Dad's heart attack. Nothing like seeing literal clogged arteries on a daily basis and then suffering a heart attack to make you cut out the saturated fat.

"You've always had a good sense of humor, Marlo," Dad said, having a seat at the head of the table and kissing my mother. "If you'd just unleash it around the young men, they'd be lining up to put a ring on your finger."

I sat on the long side of the table and put a napkin in my lap. "Yes, I can see it now. A procession of young eligible bachelors lining up into the funeral home, eager to date the undertaker's daughter." I held up my hands dramatically, lips quirking when Mom began to laugh. "I'd have to beat them away with a casket. Although you know, that might make for a great setting for the next *Bachelor*! Halloween edition, or something."

"Bah!" Dad dug into his meal—not meatloaf, sadly—and shook his head at my antics. "You joke now, but by your age, I was married to your mother already."

I chewed on a forkful of green beans, swallowing before answering. "If grandkids were your endgame, you should have had more kids to up your odds of procreation. Speaking of overpopulating the earth, have you taken a look at that projection I put together?"

Redirecting my father was the only way to escape the dating issue. This issue was far more important than the number of good eggs I had left in this body of mine. If we didn't buy some more land, we were going to run out of space. And unless we started charging recurring rental fees on the already departed in our cemetery—I could see the headache already, trying to get the deceased to sign off on membership fees—we wouldn't be making money in the future unless we had more plots to sell.

Mom darted a glance in my direction that held a heavy dose of warning. I knew that look. I'd seen it on her face every single day since Dad's heart attack. *Don't bring up work stuff with your dad. He can't handle the stress.*

But Blueball Endless Eternity was his business. Sure, he'd handed the baton over to me after his heart attack, but for major business decisions like expanding, I wanted his input. It would take a major loan from the bank to buy the plot of land next door to the existing cemetery, not a move I'd make without the full financial and emotional backing of my parents.

Dad wiped his mouth with his napkin before sitting back in

his chair. "Never thought I'd see the day. I used to think we bought too much land. I'd never fill it, but here we are."

Anxiety about this decision, on top of all the other daily stress of running a bustling business all by myself, made me lose my appetite. "Can't we just make everyone get cremated from now on? It would take up far less room."

"Marlo," Mom muttered, shaking her head.

"What? Everyone's pushing electric vehicles for the environment. I say we start a movement for mandatory cremation. Stack up the urns and use far less land. It's the ultimate way to keep the earth green. Return to ashes and forget the caskets. Oh hell, that's a good tagline!"

"Marlo." Dad simply said my name, a finality in his tone that made me sputter to a stop. He never raised his voice, but when he used that tone, everyone knew he'd reached his limit.

I sighed. "I know. I was just kidding anyway."

Mom darted into the charged silence and steered the conversation toward the latest gossip in town. Mom and Dad had been married for close to thirty years and seemed to be just as in love as the day they said I do. Sometimes I felt left out as an only child. Like they were best friends and I was the third wheel.

I let their chatter fade into the background as I ran through my mental to-do list for the evening. Ten-hour days were the norm around these parts, and even longer days when receiving a body. I'd been working so hard I'd been neglecting my friends. Perhaps I could lob a text out to them tonight and schedule a time to get together.

After helping Mom with the dishes, I headed back to the main level of the old Victorian to move Ralph to the reposing room. The family would be back tomorrow morning for the actual graveside service.

As I held the lid of the casket, I smiled down one last time at Ralph. "I hope you had a great life and I hope the next one is even better. Be well, Ralph Waldo."

And with that final sendoff I gave everyone who came

through our funeral home, I closed the lid one last time. The deceased didn't scare me in the slightest. Truly, it was an honor to take care of them in this time of transition, a privilege I did not take lightly despite my earlier teasing about cremation.

I had all the lights off on the main floor and was heading for the stairs to turn in for the night when I noticed a faint orange glow out the south window. I darted to the glass and squinted into the distance.

"You kinky little motherfuckers," I whispered to myself, fogging up the window and blocking my view of two conspirators who'd invaded our cemetery after hours.

Unless my eyes deceived me, there was a couple currently mid-snog up against ol' Mr. Landers's headstone.

I bolted away from the window and out the back door, my legs eating up the lawn. The long skirt I'd chosen today didn't help much though. I felt like I was Laura Ingalls Wilder, running down the hill in the opening credits in a neck-to-ankle dress and falling face-first into the dead grass. I pressed on because Mr. Landers had been a crotchety old man who wouldn't have appreciated teens rounding third base on his final resting place.

The orange glow I'd seen through the window turned out to be a candle flame dancing in a glass jar. I had to hand it to the teens, they'd decked out their make-out spot like true champs. A fleece blanket kept the bugs away while they were rolling around the tombstones and the candle cast an almost romantic vibe. But for me, it was the bubbles.

As I skid to a halt next to the oblivious couple—who were well on to second base, I might add—I lifted a finger in the air to pop a bubble coming from the battery-operated bubble maker they'd propped up against Mr. Landers's headstone. I almost hated to break them up. They were getting more action than I'd seen since the undertaker conference in Arizona three years ago where I'd managed to ditch my dad long enough to make out with the guy who sold the caskets with Bluetooth speakers embedded into the lining. The man had unusually long fingers.

Sadly, we'd been interrupted before I'd managed to take full advantage of said fingers.

But that was beside the point and the cemetery was closed. Additionally, it was straight negligent to have an open flame out here. *Slow your roll, Universe.* I'd been kidding when I said all of our customers should be cremated.

"Time to take that boob grab back to your car, folks," I drawled, delighting when they jolted apart and the girl let out a shriek. What did they expect? A ghost?

The guy stood up, eyes wide and hair all a mess. He reached for the girl and yanked her to her feet, both of them making a run for it like I was the grim reaper and they were my next victims. They looked no older than middle of high school if I had to guess.

"Hey! You forgot your stuff!"

Neither one bothered to slow down, look back, or show a single flicker of regret leaving their blanket, candle, and bubble machine. I briefly wondered if I could successfully incorporate bubbles into a memorial service, but dismissed the idea just as quickly.

What the hell was wrong with teens these days? Back in my day, you just looked for a dark corner and mashed bodies together. These kids had to deck out their make-out spot like a dorm room before getting it on. I shook my head at their commitment to the mood. Then I tilted my head and observed the bubbles in the candlelight.

"Huh," I said into the silent night. It was kind of pretty. Fanciful, even.

I poked a bubble and watched it splatter on my skin. Then I poked another one and another one. Pretty soon my arms were flying and I was playing a weird game of whack-a-mole, which ol' Mr. Landers would have hated simply because it had the unmistakable whiff of fun.

My foot kicked something mid bubble poke and the orange glow got brighter in a nano-second.

"Ah shit."

The fleece blanket immediately went up in flames and Mr. Landers suddenly had a front-row seat to a bonfire. Thinking quickly, I shoved my skirt down my legs and stepped out, using the voluminous material to blanket the flames. Thankfully, it worked because I didn't enjoy the idea of having to run back to the house to grab the fire extinguisher in just my black flats, gray blouse, and underwear. I'd worn granny panties today that shouldn't see the light of day or even the mooncast of night. They did not do good things for my ass.

A deep voice came from behind me. "Are you all right?"

Chills raced up my back and I froze in my panties. I wasn't scared, goddammit, I was pissed. I would have bet my life that the old motherly advice would never actually be applicable. It was like being told to wait thirty minutes to swim after you ate. Or that swallowing gum means it'll stay in your stomach for seven years. Everyone knew those were simply myths designed to curb a kid's behavior, right?

Well, the joke was on me.

I wasn't in a car accident, but I was about to be murdered in my worst pair of underwear.

CHAPTER THREE

ander

"HELLOOOOO." My voice echoed off the stone floors and empty walls of this new house of mine. The best acoustics were in the entryway where the vaulted ceilings and stone walls made me sound like Andrea Bocelli belting one out in the Tuscan countryside.

Boxes stacked up dauntingly in each room from where the movers had placed them earlier today. I should probably start unpacking but I was having too much fun making my voice bounce off the walls. Plus I was tired. Grandma Milly's spare bedroom contained a twin bed that had surely been manufactured before the first world war. Pretty sure I had a case of tetanus from that one metal spring that dug into my back all night long.

Grabbing the laundry basket that held the clothes G-Mil had so kindly laundered for me this morning while I was busy directing movers, I snatched up my gray sweatpants and a soft T-shirt. Until I found the box that held my sheets, I'd be crashing on my mattress without covers. And I had yet to find the thermostat in this place, so I hoped I didn't freeze tonight. I made quick work of peeling off my sweat-soaked jeans and shirt. Sure, I'd hired movers, but I couldn't just stand around letting them do all the work while I watched. I pulled on the clean T-shirt and nearly asphyxiated myself.

"What the hell?" I yanked harder and barely got the thing on. It hugged my chest, strangled my biceps, and ended just above my belly button. "No, no, no."

I grabbed my favorite pair of gray sweatpants and tugged them on too, realizing with horror that they ended at my shins and hugged my ass like a woman in yoga pants. The kind that wiggled right up your crack and got cozy.

"Fuck!" The word bounced off the walls and repeated back to me. G-Mil had put everything in the dryer when I'd specifically asked her to hang-dry them. I wouldn't say I was obsessed with fashion by any means, but what I did have was top-notch quality. My dry-cleaning bill was usually more than my grocery bill. I'd spent a pretty penny on these designer sweatpants that stroked my skin like silk and now they wouldn't fit a small child.

A shriek from somewhere outside had my head whipping up in alarm. I ran to the front window in the parlor and saw two people running hand in hand through the cemetery below, laughing hysterically. Another shout had my gaze dropping further. A woman flailed about like bees had taken to attacking her head. Then she kicked a candle that seemed to come out of nowhere and suddenly the entire ground around her was in flames. I didn't bother waiting to see more. I was out the front door and racing down the mountain. My old trainer in Scottsdale would be impressed. All those sprints where I cursed his name and paid him thousands of dollars for the torture had finally paid off.

I reached the fire just in time to see the woman bend over,

rip off her skirt, and blanket the flames like she was a professional firefighter with nerves of steel. She scrambled to her feet in black dress shoes attached to long pale legs that were now bare. Not even the faint moonlight could hide the sinewy curves this woman sported. Not even the moonlight could pull my gaze away from the panties oddly reminiscent of Grandma Milly's that covered an ass I would have preferred to see bare, just like her legs. Her dark hair swung as she pushed it over her shoulders and assessed the situation.

"Are you all right?" I asked, always one to lead with good manners. You could get a lot more accomplished with kindness, I'd found.

A little machine down by a headstone kept pumping out bubbles, oblivious to the gravity of the situation. The bubbles were so thick in numbers I could barely see the back of the woman's head. It dawned on me she'd been down here popping bubbles, not fending off bees. A beat of silence had my worry increasing. When she didn't immediately turn around, I paused to look around me. We were in the middle of the cemetery, not one light illuminating the situation now that the fire was out.

"Odd place for a bonfire," I drawled, stepping back and to the side to lean on the headstone. I kept my hands where she could see them. I meant no ill will.

The woman remained frozen, but I saw her eyes shift to the right to study me. A bubble floated by my face and I poked it. Damn. That was fun. I could see why she'd been flailing around earlier. I poked another one.

"Good call on putting out the fire. The bubbles are way more fun." I kept poking them until the woman unfroze, an exasperated groan wrenched from her mouth.

"Ugh! My whole cemetery could have burned down!" She bent at the waist and slapped the bubble machine. Instantly the bubbles stopped churning out.

I pouted. Why did everyone always stop the fun? This lady,

despite not having pants on which was usually a sign of a good time, seemed like she was far too serious about things considering the fire was out and there was no danger. Her dark eyebrows were drawn over pretty eyes. Her outfit, minus the granny panties, was dark and somber, much like her mood. "They're already dead, Bubbles."

That, apparently, was the wrong thing to say. I'd never seen a woman grow two inches on an inhale of fury. It was fascinating, especially when the woman was half naked and quite beautiful in an avenging-dark-angel kind of way.

She opened her mouth and I was on the edge of my proverbial chair, waiting to see what zinger of an insult she threw at me. "Nice belly button."

I blinked. That...was not what I was expecting. I glanced down at myself, finally remembering that I was in toddler clothing, and that my belly button was indeed on display. Without any warning at all, I discovered I really, really liked dark angels. If the situation in the front of my pants was anything to go by. Although that could simply be due to blood flow issues in these tight pants.

The woman bent again and snatched something off the ground. As she straightened, I took that moment to step forward and tuck her hair behind her ear so I could swipe my thumb through a soot mark on her cheek. She inhaled sharply, eyes sparkling up at me. She was tall, her gaze level with my chin. I didn't know this woman at all, but she seemed equally angry and turned on, a combination I could definitely work with. The moment my thumb touched her cheek, she flinched, bobbling the flashlight she'd picked up. I snatched it before it hit the ground, whipping it up to aim it up under my chin like I used to as a boy when my parents shipped me off to an all-boys summer camp and we spent the evenings around the campfire trying to scare the shit out of each other.

"It was a dark and stormy night," I began, pitching my voice low and menacing.

"For fuck's sake," she hissed, grabbing the flashlight out of my hands and clipping me on the chin.

She let out a mewl and grabbed her arm, the complaint about her abuse dying on my lips. The woman practically glowed, she was so pale, so I easily saw in the moonlight what caused her pain. A red streak marred her porcelain skin.

I took the flashlight back yet again and shined it on her arm. "Damn, Bubbles. You burned yourself."

"No shit, Sherlock," she spat back.

I grinned, finding her feistiness highly amusing. I'd found that most women took decades before they ripened their feistiness factor, which was probably why Grandma Milly was my best friend. She'd had plenty of decades to perfect her level of ballsiness. However, this woman was proving my theory wrong. She probably came out of the womb with a scowl and a middle finger pointed in the air. I didn't care for pushovers and this filly was steady as a headstone set in concrete.

"Let's get you up to the house so we can clean that up."

Putting my hand on her elbow, I took a step toward my house, but she didn't follow.

The woman wrenched her arm out of my grasp with a scowl. "Get lost, buddy, or I'll find an open ditch around here and push you in it."

I put my hands on my hips, barely holding back laughter. Her gaze dropped to where my pants were tightest. I returned the favor, though those droopy panties weren't tight anywhere.

"I can't in good conscience leave you burned and alone in the cemetery, Bubbles."

"Stop calling me that."

I shrugged. "I don't know your name and bubbles seems fitting. Like your personality."

She only scowled harder. "Oh good. Then I'll call you annoying."

"My name's actually Vander. Vander Booth, but you can call me annoying if you'd like. I love a good nickname."

Her eyes narrowed while she seemed to be making some kind of decision in her head. "How'd you get in here? The cemetery's closed."

I pointed over my left shoulder. "I live up there."

"No, you don't," she snapped with complete confidence despite being caught in public in her undies.

God, she was delightful. "I do. Just bought the place. Closed escrow yesterday. You can call my realtor, Audrey Hellman, if you don't believe me."

She continued to glare at me, but didn't mount another argument or continue to tell me I was a liar. This was what I'd call progress in our relationship.

"Marlo Balmero. Undertaker." She lifted one sculpted eyebrow, and if I'd had a tail, it would be wagging uncontrollably right now. "I know at least ten ways to murder a man without it showing up as foul play on an autopsy, so I suggest you don't try to murder me tonight."

I hadn't had this much fun since Grandma Milly agreed to go on that cruise with me three years ago and we'd recreated the famous Titanic scene at the bow of the boat for my yearly holiday cards.

I looked at my wrist where I did not currently wear a watch. "So, is a murder good for you tomorrow night, then?"

She didn't crack a smile, but she did tilt her head a fraction of an inch. "As long as I have better underwear on, you're welcome to try it tomorrow."

My lips lost the fight and stretched from ear to ear. "Duly noted. I'll be sure to check underwear status first. Now can we please clean that burn and get some ointment on it?"

"Only if I get a tour of the ol' Skinner house." She was negotiating with me. Like she was doing me a favor to let me doctor her burn. This woman, man. This small town. I wasn't sure if I was ready for what I'd gotten myself into, but I was damn happy to find out.

"Done."

I waved, indicating she should walk next to me up the hill between our two properties. She complied silently, neither acknowledging nor thanking me for directing the flashlight at her feet so she didn't stumble into any divots in the grass. Her head began to swivel left and right when we climbed the stairs to my front door. I didn't know what reputation the Skinners had here in Blueball, but I got the sense that my new friend Marlo had never been inside this house despite living right next door.

In the entryway, I gave her a once-over, finally able to see her in full light. The panties were even more spectacularly horrible under daylight-glow bulbs, but her face was exquisite. High cheekbones, full lashes, and eyes that held an intelligence that made this computer programmer feel dumb by comparison. I could see a blush rise to her cheeks as she took in the house, like she was excited to finally be inside of it, but when her gaze settled on me, she'd schooled her features into dismissive boredom.

When the silence had gone on long enough to make me uncomfortable—which was saying something because these pants were in crevices I did not give them permission to be in—I pointed to the hallway leading off the parlor. "Pretty sure I have Band-Aids in the hall bathroom boxes."

Her lips pulled into a sneer. "Is that where you keep the Oompa-Loompas?" Her gaze ran up and down my length, clearly finding my outfit lacking. Funny, coming from the woman with no pants.

I pointed at my chest. "These clothes? They're not mine. I mean, they are mine, but my grandma shrank them accidentally."

That explanation did not seem to improve her impression of me. Nor should it. What grown man needed their grandma doing their laundry? "How about you keep your hands where I can see them and we go get that Band-Aid, huh?"

Goddamn, she was cute. I nodded, regrouping to find

another way to make her smile. My normal charm wasn't working here. I wanted to keep cracking jokes until I found just the right one to make her smile. *Could* she smile? I wasn't sure she possessed the proper muscles to get the job done. She probably Botoxed her smile muscles instead of her frown muscles.

"Yes, ma'am."

CHAPTER FOUR

$\mathcal{M}$arlo

THE POWDER ROOM—AS I called it in my head because it was far fancier than a mere bathroom—was as impressive as the entryway. The Skinners had been our neighbors my entire life, but they rarely came out of the house. Which, of course, only fed my overactive imagination. I'd come up with all kinds of stories in my head as to what they got up to all alone in this huge castle of a house, each more gruesome than the next. I was oddly disappointed not to see any bloodstains in the travertine tile.

Vander Booth smoothed a Band-Aid over my forearm, his careful touch sending shock waves throughout my body. Considering I wasn't wearing pants, I didn't appreciate it. A girl could only handle shock waves from the touch of a handsome man when she had pants on. It was a rule in the interpersonal etiquette handbook. There were actually a lot of things you shouldn't do while a girl was pantless. Like, call her nicknames and tease her with a smile that was so handsome she was in danger of her panties going up in flames. I'd had enough flames for one night, thank you very much.

"There you go. You're good as new." Vander flashed me that smile again, and in the close quarters of the powder room, it was even more powerful than in the moonlight. He had a dimple on one side of his mouth, which should have made him look feminine, but he had the audacity to sport a granite jawline and thick eyebrows over sparkling chocolate eyes. His hair was just a touch long, swept off his forehead in the kind of messy waves a girl wanted to get her hands on. He was movie-star handsome with the swagger to go along with the ego.

And it pissed me off.

"If you're intending to skin me and wear me as a bodysuit, you'll have to wait a few days for this to heal. I don't suggest you try it though. It's a lot harder to skin a person than you'd think."

He blinked, but the smile didn't waver. "I'm not going to ask how you know that."

I snatched my arm back out of his grasp. No more touching. My panties couldn't handle it. "What are you going to ask, then?"

His grin intensified and I felt burned all over again. "You seem to have a preoccupation with me murdering you, so hypothetically, how would you suggest I successfully go about that?"

I lifted an eyebrow. "Why would I give you all the answers? You'd use them against me."

Vander held his hands up in a gesture of peace. "My grandma would be incredibly disappointed in me if I murdered someone, so believe me when I say I have no intention of murdering you."

"That's exactly what a murderer would say. They'd lure you in with cute grandma talk when they already murdered sweet grandma and fed her to the plants out front. You're probably wearing the clothes of a small person you murdered just this morning."

Vander smoothed his hands down his tight shirt. I chose to look away from the mounds of muscle that were straining to be free of the ridiculous material. I would not be the stupid girl in the after-school documentary who fell in love with her murderer. But that tight round ass on display wasn't exactly playing fair.

"I assure you that's not the case. Here. I'll show you." He stepped around me and exited the powder room. I had no choice but to follow, lest he get too far ahead of me and have the opportunity to grab a murder weapon when I wasn't looking. Mostly though, I was just looking at his ass. Annoyingly, he kept his hands in the air, as if he knew I still didn't trust him.

When we reached the kitchen—holy crap on a cracker, he had one of those fridges that was the size of a small SUV and two sinks...who the fuck needed two sinks?—he pointed down at a laundry basket.

"I'm going to grab my phone."

"Mhm."

I kept up a good front, but I wasn't actually worried he'd murder me. He'd used Audrey's name out in the cemetery and it came flooding back to me that she'd had some baller of a client she was working with. It was all she'd been talking about the last month. Some big spender wanted to buy a house here in Blueball. Naturally, this place made sense. It was the largest and priciest home in the county. Everyone knew millionaires didn't usually jeopardize their cushy lifestyle to kill a stranger.

Vander pulled a cell phone out of the basket and threw a ball of yarn at me. "Here's a sweater."

I frowned at the questionable garment but put it on. Vander looked up from his phone, mouth twitching as he took in the huge green monstrosity that now enveloped me.

His finger drew a figure eight in the air. "I meant for you to put it around your waist, but whatever."

I looked down at my bare legs, thankful I'd at least remembered to shave yesterday. The hem of the sweater reached the bottom of my granny panties, thereby covering me sufficiently. There were a few patches sewn into the sweater and I tilted my head to give them a read.

"If found dead, delete my browser history."

Vander chuckled. "Yeah, G-Mil knows me well."

I looked up at the handsome man, annoyed that he was slightly funny. In my experience most handsome men were as boring as prom, all glitter and no bang. Or maybe that had just been my experience. "Mine would say, if found dead, delete my Kindle library."

Vander sidled up next to me, a subtle whiff of cologne distracting me. He smelled like pine trees and bergamot, a combination he could have had for free just rolling about outside, but probably spent a chunk of money to spray onto his neck. "Look. As you can see, Grandma Milly is alive and well."

My jaw dropped open as I leaned into his side. There he was, standing next to Milly in the picture on his phone. He held keys in the air and he was sporting the same hideous sweater I now wore.

"Milly is your grandma?" I jerked away from muscles and cologne and temptation.

Vander went to put his phone in his pocket, but thought better of it when the material wouldn't accommodate even the tiniest bit of further stretch. "That's right. MadLib Milly. She used to do those MadLib things with me when I was a kid. God, she was vulgar!" Vander shook his head, a soft smile making him far too handsome for his own good. "Those were good times."

I nodded, brain trying to catch up. "Sure, sure. Nothing like learning about sex from your grandma to really cement foundational memories."

Milly had sewn all the costumes in the school plays, Christmas productions, and even a wedding dress or two. She'd always been super sweet, but a little off-kilter with her long-winded storytelling and her constant laughter. I'd only had to hush someone's laughter twice in my history of facilitating funerals and both times had been Milly Booth. Meeting her grandson, it all made sense. They both talked too much and laughed like it was their job.

I clapped my hands together, startling Vander. "Okay, well, thanks for the mini-tour. The powder room exceeded expectations, but you should probably start with the kitchen from now on. Real stunner. I gotta go."

My footsteps echoed through the hallway as I made my way back to the front entry. Vander's weren't far behind.

"What's the hurry? I can show you the turret."

I froze with my hand on the doorknob. Fuck. When would I ever get another chance to tour a turret? Then I remembered the time, my lack of clothing, and my original plans for the evening, which did not involve an annoying neighbor with far too many nauseating smiles.

The door swung open without a single squeak, which was fascinating, given its size and age and lack of use from the house sitting empty for several years. I'd have to ask Audrey if the Skinners left any information on where they got their door. Not that I was in the market for a new door that would set me back five figures, but I'd like to discuss their joint grease. Caskets that squeaked eerily when you opened or closed them were frowned upon in my business. I was always on the prowl for a good joint grease.

"Marlo?"

"Huh?" I spun around to see Vander looking at me quizzically. His hand covered mine on the doorknob.

"I asked if I should walk you back. Being new here, I wasn't sure if the cemetery was safe at night."

"Oh!" I removed my hand and stepped outside. "No. It's safe. Just an occasional fire to put out. I'm good." I hooked a thumb over my shoulder awkwardly. "Got a date."

Vander's smile disappeared and his eyebrows tried to frown. Even his frown looked festive. "Oh. Sure. Okay, well, good luck."

I started down the stone steps. "I'll need it," I mumbled.

That was the truth. I'd attempted a bazillion first dates. Every time the guy found out I was an undertaker, they suddenly ghosted me or found a reason to leave the date early. Even worse were the guys who didn't even bother to get to know me, instead quizzing me on all things death. It was like men were either obsessed with undertakers or repulsed by them. I wanted a guy who'd take my profession in stride, not freaked out nor unhealthily intrigued either.

When I got to Mr. Landers's headstone, I swooped down to pick up the bubble maker. That puppy was coming home with me.

"I'll sweep up the mess tomorrow, okay?" I asked Mr. Landers to dead silence.

I dared a peek up at the Skinner house, jolting when I saw Vander standing in the turret I hadn't investigated, his fantastic physique outlined in the window with a soft light glowing behind him. He raised a hand and waved. I didn't bother waving back. Seemed far too friendly.

Instead, I hustled home to take a quick shower. I laid Vander's sweater on my bed and made sure to change underwear before my date. I waited outside my house, purposely giving the funeral home address to prospective dates when we connected online. I'd rather weed out the scaredy-cats right away. It was ten minutes past the time when tonight's date was supposed to pick me up when I got his apologetic text about some emergency preventing him from keeping our date.

With a sigh, I turned right around and went inside. Another one bit the dust.

I grabbed a bag of chips out of the arrangement room where we offered snacks to the family members of the deceased and headed for my bedroom. If I pushed the curtains out of the way, I had a direct view of the Skinner house. I used to stare up at that house as a child and come up with stories in my head about princesses and castles and dragons that killed the princesses. It wasn't exactly fairy-tale material, but it had been my favorite thing to do as a child. Now I sat on my bed and stared up at the house, envisioning a tall, muscular prince with ill-fitting clothes and a dimple of distraction.

Picking up my phone, I texted my friends, studiously ignoring the house on the hill and its new owner.

Me: I need a girls' night.

Paisley: Hell yes!! I'll schedule the babysitter.

Keva: She's alive, y'all.

Me: Was I ever feared dead?

Audrey: I think we always wonder. You go deathly silent sometimes, babe.

Me: I'm just busy.

Paisley: Um, Keva and I have newborns. We understand busy. You just go into your cave.

Me: I like my cave.

Audrey: We know you do, Dracula, but it's healthy to get outside. Have you even seen the sunshine the last few days?

Me: Yes. I had to walk an old lady around to find the perfect plot for her deceased husband yesterday and she insisted on the middle of the afternoon. I did wear a hat though. And long sleeves. And sunglasses.

Paisley: Sigh. Let's meet at my place. No dead people here.

Me: Hey, don't knock my life. The dead people are actually nicer than the three dates that have bailed on me in the last week.

Keva: Ouch. I'll bring the margaritas.

ander

I'D UNPACKED EXACTLY one box in the last twenty-four hours that I'd been living in my new house. Considering my only clothing options were either my dirty moving clothes or a few outfits that were now currently only fit for a kindergartener, I had to unpack a box of clothing. I should be unpacking the kitchen too, but I had more important things to do. Grandma Milly was expecting me to pick her up and take her to the grocery store today. She insisted she had enough food, but I snooped when I stayed the night with her and she had bare cabinets and a wilty head of lettuce in the fridge. That simply would not do. If she was going to live past one hundred, I needed to get more nutrients into her.

Turned out, the GPS on my truck was overkill. There was only one turn and one stoplight between me and G-Mil. If I got lost in Blueball, I had no business driving in the first place. I was accelerating through the stoplight intersection when I saw an odd sight on the shoulder of the road. I slammed on my brakes and pulled over in front of a hideous purple car. It was an oddly shaped car, like a cardboard box on wheels, but it was the legs sticking out from under the car that held my attention.

I'd recognize those pale legs anywhere.

The grin was already stretching across my face when I slid out of my truck and approached with caution. I'd spent most of last night thinking about my new neighbor and being highly amused. Then I'd remember her date and I'd be left annoyed with myself for caring. I was in Blueball to help Grandma Milly, not flirt with the oddly beautiful woman next door.

I would have worried Marlo had actually been murdered— not by me like she thought—if it weren't for the string of creative curses coming from under the car.

"It's the wicked witch of the west!" I exclaimed, leaning against the hood of her car and folding my arms across my chest. I watched her legs jolt and then get deathly still. "Wait. Or is it the wicked witch of the east? I can never remember."

With an admirable grunt, Marlo crawled out from under her car, looking adorable in a black band T-shirt that had seen better days and cutoff jean shorts. The Band-Aid I'd given her last night was still on her forearm. Her nails were painted a dark purple today and she wasn't sporting any makeup. Her dark hair blew around her face in the gentle breeze. I saw a leaf or two caught in the strands, probably from lying in the dirt while she cursed at her vehicle.

"Oh look, Annoying is back," she deadpanned with a straight face.

I grinned. "Nice to see you again too, Bubbles." I pointed to her car. "Having difficulties?"

She shook her head. "No, I like to stop and smell the under-carriage some days."

A laugh bubbled up and I didn't miss the way Marlo had to fight to keep her lips from tipping up at the corners. "May I offer my assistance?"

"No."

I held out my hand. "Give me the crowbar."

She lifted the piece of metal and brandished it like a weapon. "No. You might murder me with it."

I rolled my eyes and easily snatched it from her hands. "Are we doing this again? Pretty sure I wouldn't choose daylight hours in the middle of bustling downtown Blueball to commit murder."

Marlo frowned so hard her dark eyebrows had crawled together. "A woman can never be too careful." She tilted her head. "And I have clean panties on today, so my head's basically on the chopping block."

My brain instantly zeroed in on the panties statement, envisioning those long legs in lacy black panties, because of course Marlo would have a black pair on. No sparkly pink for this woman.

"Oh really," I muttered suggestively, leaning in to watch the way color stained her cheeks. I was starting to see that Marlo was good at maintaining that straight face, but there was a lot more going on under the surface. It might have been wishful thinking, but I could have sworn Marlo swayed toward me before her spine snapped straight and her eyes narrowed.

"Do you know how many people die each year on the side of the road when their car breaks down?"

I stepped closer to the back tire that was clearly flat. "Can't say I do. I prefer to look at the brighter side of things. Know how many people meet their future love interest on the side of the road each year?"

Her cheeks went redder and her mouth snapped shut. I chuckled, crouched down, and loosened the lug nuts with the crowbar. "Got a jack in your trunk?"

She huffed but got it for me, handing it over. "I thought the lug nuts were on the back side of the tire," she muttered.

"Common mistake, Bubbles." With the car up on one side, I took off the lug nuts and removed the tire. "Hand me the spare."

She growled but handed me the spare a moment later. My

new neighbor did not like a man telling her what to do, that was clear. Made me want to bark all kinds of orders at her just to hear her hiss and spit.

Lug nuts in place, I lowered the jack and removed it. "Should be good to go, as long as you're not going far. Blueball have a repair shop?"

"They do."

I put all the tools in the back of her car and rubbed my hands together to wipe off some of the black streaks. "Okay, well, I'll follow you to make sure you get there safe."

"No, thank you." Marlo moved to the driver's side door, frown firmly in place.

"I wasn't asking," I drawled.

"I'm not waiting," she drawled right back.

She slammed her door shut and cranked the engine. I realized her intention right as she gave the car some gas. I had to jump out of the way to keep from being sideswiped as she rocketed back into traffic—though a single solitary car on the road was hardly what I'd consider traffic.

I ran for my truck, hopping in and following her before she got too far away. Two blocks later, she turned and bounced over the curb into a repair shop parking lot. I winced, hoping that dinky spare would hold. Pausing in the middle of the street, I gave her a friendly wave, which she ignored by turning her head the other way and pretending I didn't exist.

My laughter was loud and abundant alone in the cab of my truck as I pulled away and headed for Grandma Milly's place. Marlo had something against waving, along with a general grumpiness that fascinated me. It was a challenge to get a genuine smile out of her. Two interactions and I hadn't seen it yet.

Good thing Vander Booth never backed down from a challenge.

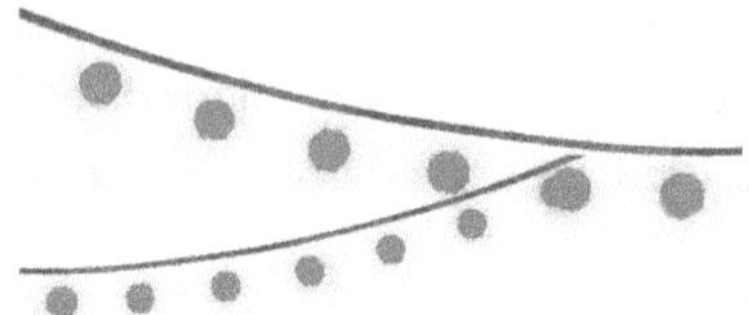

"Why are you smiling? The price of organic blueberries is enough to send an old woman into cardiac arrest!"

G-Mil looked ready to throw her heavy purse down and fight me over my insistence on organic fruits and vegetables. The young guy stocking the pineapples tried to look like he wasn't eavesdropping but he kept giving us obvious side-eye.

I put my hands on her shoulders and made her look me in the eye. "Grandma, you need healthy food to live a long time. I can't let you buy muffins for breakfast."

"They have blueberries in them!" She glared at me so hard I actually started to worry about that heart attack.

"Along with a lot of sugar and gluten."

"What's wrong with gluten? You young people, I swear. I've eaten gluten my whole life! I didn't live to my eighties to be told I can't have a goddamn bite of gluten for breakfast. Bring back the gluten, I say!"

Oh boy, this was unraveling fast. "Okay, how about this? I'll bake you some homemade blueberry muffins with organic blueberries. Would you like that?"

G-Mil lifted her nose in the air. "I might accept that."

"Great. Let's move on to snacks."

I pushed the cart out of the produce aisle, hoping we could make it through the snack aisle without another tantrum. This was like shopping with a toddler. I'd seen the women wrangling multiple children while trying to fill a cart with decent food. Seemed like maybe grocery delivery would be a better option in the future for both me and moms of toddlers.

"Why were you so late anyway?" G-Mil asked, suddenly happy and dumping every single bag of chips into the cart that she could get her hands on. Thankfully she couldn't reach the two top shelves or I'd have to get another cart.

I decided to pick my battles and kept my mouth shut about the chips. "Oh, I saw Marlo on the side of the road, so I stopped to change her tire."

G-Mil froze in her tracks, then spun around, forgetting all about the chips she'd had her claws on. "Marlo? From the funeral home? I wasn't aware you two knew each other."

I nodded, not yet seeing the trap I was walking into. "Yeah, we met last night actually. She had a little incident at the cemetery and I came out to check on her. Ended up bandaging her arm and giving her a quick tour of my new place."

Grandma rubbed her gnarled hands together. "Oh, the Balmeros are such a lovely family. Shame no one has turned Marlo's head yet. I must say, young men are just built differently these days."

As one of those young men, I was affronted. "What's that supposed to mean?"

Grandma shrugged and pulled the cart down the aisle toward the shiny packages of cookies. "Just that young men these days want a girl with a juicy booty and a huge social media following. They don't realize that booties droop and social media accounts get shut down in the blink of an eye. What you boys need is *substance*."

I thought back to my last date. She'd had a shapely backside and a cult following on her style account. Well, shit. I hated being predictable.

"And what is your definition of substance?"

Grandma put a packet of Oreos in the cart, which I took out and put back when she turned to grab a box of chocolate chip cookies. "A solid work ethic, a focus on building a family, and a personality that lasts even when the physical crumbles." She shrugged and reached up high for gingersnaps. "You know, like Marlo."

I realized my folly immediately. I never should have brought up a woman in front of G-Mil. She would forever be trying to play matchmaker. She'd once seen a picture of me with a date at a charity event in an obscure gossip column right around the time I sold my company and mailed the woman a care package of my favorite foods. I couldn't remember the woman's first name and G-Mil had been ready to mail the wedding invitations.

Distraction. That's what I needed.

"So I was thinking of opening a business here in Blueball since you won't let me spend my fortune."

Grandma spun back around, interest in those sharp eyes. Her food choices were that of a toddler, but her mind was sharp as a tack. "Oh? What kind of business?"

I pushed the cart away from the snack aisle and toward checkout. "I'm not sure yet, but I want it to be something fun that brings friends and family together. Something that enhances Blueball."

G-Mil put her hand on mine and patted it. "Oh, I quite like that, Vandy. Having a purpose is good for a man. You can't be retired at thirty-two. You'd go mad!"

I gave her a squeeze and moved to put the groceries on the conveyer belt. "My purpose is to take care of you."

"Ohh." She waved her hand through the air, as if to bat away my suggestion. "I don't need help. I get by just fine on my own. What you need is a girlfriend." She paused, staring at the groceries I was unloading. She was probably counting the cookie boxes and coming up short. I hurried to put the rest of the groceries up and move her and the cart to the register.

She snagged my hand and squeezed until I looked down at her. Her pale blue eyes sparkled up at me.

"I do love having you here with me though."

"Same, G-Mil. You're my best friend." I leaned down and kissed the top of her head, breathing in the powdery scent of the woman who'd always loved me unconditionally.

I didn't get home until late that night. After putting away all the groceries, I'd spent the rest of the day baking and cooking, making sure G-Mil had ready-made meals for the week. The homemade muffins may have been gluten-free, but I noticed she ate two of them before I left her to watch her nightly show.

"Night, Grandma."

"Night, Vandy!" she called from her chair, cozied up in her nightgown and a blanket over her legs. Her gaze was already on the reality show.

"I'll see you tomorrow."

"Think about that girlfriend idea!"

I waved her suggestion away and headed home to my boxes. There, on the front step of my house, was a package. I got out of my truck and approached, realizing it was my sweater as I got closer. The one Marlo had been wearing when she left my house. There was a note on top of the folded sweater, chicken scratch writing on Blueball Endless Eternity letterhead.

I'd make it look like an unfortunate accident, and I'd make sure I had a solid alibi for that timeframe.

I tossed my head back and roared with laughter.

The woman had told me how she'd get away with murder.

Weirdest. Town. Ever.

CHAPTER SIX

*M*arlo

THE RETIREES of Blueball and surrounding areas were awfully quiet this week. And by quiet, I meant not dying. I had the morning off. No funerals or embalmings or even appointments for buying plots. I was blessedly free to do whatever an almost thirty-year-old single woman did. I would have lazed around in my bed with copious salty and sweet snacks, followed by a Netflix binge, but the girls had designated today as our girls' night. Girls' morning just didn't have the same ring to it, but that was when we all could manage time off.

I stopped by Crazy Beans for a coffee, black as my soul, and a hit of sugar. I had a tray of brownies in the car to share, and if I didn't pick up a nail in one of my tires again, I'd be over to Paisley's before ten. Normally, I kept my head down and did my business around town to avoid annoying conversation, but I found my gaze sweeping the inside of the shop, looking for a tall golden man with a fucking smile stamped across his face. On principle, I didn't trust people who smiled so much, but I could admit that I found myself intrigued with Vander. And knowing I was intrigued pissed me off and added to my bad mood.

My parents would be dismayed, claiming they raised me better, but my friends would understand my lack of manners upon arrival. With the tray of brownies in one hand and my coffee in the other, I couldn't knock on Paisley's door. It only made sense to kick it to let her know I was on her doorstop. And it felt good to kick it. Like I was getting out some frustration that had been bubbling inside all week long. I really had nothing to be frustrated with, except for myself.

I'd been eyeing the Skinner house day and night since I'd been up there with Vander. He irritated me to no end with his endless jokes and his disturbing smiles, and yet my eyes tried to search him out. It was ridiculous. It was absurd. And if this shit with my eyeballs didn't stop soon, I was going to take matters into my own hands and strap horse blinders to my face.

"You going to just scowl at your feet all morning, or actually come inside?"

Paisley's drawl had my head whipping up. See? I was off-kilter, losing control of my thoughts to a person I didn't even like. She had the door wide open and an amused grin on her face.

"Did Audrey bring mimosas?"

Paisley waggled her eyebrows, which was all the confirmation I needed. "Then I'm coming in."

I swooped past her and dumped my brownie tray on the kitchen counter before turning and hugging Paisley and then Audrey. Keva wasn't here yet. Boston, Audrey's fiancé, waved and bent down to kiss my cheek before turning to sneak out the back.

"He's got to get back to work but he saw my car pull up," Audrey explained.

Boston worked here at Glamper's Paradise with Gannon, Paisley's husband, and Lincoln, Keva's husband. My three best friends had found men and true love this last year and a half. I was happy for them. Really. Just look at my face. Totally happy.

Keva burst through the front door, calling, "Sorry I'm late! I leaked onto my shirt and I had to go change."

I grimaced. For someone who dealt with dead bodies all the time, I was oddly squeamish about alive ones. In the last few months I'd heard more than I ever wanted to know about episiotomy stitches and leaky nipples. For fuck's sake, let a girl find love before you tell her about the dark side of things.

Audrey grabbed my hand and pulled me down on the couch with her. Paisley sat on my other side and Keva sat on the coffee table directly in front of me.

"Did you want a chair?" I asked, quite politely, I thought.

Keva shook her head and leaned closer, elbows on her knees. Warning bells erupted in my head. Everyone was staring at me. Well, fuck. I knew what this was. I'd been on the other end of this situation before.

"We're having an intervention, honey," Audrey said so nicely I wanted to smack her.

My head was already shaking an insistent no. "I don't need an intervention unless you're talking about what to do with my land problem."

"You've been very distracted lately," Keva threw out there.

"We were actually pretty shocked to get your text about a girls' night." Paisley patted my hand. I hated pats to the hand. Why did people need to touch when they spoke?

I snatched my hand away to flail it about in the air. "I've been busy. Working. Taking over the business. You guys know this."

"We do know this, but this is more. You've made multiple remarks about men lately, and as your besties, it's up to us to pry the bullshit out of you." Keva looked like she was ready to grab the crowbar.

I grimaced. "That sounds terrible."

"What's up with your recent dates?"

"Did they ghost you? Or were they just terrible humans?"

"Are these all from that one app I told you about?"

"You know, I think maybe we need to find someone local.

Online is a cesspool."

"Girls!" I had to raise my voice to be heard over their peppering of questions and comments about my love life. "Yes, I have gone on some bummer dates and been ghosted by some others. But I'm fine. Just working and dating. It's all good."

Audrey leaned into my side. More goddamn touching. "You're not crying yourself to sleep at night?"

I scoffed. "Do I look like a crier?" I pointed to my chronically dry eyes, the ones that didn't cry even at the most emotional funerals. You didn't grow up literally in a funeral home without developing some thick skin and empty tear ducts. Crying just wasn't in my wheelhouse.

Paisley tutted. Keva sighed. Audrey tried and failed to suppress a giggle.

"What I really need is a solution to my business problem."

"What's that? A non-toxic embalming solution?"

Paisley was such a smart-ass. "No. When embalming you want all the toxins possible. I mean my land problem. We're running out of plots."

"Oh shit," Keva whispered, eyes wide. "Could you expand with another funeral home in Hell?"

I couldn't help it, I chuckled a bit. Wouldn't that be something? To own a funeral home in a town affectionately called Hell? That might be the pinnacle of undertaker success actually.

"No, I don't want to duplicate the funeral home in another town. I don't have anyone to run another location. I just need more land."

"I can help you," Audrey said quickly. "I can run a search for properties with over five acres in Blueball and see if anyone wants to sell. Girl, I got you. This is what I do!"

I was nodding along, mentally kicking myself for not going to Audrey right away. She was a realtor and could steer me in the right direction, and she'd do it with the best friend discount. Maybe my friends were correct in their assessment of my personality fault: I really did need to reach out and ask for help, even when it pained me to do so. There was undeveloped land right behind the cemetery already. Maybe the owner wanted to sell, but I wouldn't know that until I got my realtor bestie to help me.

"I actually have a parcel in mind. It's perfect, actually." I sat up straighter, getting into it now that my friends had forced me to open up. "You know that—"

A loud knock on the door had all of us turning in that direction. Audrey jumped up.

"Oh! That's probably my client. I invited him over to meet the boys. He's new in town and needs friends." She rushed off to the door while my brain came to a screeching halt. I stared at the scuffed toes of my Doc Martens and wished for the floor to open up and swallow me whole.

It couldn't be, could it?

"Ladies, this is Vander Booth. Vander, these are my friends, Paisley, Keva, and Marlo."

I looked up to see Audrey with her hand on Vander's elbow as she pointed to each of us. He stood there looking disturbingly handsome in dark jeans that came to his ankles, a loose-fitting T-shirt that probably cost more than my car, and his grandma's handmade green sweater. He'd added a patch since I'd worn it —*In my defense, I was left unsupervised*—which was also funny, damn him. Vander tossed that flirtatious smile to each of my friends before his gaze landed on me. If anything, the smile grew, as if it knew how much I disliked it and it simply fed off my negativity.

"Well, well, well. Are you wearing nice panties today, Bubbles?" Vander asked immediately, creating a wide variety of reactions from my friends. Audrey looked shocked, Keva appeared pissed, and Paisley seemed disappointed that yet another handsome single man turned out to be a douchebag. *Join the club, sister.*

"It appears you found clothes that fit today, Annoying," I snapped right back.

"I murdered a normal-sized man today."

"What? You couldn't find more Oompa-Loompas?"

"Blueball is fresh out, though I hear you can often find women out late at night in just their underwear."

My face burned hot and I snapped my mouth shut before I could tell him to go to Hell. It was literally right next door. Not that hard to find. Heads were swiveling back and forth and I knew my friends had a thousand questions they now wanted to ask me.

"Okay..." Audrey said tentatively into the charged silence before pasting on a bright smile. She did remove her hand from Vander's arm, however, a move that brought me relief. And pissed me off. "Looks like you two know each other, huh?"

Vander, who possessed better peopling skills than me—didn't take much—smoothed things over. "Yes, in fact, we met a few nights ago at the cemetery. Our Marlo here is quite the funny woman."

"Oh, is she?" Keva asked, leaning closer to Vander like he was the source of all the town gossip. "Do tell."

I stood up from the couch. "I'm sure you have somewhere better to be. Maybe up in your castle, lording over us little folks?"

Vander's dimple winked at me. "Oh, I only lord over Oompa-Loompas."

"I'm still wondering about the panties comment," Paisley interrupted. "Do I need to kick your ass to defend Marlo's honor? Because the baby's going to be up from her nap in like ten minutes. My time for ass-kicking is limited."

Vander had the audacity to light up like a cremation furnace. "Baby? I love babies! If you need a babysitter, I'm your guy."

Both Keva and Paisley were already nodding, won over by a total stranger for simply offering to babysit.

"He's a stranger, y'all. And possibly a murderer. You can't let him babysit Aster and Cora."

Audrey frowned at me. "He's not a murderer, Marlo."

"Yeah, Bubbles."

I shot Vander a scathing look. I did not appreciate him ganging up with my friends. "He has money, Audrey, but you don't know that he came by it legally."

Audrey opened her mouth and then snapped it shut. Ha! Got her there. She was so blinded by the dollar signs that came with the house sale, she'd forgotten that she didn't actually know Vander Booth. None of us did.

Vander put his hands up. "I'm not here to murder anyone, and thank you for the offer, Ais, but I'd prefer an ass-kicking on another day. I actually came to meet the guys, but also to talk to Rey about another real estate deal."

"Ais? Rey?" Paisley muttered, looking confused.

Audrey, on the other hand, pounced, putting her hand back on Vander's elbow. "Sure! Whatever you need, I can help you with. Want another house? Maybe one up in the mountains? Like a vacation-type place?"

What the hell was happening here? How had Vander been here all of three seconds and made friends with my besties? It had taken me kindergarten through fifth grade to make Paisley and Audrey like me. Keva only put up with me when she first moved here because I stuck around like an annoying barnacle of loserdom.

"I'd like to buy a plot of land for my new business," Vander announced as I glared at the side of his head.

"Great! Let's go take a look and we can put in an offer this afternoon." Audrey was seriously pissing me off with the hand squeezes. Why did everyone have to touch so goddamn much?

"Sweet. It's the plot of land behind the Skinner house and the cemetery."

Fury climbed up my spine and out my mouth like some kind of alien explosion in the form of a garbled gasp. Vander wanted the same plot of land I'd already scoped out to be mine. And he had the deep pockets to outbid me, several times over.

"You flirty little weasel in doll clothes!"

CHAPTER SEVEN

ander

"MARLO!" Audrey gasped, probably shocked at Marlo's inability to form an adult-level insult. Doll clothes? Damn, that shit was funny.

Marlo, though, didn't seem to find anything funny right now. Or maybe ever. Her cheeks were the color of G-Mil's lipstick and her hands were clenched into fists at her side. But mostly it was the eyes that gave her away. She looked like she was summoning fire-breathing beasts from the depths of hell to come earthside and wipe me from existence. Her eyes were fucking terrifying.

She opened her mouth and I expected bats to fly straight at my head. "No, *I'm* buying that land." Thankfully, the bats didn't materialize, but her meaning was clear.

If she could influence the sale of that plot by sheer force of will, that land was already Marlo's.

But that just wouldn't do. I couldn't live out my life up in the ol' Skinner house, retired at thirty-two and eventually dying of boredom only to be buried in Marlo's cemetery and have her desecrate my grave on a daily basis just for funsies. I wanted to have the funsies. I wanted to build a new business in Blueball all about funsies. And I needed that land to do it.

I crossed my arms over my chest, trying to look just as scary and probably failing. "I think you must have hit your head trying to change your tire. *I'm* buying that land."

Marlo somehow stood in front of me without her legs actually doing any walking. She probably threatened the space-time continuum until it caved and let her move freely about the space unlike us mere mortals.

She glared at me, extending her spine like her five foot eight was somehow intimidating. She should stick to the eye glower. "You just moved here. You're an outsider."

I leaned into her space. "You make such an excellent welcoming committee, Bubbles."

She moved lightning fast, a single finger now drilling into my chest as she practically vibrated with anger. "The town needs that land. You can't swoop in here on day one and steal land that we need. I promise you you'll be run out of here with your tail between your legs."

The outrage I demonstrated was all pretend. "How do you know I have a tail?"

"Believe me, I saw everything in those toddler clothes you like to wear!"

I grinned, watching her anger flame even higher at my amusement. Sounded like Marlo liked checking me out in that tight outfit. "You were checking me out, Bubbles? Very interesting. G-Mil will be so happy you're interested in her grandson."

Her eyes lit up and she sputtered. "Speaking of Milly. You want to be the asshole who steals land from the town? You think that'll paint her in a good light?"

Humor vanished in an instant. Poke fun of me all you want, but nobody talked about Grandma Milly in threatening tones like that. Veiled or not, the threat was there. And I wouldn't stand for it.

I smacked her finger off my chest, absolutely done with the teasing. I was pretty sure Marlo knew it too because she suddenly didn't look like she was about to spit fire. She shrunk back. "Don't you dare speak about G-Mil."

I opened my mouth to unload, but Audrey interrupted, wedging herself between us. "Guys?" She swiveled her head between us, but Marlo and I were too busy glaring at each other and breathing hard. "No one is buying that land today. We don't even know who owns it and if they're willing to sell. How about we all just settle down before we say something we'll regret?"

"I regret nothing," Marlo snapped.

"Not even the granny panties?" I snapped back.

Marlo inhaled sharply through her nose and then spun, walking away to sit in the chair in the far corner of the room. I stepped back also, giving Audrey some room. I hadn't come here to start a fight. I'd come to make friends. The irony was not lost on me. Making friends was not exactly my strong suit and here I was getting in a fight and fucking things up already.

"I'm sorry, ladies. I'll start over. I'm Vander Booth, newest resident of Blueball and grandson of Milly Booth. I just bought the Skinner house, thanks to Rey here."

I shook hands with Paisley and Keva, both of whom did not look at all put off by my verbal sparring match with Marlo. If anything, they were giving each other sly looks. That weird thing women did when they had a whole conversation with their eyes without saying a single word. Marlo continued to glare at me from the corner while the ladies asked me questions about where I was from and why I'd moved to town.

"I came to take care of Grandma Milly. She's my best friend."

All three ladies got puppy dog eyes and filled the room with soft sighs. Pretty sure Marlo hissed at me.

"I'm retired from my first career, but G-Mil and I have been talking. I'm too young to sit at home bored. I want to start a business here in Blueball. Hence the search for land."

"For what? A place to bury your murder victims? Storage for your Oompa-Loompas?" Marlo's voice could have cut glass with all its sharpness.

God, I loved her insults. I hated to say it, but they kept me amused. "Nah, I can use your cemetery for that. The land's for a paintball field."

"Oh! I love paintball!" Paisley gave me an encouraging smile.

"Can't say I've tried it, but I'd be up to give it a go." Keva shrugged.

"Are you fucking kidding me?" This was from Marlo, of course.

"I don't kid around," I drawled, which was clearly a lie. That's mostly all I did.

Marlo shot out of her chair. "What this town needs is an expanded cemetery. That takes precedence over some silly paint-ball field."

"I don't know. Have you asked Blueball? Maybe they don't want an expanded cemetery. Maybe they want some fun!"

Marlo scoffed, looking at her friends for support and not finding much. "All you care about is fun."

I winked at her, watching her blood pressure climb to unhealthy levels again. "Some of us know how to have fun, Bubbles."

Marlo got scary quiet, eyes like laser beams as she glared at me. I wasn't sure what someone putting a hex on another person looked like, but it was probably a lot like how Marlo looked right now.

A door somewhere in the back of the house slammed and boots traipsing across hardwood floors filled in the awkward silence.

"Hey, what's with all the shouting?" A guy with a baseball cap on and enough muscle to make me rethink my gym schedule, or lack thereof, entered the room from the hallway. His gaze skimmed over the ladies before zeroing in on me. The blue tone of his eyes went frosty. "And who are you?"

I held out my hand. "I'm Vander Booth. Newest resident of Blueball. Audrey invited me over to meet everyone."

If that guy wasn't scary enough, an even taller and beefier guy came into the living room and immediately went to Audrey's side. "Is he a good one?" he rumbled loud enough we could all hear.

Audrey smiled. "Yes! He's the one who just bought the Skinner house. He's new in town and I thought y'all would like to meet him. Play nice, boys."

A third man entered the room, shorter than the first two, but more ripped and tatted out. He pulled Keva out of her seat on the couch and sat in her spot, pulling her back down on his lap. The meaning was clear: this is my woman, don't look or touch.

The first man grunted. "Can you play a musical instrument?"

Clearly, there was a right answer here, but instead of over-thinking it, I spoke the truth. "Nah, but I can sing. Been known to rock karaoke a time or two."

The tension in the room broke and the first guy broke out into a smile. "Hot damn! Okay, cool. You free next Friday?"

"He's busy," Marlo deadpanned.

Thankfully, my new friends talked right over her. "I will gladly pass the microphone to you, buddy. I'm Boston." The biggest guy in the room leaned around Audrey to shake my hand.

"And I'm Lincoln, the drummer in our little band." The guy on the couch smiled, suddenly not intimidating at all.

I nodded, feeling excited about the possibility of real friends. Also a little nervous if I was being honest, but I'd fake my way through it, even if it killed me. "Do we have a name for our band?"

"I'm Gannon, by the way. Original owner of Glamper's Paradise." The man in the hat shook my hand. "We're bouncing the idea around for Blueball Band of Brothers."

"The BBB." I nodded. "I like it."

"For fuck's sake," I heard Marlo mutter.

A baby started crying from somewhere in the house and Paisley jumped up. "Well, I guess it's settled. We'll see you next Friday at the fire pit, Vander. Try not to kill our friend before then."

My gaze shot to Marlo as Paisley exited the room. My nemesis looked so darkly pretty sitting there. Her hair always looked like she'd forgotten to brush it but it somehow worked for her. It looked alive with energy, contrary to the black she always wore.

"We're not very good yet, but we're working on it." Lincoln interrupted my thoughts.

Keva backhanded his arm. "Yes, you are! You always draw a crowd."

"Mostly because you're all hot," Audrey drawled, earning herself a kiss on the top of her head from Boston.

"Why, thank you," I preened.

"Not you, jackass," Marlo muttered.

I had to roll my lips in to keep from laughing. I figured I'd pushed her buttons enough. "I'm off to G-Mil's."

"Is she making you another sweater?" Marlo snarked from her throne of disdain.

I gave her my best smile. "I certainly hope so. She only makes sweaters for people she loves. People who deserve her sunshine in the form of yarn. Probably why you don't have one."

Marlo's tongue shot out so unexpectedly and childish, I barked out a laugh. My new buddy, Lincoln, looked to Keva with confusion written all over his face.

"What's gotten into Marlo?"

"Marlo's finally found a sparring partner," Keva responded.

Audrey left Boston's side to walk me to the front door, but not before I heard Lincoln's voice, full of laughter.

"Was that actually sparring or flirting? With Marlo you just never know."

Marlo's bark of disgust had me laughing all the way to G-

Mil's place. The warm glow filling my chest the rest of the day had everything to do with Grandma finding a new patch to sew on to my sweater. It had nothing at all to do with thinking my disgruntled next-door neighbor was flirting with me.

Not. At. All.

CHAPTER EIGHT

arlo

I WAS NOT ashamed to say I'd seen my fair share of bad moods. Sometimes I woke up and chose violence. Or at least in my head. I'd killed off most of the people of Blueball in my imagination at some point in time. Did that make me a psychopath? Or maybe I was the only self-evolved adult out here, using my imagination to take the edge off my frustrations instead of actually doing something about it.

In reality—and don't tell another soul about this or I will have to take those imagined killings to the very real streets of Blueball, and frankly, I don't have time for that—I was a softie inside, wanting to be of help to those I loved. I didn't love very many people, but those I did, I loved hard.

And currently, I was failing them all. Including myself.

Dad, in his perfectly creased slacks and polo shirt, sat at the breakfast table eating dry toast while Mom bustled around him, all fake chipperness as she talked about today's latest doctor appointment. This time would be with a specialist in the big city.

Hope was a flimsy bubble, just begging to be popped. I watched the way they snuck in a hand squeeze as she brought him another cup of decaf coffee. Or the way he patted her butt whenever she walked close enough for him to reach. They were adorable. So damn cute I wanted to puke.

Instead, I took out the trash, going through the kitchen, down the back stairs, across the garage, and out the side door to heft the overfilled bag into the trash can. I got it in there right as I caught movement up the hill. My gaze lifted and who did I see but Vander Booth, half naked, out on his terrace, surveying his land. Okay, he wasn't naked, but he didn't have a shirt to go along with that dark pair of pajama pants. His chest was broad and muscular, far more attractive naked than in a shirt ten sizes too small. Muscles were well defined but not overstated. He held a cup of coffee in his hand while his other hand was in his pants pocket. He appeared carefree. At peace. Like a man who had no idea the old ladies of Blueball would be staring through binoculars trying to get a good look at him.

The trash lid slipped out of my hand and crashed down on the can, creating a racket that might have even woken up my sleeping friends in the cemetery. Vander's head whipped over in my direction. I did the same, but whipped my head in the direction of my house like the siding had somehow become incredibly interesting.

"Miwtoossbub?" Vander called down to me.

I squeezed my eyes shut. He'd already seen me looking, so to run away now would just be childish. Not that our entire exchange yesterday at Paisley's house *hadn't* been childish. It's just that I'd wanted to turn a corner today, moving firmly into the realm of just wishing Vander death in my head. Not actual death-wish words coming out of my mouth. Still, there was nothing for it now. I was a rabbit, caught in a snare and forced to look her predator in the face. So I made myself turn and put a hand to my ear.

"Huh?" I called back, clearly still entrenched in the idea of acting like a child.

"Like what you see, Bubbles?" he shouted. Clearly. Loudly. Annoyingly.

I was raging inside, but I made sure my shrug was long and slow. "Not much to see from here," I shouted back.

Instead of slinging another insult at me, the man began to dance right there on his stone terrace without a single note of music playing, coffee mug held high in the air. And boy, could he dance. My gaze immediately dropped to the hip swivel, wondering how he knew that TikTok dance Audrey had tried to get all their men to learn. She claimed they'd go viral if all three of them did it, and now I knew why she thought that. Vander did a slick twist and ended up with his back to me, shaking his ass like he was being paid for it. I couldn't stand here and watch any more of this.

It was too early in the morning to be nauseous.

Or turned on.

"Okay. Well, thanks for that," I hollered back. Softly. Soberly. Lamely.

I was in a full sprint heading back up the stairs into the house. I needed less thinks-everything-is-funny Vander and more business-Barbie Marlo. I had a cemetery land crisis to figure out. And I had to do it before Mr. Dance-a-lot swooped in with his deep pockets and smooth moves.

"Hey, Dad?"

He was grabbing his keys off the hook in the kitchen. "Yes, dear daughter of mine?" As far back as I could remember, Dad always made time for me, and this morning was no different.

"Can I talk to you later today about my plans for expanding the cemetery?" I could hear Mom in their bedroom trying to find her shoes. She wouldn't appreciate me even mentioning work to Daddy, but I had to talk to someone. Who better than the man who'd run it successfully for decades? I had no plans to stress his heart. I just needed to run things by him and get his opinion.

"Sure, girlie. We'll be back a little after lunchtime, but my afternoon is yours." Dad pulled me into a hug that made me forget about work troubles, feeling like the third wheel with all my friends, and annoying neighbors.

"Found them!" Mom exclaimed, coming into the kitchen in a pair of ballet flats she liked to wear when she was dressing up but didn't want her feet to hurt from wearing heels. She screeched to a halt when she saw us hugging. "Did someone die?"

Mom started cackling and we both joined in. It was a long-standing family joke that wasn't really all that funny, I suppose. But when you were surrounded by death every day, you had to find ways to diffuse the sadness.

Dad let me go and plucked Mom's faded brown leather purse off the counter, handing it to her. "My chariot awaits, my princess."

Mom faked a frown. "Hey, I thought I was your queen."

I rolled my eyes and hightailed it to my room before I heard or saw Dad's answer. I didn't need to stay and watch those two flirt. Talk about gross. I flopped down on my bed and refused to look outside my window to see if Vander was still outside. I was stronger than that, goddammit. I tilted my head back and thought about what I needed to get done today. The whole downstairs needed vacuuming and dusting. No one liked to pick out a casket for their dearly departed loved one lined with dust.

Before I was ready to face the day, I rolled off my bed and forced myself to put on some decent clothes and take care of basic hygiene. Audrey was coming over soon to walk the parcel south of us with me. I'd texted her last night and she promised to do some research to find out who owned it. Just as I was replaying that show Vander gave me this morning for the tenth time, the doorbell rang outside the downstairs office.

"I'm coming!" I called out, racing down the stairs and to the front door.

"Hey, Bubbles," Audrey trilled, standing on my doorstep in the cutest sundress and matching light sweater you've ever seen. If you liked pink and ruffles and shit like that.

I screeched to a halt, refusing to hug her now that she'd called me that. "No. Absolutely not."

She burst out laughing. "I'm kidding. Too soon?"

"Always too soon," I grumbled.

Audrey threw her arms around me and hugged me far tighter than necessary. "I'm sorry. I'll leave the cutesy nicknames to Vander." She pulled back and shot me a wink, like we were two friends sharing a secret about a boy.

I was already shaking my head. "No. It's not like that. I don't like the man."

Audrey looped her arm through mine and tugged me out the door. "Doesn't matter if you like him or not. The man is hot."

I snorted, climbing into her new car, the one she'd bought just last week, partly because of the commission she'd made off of selling Vander the Skinner house. The new-car smell pervaded my senses and I let myself enjoy it the whole way to the far side of the empty parcel of land. I'd probably never afford a new car myself, so I'd have to live vicariously through Audrey.

She pulled to the side of the road by a little gate with a *Private Property Keep Out* sign. Clapping her hands, she smiled from ear to ear.

"Okay, this is it. You ready?" she asked with her usual excitement when talking about land or square footage or setbacks. I understood. I got excited about new body coolers, adjustable embalming tables, and the newest lightweight urns that were practically indestructible but still looked fancy.

I pushed the passenger side door open and stepped out into the brisk morning air. "Ready to see my future."

Audrey squealed and came by my side. It wasn't often I talked with such passion about my prospects in life. I just had a feeling about this place. Green shrubs looked like they wanted to take over the little gate, but someone had cut them back at some point in the last year. Audrey still had to pull a few vines out of the slats of wood to get the gate open enough for us to walk through. A butterfly flitted right by my face, a gesture I tried not to take as a good omen. I didn't want to get my hopes up quite yet.

Green fields with wild flowers growing in bunches almost as far as the eye could see greeted us. Audrey sighed and I knew what she meant. This place was gorgeous.

"Come on. Let's walk the whole thing and make sure it'll work for you." Arm in arm, Audrey and I walked the perimeter, stopping to check out trees and even a little stream that cut through the far corner of the lot. I could just see the corner of my house past the cement block wall that circled the existing cemetery. We'd have to knock down one section of the wall, but this place would be a natural extension of the existing cemetery. This parcel would be an even more tranquil place to bury loved ones. Visitors could come and commune with nature while they were assured they buried dear old grandpa in the best spot in all the county.

When we circled back to the front gate, I felt the yearning in my gut. Something about this land had settled into my body and grown, pushing to take up space and be noticed. I wanted this place. I wanted it bad.

"Audrey?" I said as I looked out at it one more time.

"Yeah, babe?" She, too, was mesmerized by the peaceful field, gazing at it like she didn't want to leave just yet.

"I want it," I said softly, afraid to put my wish out there in full volume lest it be taken away from me. I wasn't familiar with making stretch goals. Having fallen into my father's career footsteps, I mostly just took every day as it came. Having a big audacious goal was fucking terrifying.

"I know, babe." Audrey turned to me, tugging on my arm. "There's just one thing you need to know."

My gut twisted immediately. All that peace I'd felt walking around? Gone.

"Tell it to me straight."

Audrey winced, sympathy in her eyes, which only made my stomach hurt worse. I had to give her credit though. She plowed ahead, ripping off the Band-Aid like a true friend.

"Milly Booth owns this land."

CHAPTER NINE

ander

"I'T'S GOING to turn out better than any of our Christmas cards before!"

G-Mil grinned in the dim light of the few-and-far-between streetlights as we headed back to my place, looking entirely unlike herself, except for the glint of mischief in her eyes. I'd had the very best idea this morning and had ignored my unpacked boxes yet again to run all over multiple towns to collect the supplies I needed to make this idea come to fruition. Thankfully, G-Mil had not only gone along with it, she'd embraced my crazy with open arms. Takes a crazy one to appreciate an even crazier one.

"It's a little early in the year to be doing a Christmas card," she reasoned, holding on to her bouquet of fake black roses.

I waved away her concern. "I get that, but we want to be the first cards that hit mailboxes this year. And I firmly believe good ideas need to be pounced on or they evaporate. Which is why I want to tell you about my idea for a business here in Blueball."

"Please tell me it's not another smarty app."

I sighed, but I wasn't mad. I'd explained to my grandma about a hundred times what an app on a smartphone was and specifically what I'd created, but it had gone right over her head. Or maybe she was purposely being obtuse. One never knew with G-Mil.

"It's not an app." I pulled into my driveway, but stopped the truck just a few feet in. The stone wall around the cemetery ended at the tree line that separated our properties. As I'd learned the night I tried to save Marlo from the fire, one could slip right between the trees and find themselves in the cemetery after hours.

I hopped out of the truck and shut the door silently, coming around to help G-Mil down. I'd had an automatic running board installed on the passenger side of my truck that created a step-stool type situation just for Grandma Milly. While I'd gotten all of my personality from her, I'd clearly gotten my height genes from somewhere else in the family tree. Once she was finally on her feet and steady, I gently shut her door and took her by the hand, holding our equipment in the other.

"Are we allowed—"

"Shh!"

For barely being five feet tall, the woman had a voice that carried. She glared up at me, footsteps hesitating.

"Is this a stealth mission?" she asked, mostly in a whisper.

I couldn't lie to G-Mil. "Yes."

Her face broke out into a grin. "Hot dog!"

"Shh!"

She growled at my reprimand but there was an extra spring in her step as we picked our way across the uneven ground to the cemetery. Swiveling my head left and right, I made sure the coast was clear. Last thing I needed was a security guard chasing my eighty-three-year-old grandma. Though based on the way Marlo had to break up the teenagers not long ago, I was betting on Blueball Endless Eternity not having security.

When I found a tombstone that was tall enough for what I had in mind (Otis P. Whitman, deceased in 1913), along with another one nearby that would be the right height for propping up my phone (Bertie Katherine Smith, deceased in 1967), I got G-Mil in place before setting everything up. I had no idea who these two people were but I appreciated their assistance with this photoshoot and I'd be sure to send them one of our finished Christmas cards as a thank-you.

"Okay, here's what we're doing. No smiling. Just hands on the gravestone and look at the camera. I'll have it on a timer, so just hold the pose until the flash goes off." I set up the portable step that would make her taller than me and helped her climb up.

"Is my hair okay?" G-Mil was fussing with the wig I'd gotten her instead of holding on to the gravestone for balance. The wig was pitch black, straight hair, coming down to her waist and covering the black velvet dress I'd picked up at a secondhand shop.

"It's perfect, but stop messing with it or it'll be crooked."

I came to her side quickly, standing next to her, one hand on her shoulder, the other on the tombstone. "Okay, don't smile!"

The flash went off and I stepped over the grassy mound to check the photo. "You smiled."

"I did not!" G-Mil hissed.

"Then why do I see your teeth?" I showed her the picture on my phone.

"I was baring my teeth. Seemed more scary."

I put the phone back on Bertie's stone and reset the timer. "Your Morticia outfit is scary enough. Just be regal in your darkness."

"Regal," she muttered, lifting her nose and posing as I got next to her and assumed my position as Gomez Addams. This three-piece suit was itchy as hell, but I'd make the sacrifice for the best picture we'd ever taken together.

After several more iterations of poses, I had one more in

mind we needed to take so we had things to choose from when a scary voice interrupted us.

"What the hell do you think you're doing?

G-Mil and I both spun around to find Marlo storming toward us, her hair piled on top of her head with strands escaping all around her face. She, too, was dressed in all black, making her and G-Mil a matched set.

"Oh, Marlo!" G-Mil exclaimed, forgetting she was on a step and lurching forward in Marlo's direction.

I reacted, reaching for her and catching her as she tumbled. I heard Marlo gasp, but all I cared about was setting G-Mil back on her feet safely. Her wig was highly askew and her dark lipstick had left a six-inch smear across the vest of my suit.

"You good?" My heart was pounding inside my chest, but I tried to act calm.

"Whoopsie," G-Mil mumbled, stepping on my feet before getting her own firmly planted on the ground. Next thing I knew she was swatting at my chest. "Put me down, you mad Castillian."

I let her go, shaking my head at how far into character she'd gotten. "You're welcome, by the way. For saving your life."

G-Mil winked at me before turning away to address Marlo. "Hello, dear."

"Hello, Milly. Lovely to see you as always."

My jaw dropped. I didn't think Marlo capable of pleasantries. I snapped my mouth shut when Marlo swung her gaze to me, immediately shifting into a disagreeable expression.

"May I ask why you're trespassing again?"

"Again? May I remind you that you have a penchant for flammables? This is only my first trespassing offense. Rushing in to save you like a real-life hero was not trespassing."

Marlo folded her arms across her chest, looking like a cute toddler in the middle of a tantrum. She was wearing pajamas. The kind that button down the front.

"First offense or second, why should I not call the cops and have you arrested?"

I faked outrage, my hand coming to my chest. "You'd have my grandma arrested? Sweet little Milly?"

Marlo's lips wobbled and I thought perhaps the earth had shifted in its rotation. Was she about to smile? She looked over my shoulder and that's when I realized G-Mil was currently sneaking away to the truck without me.

"Did your sweet little grandma just ditch you at the scene of the crime?"

Now it made sense why Marlo was tempted, even for a moment, to smile. Her getting the best of me only made me giddier. Nothing I loved more than a challenge. I'd get Marlo to smile before I died of old age. I was sure of it.

"I'm tired, Vandy. Can I nap up at your place?" G-Mil called out over her shoulder, sounding older and more frail than she had all night.

Marlo and I both followed her, easily catching up, one on either side of her. If I'd taken a second to think about it, I'd want to hug Marlo for caring about my grandma's well-being. G-Mil's wig was hanging so far down her right side, she was in danger of tripping on it. I yanked it off her head and bent down to carefully lift G-Mil into my arms. She yelped at the elevation change.

"Come on. Let's get you up to the house."

G-Mil flailed about for a second, trying to get a line of sight on Marlo. "Oh, Marlo, dear? Will you help my Vandy? I'm too heavy for him to get me up there without help."

"Of course, Milly." Marlo fell into step with me, taking the wig from my hands and running back for the step stool and my cell phone.

While I waited with G-Mil in my arms—who was light as a feather, by the way—I narrowed my eyes at her. The old bat smiled back serenely. I knew that look all too well. She was up to no good.

"Okay, got everything," Marlo said breathlessly, walking next to me as we climbed the hill to the house.

We got to the house and Marlo opened the door for me. "Feel free to grab a drink in the kitchen." At least I'd opened the box that held my tumblers and expensive scotch.

By the time I got G-Mil settled on the couch in the parlor room with a throw blanket over her, Marlo had stacked everything on my kitchen island and leaned against it, foot tapping on the stone floor. She was biting her thumb nail and staring at her shoes. A splash of scotch sat untouched in a glass behind her.

"She okay?" she asked quickly, head popping up when I came into the kitchen. "I didn't mean to startle her. I saw you and came storming over. I didn't realize—"

I held my hand up and she quit talking. "She's fine. You didn't do anything wrong."

Marlo didn't look convinced.

"Milly will outlive all of us, don't you worry." I took off the itchy suit coat and laid it on the counter. Then I attacked the long sleeve shirt, rolling each sleeve up my forearm. "I need to apologize for trespassing."

Marlo swallowed hard, her gaze tracking my movements. "The cemetery closes at nine."

I was suddenly aware of how quiet it was in the kitchen. Even speaking at full volume, in a house this large, Grandma wouldn't be able to hear us. Testing a theory that popped into my head and couldn't possibly be true, I reached up to unbutton the top button of my shirt. Marlo's eyes shifted, zeroing in on my throat. I studied the way her cheeks held color that the rest of her pale skin did not. The way her breathing had kicked up just standing there.

Holy hell, Marlo wants me.

The thought of Marlo, the queen of frowns and insults and general disagreeableness, wanting me, filled me with a joy I couldn't quite understand. I flicked another button open, watched her tongue dart out to lick her lip, and I nearly went rock hard in an instant.

I took a step toward her, watching her like a hawk. Suddenly I wanted to feel the heat of her skin below those satin pajamas. Flick open one of her buttons and see what she did. Would she swipe at me with her nails or beg me to kiss her? I had a feeling whatever she chose would involve pain with the pleasure.

"Maybe I was hoping to run into you again," I said softly, not wanting to break the spell that existed between us here in this kitchen.

Marlo leaned forward, one hand clenching the edge of the aisle counter. "I live right next door. You didn't need to resort to trespassing to see me."

I lifted my hand ever so slowly, finally touching her hair and tucking a wayward lock behind her ear. "Maybe I like seeing you in the moonlight, rage behind those dark brown eyes."

Her long lashes fluttered. I didn't move my hand away from her face, instead tracing the line of her jaw with the side of my thumb. She was soft. So opposite of her personality.

Marlo sucked in a breath and then her head tipped back. Her gaze locked on mine and the rage there turned into something more. Something hotter. Something that would singe us both.

And I was up for a good singeing.

I leaned down, our lips now just a mere inch or two away from each other. I paused, giving her a chance to pull back. To call off this ridiculous kiss between two people who didn't even like each other.

Though that was a total lie. I'd liked Marlo from the beginning. However, the like was entirely one-sided, so if she didn't want my kiss, she needed to tell me now.

Her hand came up and her fingers became iron bars around my wrist. I didn't know if she was pulling me to her or pushing me away. Frankly, I celebrated even these short seconds of being near her.

"Are you going to buy that land?" she whispered, fingers tightening.

My mind began to race. Was this some sort of test? A threat? A way to blackmail me into doing what she wanted?

"Absolutely."

Her eyelids fluttered closed for a brief second and then she was moving. Backwards. Away from me. Her back finally hit the refrigerator and then she was spinning and marching out of the room like there was a ghost after her. I took a brief second to mourn the kiss that never was before racing to follow her.

I caught up to her in the entry, snagging her wrist like she had mine just moments before and spinning her around. She snatched her arm back, eyes now flashing with the rage that had always been there and I mistook for something more.

"Don't you dare try to manipulate me!" she hissed, keeping her voice low for Grandma's sake.

I frowned. "I don't know what you're talking about."

"I know you and Milly are tight. You don't need to flaunt that for me to get the message. And you certainly don't need to pretend to want the weird undertaker woman to get what you want. Just flash the cash and everything you want is yours. I get it. Message received."

And with that confusing bag of words that made absolutely no sense, she ran out the door, down the stairs, and back to her house. I stood on the porch and watched her, making sure she got there safely before coming back inside and trying to piece together what the hell had just happened.

CHAPTER TEN

*M*arlo

A BLACK CLOUD followed me for several days, fueling a pissy mood to the point even my father, who gave me this genetic disposition and understood my cantankerous nature, was giving me a wide berth. Dad carried his grumpiness under a veneer of somberness that suited a second-generation undertaker. I carried mine like a sword of anger and a shield of crankiness.

All I could do was replay every interaction with Vander Booth in a whole new light, looking for the exact moment he'd one-upped me. Knowing that he'd known his own grandmother owned that land, and also knowing I wanted it, made every prior conversation come alive through a red haze of anger. That motherfucker had been playing the long game while I'd been busy hurling elementary-level insults his way.

The phone rang—yes, they still made landline phones— waking me from a particularly wonderful dream where I had a Vander-shaped ditch dug in the cemetery all ready and waiting for him.

"Motherfucker," I muttered, trying to pry my eyes open enough to answer the damn phone.

No one called the cemetery this late—wait, no, this *early*... the sun was just barely brightening the sky outside my window— unless there was a death in the family. Being woken from sleep was simply a reality of being an undertaker. Ever since Dad's heart attack, we'd moved the after-hours telephone into my room.

"Blueball Endless Eternity, may I help you?" My voice sounded hoarse, probably from yelling at Vander in my dreams all night.

"Hey, this is Julie from Sunnyside. Sorry to call so early but we need to schedule a transport from the hospital to the funeral home."

I sat up and scrubbed a hand over my eyes. "I'm sorry to hear that, Julie." Sunnyside was a small retirement home in Blueball. That was the trouble with a small town, I knew everyone who came through my doors. "Who is it?"

"Old man James." Julie sighed.

I frowned. I'd been called twice to collect his body from Sunnyside just in the last six months. James had gotten bored in his golden years, probably because he didn't have any family left and had to entertain himself somehow. He'd faked his own death so many times the staff didn't blink an eye when they walked in his room and found him lying on the floor in a heap. He'd even thinned down ketchup one time to add to the drama.

"Did they check his pulse?"

Julie let out a noise like she laughed, but was trying to muzzle it. "Yes. I asked that too and they told me they even put the elec- trodes on his chest to make sure he hadn't just practiced how to lower his heart rate temporarily."

I threw off the covers. Looked like I had a body to collect. "Okay. I'm on my way."

"Thank you, Marlo. I know I can always count on you."

We hung up and I got ready, pulling on flowy black slacks, my trusty Doc Martens, and a fitted black T-shirt that only showed my white stomach if I raised my hands overhead, which I wasn't planning to do. I ran my fingers through my hair and brushed my teeth, which was the extent of my hygiene. It was too early to fuss with a mascara wand that close to my eyeball.

The drive to the hospital on the other side of town gave me time to examine my bad mood. Mostly because the old transport van didn't go above forty miles an hour. Sure, I had stress on my shoulders about keeping this cemetery running. I was a third-generation Balmero undertaker, tasked with keeping the family business going, but it was more than that. I was feeling left out of the personal side of my life. My best friends were all paired up and starting families while I couldn't get a single date to show up. I tried not to let the comparison poke at old wounds, but it did.

And then there was Vander. The next-door-neighbor pain in the ass. As annoying as he was, that ass was also very nice. For one quick second there in his kitchen, when it looked like he was about to kiss me, I'd let myself dream. I'd let myself believe that a guy like him could be interested in a girl like me. Of course, the truth of the situation came crashing down on me before I'd gotten to experience a kiss from Vander Booth.

He'd been playing me.

I honestly hadn't taken Vander for being one of the weirdos that gets turned on by my profession. Or to be so cruel that he'd try to get me to fall for him just so he could throw it in my face that the land I wanted was one step away from being his already.

I'd wanted to be wrong about him so badly, I'd almost fallen for his charm.

I pulled up outside the back entry to the hospital, putting the old van in gear and hopping down. Charles, the respiratory therapist on staff, was outside having a smoke break, leaning against the building.

"Hey, Charles. Haven't quit that shit yet?"

He did that head-nod thing men do as a way of saying hello.

"Nah. Figure this habit is the only way to end up naked on your table."

I barked out a laugh. Charles was pushing retirement age and happily married, but was never afraid of a little workplace flirting. He was harmless. "Well, I guess if they haven't killed you yet, why stop now, huh?"

He pointed his finger at me, cigarette smoke billowing in the air. "Exactly!" Then he proceeded to hack and I grimaced, walking past him into the hospital corridor.

I knew the hallways like the back of my hand, finding my way to the elevator that would take me to the basement where they kept the morgue. Not a lot of staff were here yet, just the bare-bones night crew before their shift replacements came in at seven. I hit the down button and waited. The elevator doors slid open and I almost walked inside when a man came flying around the corner and skid to a halt, his head on a swivel. Well, fuck. I'd recognize that ass anywhere.

"Vander?"

His wide-eyed gaze landed on me and it only took him a second to start talking. "I'm lost. I need to find the ER. I think I came through the administration offices and now I can't find the ER or a way out. Do you think it's down this way?" He pointed down the hallway from where I'd come. "Or down this way?" He pointed from where he'd come. Then his hands went in his hair and I thought he might cry.

I dealt with a lot of emotional people in my profession, and while I was quick to pass out tissues, I was not used to consoling people wearing gray sweatpants that outlined all the things I'd wondered about my neighbor when I should have been sleeping.

"Vander? Are you okay?" I stepped away from the elevator and put my hand on his arm, tugging his hand away from pulling out his thick hair. "Why do you need the ER?"

I scanned his body again—the first time was like a leftover reflex, I swear—this time for injuries. He looked fine...like really fine, if you know what I mean. I squeezed my eyes shut and berated myself for getting distracted by his body. He was a manipulative asshole and it would do me well to remember that.

"G-Mil. The hospital called me. I raced over here, but I can't find her."

Putting aside my anger toward Vander was natural, given the circumstances. I'd seen people in panics before, and I'd bet my trusty van this guy was on the verge of a breakdown.

"Okay, let's go to the ER." I increased my grip on his forearm and towed him behind me. Thankfully, he wasn't so far gone he couldn't get his feet to cooperate. A few quick turns and a long march down a hallway, and we found ourselves in the waiting room of the ER.

Vander turned the tables on me, and when I released him, he grabbed my forearm and dragged me to the nurses' station. "I'm here to see Milly Booth."

"I'm here for James actually. Last responder," I mumbled, introducing myself and not surprised at all when no one paid me any attention.

"Oh good, she was calling for you earlier. Let's get you back there. You're Vander, I assume?" the nurse asked, standing up and ushering us to one of the exam rooms.

I tried to pull away, but Vander wasn't having it. I found myself by his side as we stepped around a curtain in exam room three and finally saw Milly. She looked tiny in the hospital bed with a mound of blankets on her, oxygen in her nose, and an IV attached to her arm.

Vander finally let me go and sank to his knees, sliding right up to her side. "Grandma! What happened?"

He pulled her hands in his and kissed the backs of them. The gesture was beyond sweet. If I hadn't already known he was an asshole, I would have fallen for him right then and there. Thankfully, I was smarter than that.

Milly pulled a hand away to pat his head, giving him a weak smile. Then she turned her gaze to me and positively beamed. "Oh, hello again, Marlo. I'm so glad you're here."

I raised my eyebrows. Why was she glad *I* was here? I just wanted to pick up a body. Preferably not hers.

"G-Mil, what happened?" Vander asked again. Milly kept stroking Vander's head, and I tried to back out of the room. This wasn't my family. I shouldn't be here.

"Oh, Marlo, dear. What do you call those things old people wear around their necks?" Milly was looking right at me.

I halted my retreat. "Um, a medical alert?"

Milly smiled again. "Yes, that's right. Such a smart girl. Vandy here got me one and I got to use it today! Did you know that the Blueball Fire Department has some hunks on staff?"

"Grandma," Vander groaned. "Forget the firefighters. What happened?"

Milly shot me a wink and I wondered how much morphine they'd given her. She turned her attention to Vander, but I didn't risk leaving the room. I felt awkward staying but I didn't want to sneak out and hurt Milly's feelings either. I was in a bad mood, but I wasn't a monster.

"I was getting dressed this morning and my foot must not have been all the way through the leg hole of my underwear and I tried again to get it in there, but then my toe got caught and I lost my balance. Next thing you know, I'm on the ground with my undies around my ankles. Good news is I fell on my right hip, which they replaced two years ago with titanium or something, so the damage isn't so bad. I'm practically Iron Man."

I walked back into the room fully, wanting to hear this. Morphine Milly was hilarious.

Vander groaned again, standing up but not letting go of her hand. "And the bad news?"

Milly scoffed. "I would think that's obvious. The firemen showed up and I didn't even have my underwear on! Talk about embarrassing!"

Vander's chin dropped to his chest. I was busy shaking with suppressed laughter. Milly was oblivious to it all.

"So, that's it. It's too dangerous," Milly announced, louder than a freight train whistle in the dead of night. "I'm going commando from now on!"

There it was. There was the bad news we were waiting for.

Vander leaned over and whispered in my ear. "Let that sink into your soul."

My lips wobbled and my shoulders shook. I squeezed my eyes shut yet again and reminded myself why I hated Vander. I would not be swayed by his sweetness toward his grandma. I would not let Grandma Milly charm me just like her grandson. I had valid reasons to dislike the rumpled and frantic man beside me. I could sympathize and extend my well-wishes without feelings becoming attached. With my resolve firmly in place, I opened my eyes again.

I leaned down to kiss Milly's cheek and whispered my goodbyes and good lucks.

"I do hope you'll come visit me, dear." She smiled so sweetly I couldn't say no.

"Will do, Milly. You just focus on healing."

Then I turned to Vander, staring at his chin instead of his sparkling eyes or the dimple of distraction. "Gotta go, have a body to get in the van."

I swept past him, but he snagged my arm at the last minute, shifting away from Milly to say in a low tone, "Thank you, Marlo. I was panicking back there and you helped me. I won't forget that."

My heart pitter-pattered at the use of my real name for the first time like he'd confessed something significant, but my head knew better. I simply nodded and pulled my arm away from his grasp. No more touching Vander. No more visiting his house. No more looking for him outside my bedroom window. Vander was officially dead to me now.

Thankfully, I was used to dealing with dead people.

ander

THE REST of the week had flown by, mostly because I'd spent my time driving back and forth from the hospital to check on G-Mil and my own house where I'd hired a team to unpack my boxes and set up the guest room. At the rate I was going on my own, I'd be fully moved into my house sometime next year, and that timeframe just wouldn't do now that Grandma was injured. We were lucky she'd evaded a hip fracture, but she was still sore and bruised. The doctors had firmly suggested ongoing physical therapy, to which Grandma had asked if the therapist was cute. I'd narrowly escaped banging my head against the wall.

This morning, I'd broached the subject of her moving in with me temporarily and she'd taken it well. Her existing house was small, but cute, set in a great part of town. I knew she'd miss her neighbors, but this recent injury had highlighted that she needed a caretaker. And nobody would take more care of my grandma than me.

As I smoothed my hands down my sweater and second-guessed my outfit for the tenth time, I reminded myself that tonight was supposed to be fun and casual. Just a hangout with new friends. Nothing to be anxious about. Certainly no reason to wonder if a pair of three-hundred-dollar jeans would be frowned upon here in Blueball. Should I have bought a pair of Levi's with the crease in it? I tried to remember what Gannon, Lincoln, and Boston had been wearing when I met them, but my mind was blank.

"You're likable, Booth," I muttered to myself as I climbed in the truck and headed into town, trying to calm my nerves with positive self-talk. "Just be yourself."

As was common with my self-talks, I talked back to myself. I firmly believed that was a sign of intelligence, not mental illness.

"That strategy is working so well with Marlo." I huffed. "Although I don't think she's exactly typical. At least, not where I'm from. Maybe Blueball does things differently."

Now I was more nervous, wondering if I should have brushed up on some *day of the dead* jokes to fit in, or maybe they wouldn't understand my sweater's importance and judge me for wearing homemade goods, or maybe even my haircut was all wrong. I was good at being the life of the party when I didn't care about the people at the party. When it came down to actually making friends, I was horrifically awkward. I parked down the street from Paisley's house and told my shaking legs to do their thing. My rapid heart rate would just have to keep up.

"Face it, Booth. You suck at making friends," I muttered. Hey, I never said I was good at these pep talks.

The sound of a door closing had me spinning around. A purple box on wheels had parked right behind me. Marlo. Our gazes snagged and we both rolled our eyes.

"Talking to yourself again?" she drawled. I could barely see her. With black clothing and dark hair that blended into the night behind her, all I saw was a floating white face coming toward me.

"Already cracking the jokes," I replied, trying to sound casual and failing. At least to my own ears.

Marlo's head tilted as she came right up to me. From that close I could see the eyeliner she'd added to her top lids, along with the mascara that made her eyelashes impossibly long. Her dark brown eyes were pretty on any given day, but dressed up like that, they were haunting.

"Are you..." Marlo trailed off, still staring at me intently. I wanted to turn and run, but I didn't want to leave her in the dark. "Are you *nervous?*"

She practically shouted the last word. I swiveled my head but didn't see anyone else out and about, eavesdropping on our conversation. "Of course not," I scoffed.

Marlo's eyes squinted. "Swear on your grandma Milly's life that you're not nervous."

My spine snapped straight. "Hey. Nobody messes with G-Mil."

Marlo's smile bloomed like a rose in the afternoon sunlight, slow and methodical. When it took over her face completely, it took my breath away. Fuck me, this woman was prettier than any celebrity I'd ever seen. She was gorgeous when she frowned, but her smile put her somewhere in the stratosphere of angels. I was witnessing a miracle.

"You *are* nervous."

I blinked, still trying to form a coherent thought while basking in the first Marlo smile I'd ever witnessed. "Don't ever stop that," I whispered.

Her smile stayed but her eyes lost the glimmer. "What? Giving you shit?"

"No. Smiling."

Her smile faltered then, falling by degrees. Mentally, I kicked myself in the ass for making her lose the smile. I felt like I'd snapped the stem of a rose and threw it to the ground, making the perfect petals wilt and die. My brain spun and I tried to come up with something to say that would bring it back.

"I actually am nervous," I rushed. "I don't make friends easily."

The faded smile dropped into an expression of shock. "You? Vander Booth? The same guy who ran up to help a stranger in the middle of a cemetery? Or again on the side of the road? You don't make friends easily?"

I shot her a grin. "Whoa. That's a lot of questions, Bubbles."

She snorted and began to walk down the sidewalk. I dashed after her, falling into step. "People who give other people nicknames immediately upon meeting them don't have problems making friends."

She sounded so sure of herself I almost believed her. Except I'd lived the opposite my whole life. "Oh really? What if I told you I give people nicknames because I'm desperately trying to get them to like me and think of me as a friend?"

I winced, even as her footsteps faltered. She spun toward me and snagged my sweater sleeve. I stopped, but kept looking down the block at Paisley's house, wishing I'd just kept my mouth shut. Precisely one other person knew about my social phobia and she was currently back at my house sleeping after the pain pill I'd given her.

"Are you being serious right now?"

I dropped my head to look at the toe of my shoes. See, this was why I never brought this shit up. Everyone took one look at me working the room and assumed I had a long list of friends. They had no idea that under all those jokes and in-your-face charisma was a lonely guy without a single friend of substance. Well, other than G-Mil.

Turning to Marlo, I made myself look directly at her. She'd looked me in the eyes without pants on. I could at least be that brave in return. "Listen. I want to make Blueball my permanent home, which means I want real friends. And I'm not good at that. I can be the life of the party, but deeply connecting with people is not my forte. Make fun of me all you want, but that's the truth."

I pulled away from her and began to walk again. I heard the heavy thud of her boots as she caught up. She didn't say a word the rest of the way, but she stayed by my side during the initial introductions and small talk until I got pulled into the kitchen by Gannon with promises of another beer. I tried not to think that maybe she felt sorry for me and thought I needed assistance, but I couldn't lie to myself. Having her next to me as we entered the house and got reintroduced to everyone had helped me be less nervous.

"Okay, so how many country songs do you know?" Gannon asked, handing me another longneck beer after he popped the top off of it.

I shrugged, wishing I could give him the answer I thought he wanted. "Um, well, a few, On. I know about friends in low places and waiting in the truck and letting the liquor talk. But I mostly know classic rock."

Boston was nodding along sagely. "We can work with that."

Lincoln nudged me, looking excited. "Dude, tell me you can do some Led Zeppelin. They have some wicked drum solos."

Gannon hooted out a laugh. "You want a drum solo? How about Phil Collins?"

"What?!" Lincoln looked offended.

Gannon bopped him on the back of the head. "'In the Air Tonight,' dummy. That song is straight fire for a drummer."

"I don't know. Inc and I don't really jive with Phil Collins." I came to Lincoln's defense.

Boston scratched the side of his head. "I'm confused. Is Inc Lincoln?"

All heads turned to look at me. I thought back to what I'd told Marlo. "Yeah, sorry about that. I tend to give people nicknames in my head. On is Gannon. Inc is Lincoln."

Gannon cracked up while Boston looked curious. "What's mine?"

I grinned. "You can only be Sto."

The guys cracked up and I felt like maybe, just maybe, they'd accept me into their tight circle.

Gannon pointed his beer at me. "Only if you can be Der."

All of us cracked up again.

"What's all this laughing for?" Paisley walked into the kitchen, red Solo cup in hand. The other ladies were right behind her, but my gaze zeroed in on Marlo. She was looking at everyone's faces, before settling on mine. I wanted to think she was worried about me.

"Vander's got nicknames for all of us," Gannon explained.

Paisley snuggled into his side while looking over at me. "Is that why you called me Ais the other day?"

I nodded.

"And Marlo gets Bubbles?" Keva interjected. "That seems to break the trend."

I couldn't hold Marlo's gaze. "She's special."

The girls all started talking at once, but Gannon cut through the hubbub. "Let's head to the stage outside and practice, boys!"

The group headed out, traipsing through the glampground Gannon had opened just over a year ago. I didn't know much about the glampground business, but this place was what G-Mil would describe as adorable. The trailers were mostly throwbacks that had been restored. Fire pits, horseshoes, volleyball courts, and hot tubs dotted the areas in between glampsites. I could see why couples and families would want to stay here for their get-back-to-nature vacations.

Beneath a huge oak tree, there was a wooden dance floor in front of a makeshift stage. It wasn't fancy, but it was cozy with white string lights crossing over the whole thing. Heat lamps and speakers dotted the edges of the dance floor and picnic tables had been built around the perimeter for those who chose not to dance. The guys took to the stage and Gannon waved me over.

"Just sing any of the lyrics you know. We can get a monitor out here at some point if you want to do it karaoke-style."

I looked around and saw that no one else had a microphone. "Am I the only one singing?"

"I can do backup if necessary, but I prefer to just jam on my banjo," Boston said, voice a deep rumble that brooked no argument. The guy was huge. I'd bet no one argued with him. Ever. Plus who was I to deny a guy his precious banjo time?

The ladies sat at the tables and kept up a steady stream of conversation amongst themselves. No one was really looking at us, which helped my return flare of nerves. I didn't normally care about looking like a fool, but I wanted to be friends with these guys. They obviously cared about their little band and I didn't want to ruin it for them. So I kept my back to the dance floor and focused in on the music they were playing, singing without the microphone when I knew the songs.

"Hey, we want to hear it too!"

A feminine shout brought up all our heads. Looking over my shoulder, I could see that more people had joined the party. All the picnic benches were filled and even more people milled about. Everyone had a drink in their hands, ready to celebrate the week being over.

"All right, boys. You heard the ladies, let's give them what they want," Gannon said with a cocky grin.

"Uh, you sure we're ready for that?" I asked. Normally, bands had a play list, or at least a few private practices first. Right?

"Totally ready," Lincoln answered, hitting his sticks together before beating a steady rhythm on the drums that got everyone cheering in anticipation.

"Just sing the stuff you know. If you don't know it, body surf or something," Boston added unhelpfully.

Body surf? I mouthed.

Gannon cracked up and the bastards all started playing a country song. Thankfully I recognized it quickly and even knew most of the words, so I sang. When I didn't know the words, I made them up or danced around the stage, the cheer of the crowd egging me on. Pretty soon I forgot I was trying to make friends and just lost myself in performing for a crowd. I was good at that shit.

One song turned into another and then another. I couldn't find Marlo amongst all the people dancing, but I hoped she was still there. When we were sweaty and parched, Gannon called for a break. We jumped off the stage, and before I could get lost in the crowd, Gannon grabbed me by the sweater and led me to the coolers of beer, handing me one before taking a long pull on his.

"It's official. You're part of the Blueball Band of Brothers."

Boston let out a *hooah* in my left ear that promised hearing damage and Lincoln clapped me on the back so hard I choked on my beer. As for me, I was grinning from ear to ear. I'd made friends. Real friends. I lifted my beer bottle in the air.

"To the BBB!"

CHAPTER TWELVE

$\mathcal{M}$arlo

I was not staring at Vander.

I was not staring so hard I missed half the conversation at the picnic benches while the boys played their little instruments.

"So, you're in agreement, Marlo?" Paisley nudged me, patting Aster on the back as she lay on her mama's shoulder and fought off sleep.

"Uh..." My brain scrambled, trying to come up with what she was talking about. "Sure?"

"She said yes!" Keva shouted so loudly Cora began to cry from the pouch strapped to Keva's chest. Keva rubbed her back and swayed side to side, resorting to whispering again. "No take-backsies!"

I rubbed the spot between my eyebrows that was starting to ache. Normally these jam sessions were fun and relaxing, a time to sit back with my friends and forget about my troubles. But half my troubles was now on the damn stage looking mighty fine in those stupid expensive jeans and the Mr. Rogers sweater that was hideous but secretly adorable. What man wears a sweater in public that his grandma made him??

"What are we? In second grade?" I snarked back.

Audrey reached across the table and grabbed my hands. "It's a great plan. Honestly. We voted and you agreed and now it's a done deal."

"What's a done deal?" My friends were starting to piss me off, and if I had to hear one more song with Vander crooning the words in that velvety growl of his, I was going to jump off this bench and walk home, just to burn off this excess energy. And then I was going to have a long session with my vibrator because things were unsettled in my gut. Very, very unsettled.

Paisley smirked. "If you'd been listening, you would know."

I shot her a look that had her making the motion of zipping her lips. Paisley was stronger than me, but I knew more ways to kill a person.

"You agreed to make a move on Vander," Keva whisper-shouted.

"What?" I scrunched up my face even though every other body part of mine let out a tingly, exuberant yes. "No. Absolutely not."

Audrey sighed, patting my hands. "Don't you miss orgasms?"

"I have orgasms, thank you very much." That's what toys were for. Duh.

They all looked at each other and I wanted to vomit. I knew that look. That look came right before they gushed about how great their sex life was while I sat here like a sexless fucking bump on a log. I went to stand, but the picnic bench seats were problematic with the number of beers I drank tonight to distract myself from Vander up on the stage. That and Audrey yanked me back down. She was stronger than she looked.

"We all can see the electric energy between you two anytime you're in the same room. Why not act on it?"

I pulled my hands from Audrey's grasp and addressed the group of women that didn't seem to care that they were crossing the line into something that was none of their business. That was what besties were for I guessed.

"I'm not going to act on it. I don't like him. And he's going to take the land I want. Doing anything beyond giving him the evil eye every chance I get would only complicate matters."

"Yeah, but complicating matters leads to some hot sex," Audrey drawled.

"Ew. Please. Not this again." Keva shook her head violently until Cora began to stir. "That's my brother you're talking about."

They all started talking at once about things I didn't care to hear, so I finished my beer and tried again to get up from the table. "Thanks for a lovely evening, but I have an early morning appointment and then an embalming. Big day. Need my rest."

I only made it a few steps away before they were hollering some last-minute advice.

"Think about it!"

"Nothing wrong with eking out some enjoyment in life!"

"Quit observing life and jump in, girl!"

That last one hit me between the eyes and burrowed into my brain as I walked through the glampground to my car. I liked blending into the background and observing life around me. It gave me the peace and quiet to figure things out. Sure, every now and then I felt left out. Sometimes life seemed to move along without me. Hell, that was happening more and more lately, but that didn't mean I should jump into something unwise. Right?

Footsteps sounded behind me and I startled, realizing they'd been behind me for awhile. I pulled my keys out of my pocket and flicked open the switchblade. When the footsteps sounded about ten feet away, I twirled, brandishing the weapon.

"Jesus!" Vander slid and hit the ground, before tucking and rolling into a crouch with his hands up in peace. It was fairly athletic, to be honest, which was so on point for him. Was there anything he couldn't do?

I dropped my arm and put the blade away. "What the hell, Vander?"

He slowly stood back up, but kept a respectable distance. "I was calling your name."

I frowned, realizing I must have been deep in thought to not hear him. "Oh. Well. That'll teach you to sneak up on a woman in the dark."

His face transformed into a grin. "See? I'm not good at this murder thing."

He was right. He'd sounded like a herd of elk coming up behind me. "Stick to your singing career maybe."

He took a step and was suddenly right in front of me. The features I could barely make out a moment ago in the darkness were now so close I could see how he had a bead of sweat on the side of his temple. His hair was wild and adorably messy from running his fingers through it while he sang. Not that I'd been staring.

"You like my voice, Bubbles?" he asked, voice so low and raspy I shivered.

"Sadly, yes." My friends' insane advice ran through my brain, but I rejected it.

His grin only intensified. "I was hoping you stayed."

I frowned to combat all the warm and fuzzies that were trying to snatch up space in my body. We didn't do that shit around here. "What for? To finally murder me?"

Vander kept smiling, shaking his head slowly. "No, silly. To thank you. You helped me at the hospital and then you stayed by my side until I felt comfortable tonight. You didn't make fun of me for being nervous."

I shrugged, feeling uncomfortable accepting his thanks for something I did begrudgingly. "I hate social interactions too, so I get it."

Vander's hand came up and pushed my hair behind my shoulder, then skimmed my arm as it came down. I swallowed hard and refused to let myself shiver at his touch. One shiver a day was my maximum.

"You have some great friends. I envy you."

How had he gotten even closer? I could smell the cologne mixed with sweat and it was the best thing I'd ever smelled in my life. I mean, his smell beat out bacon.

"They'll be your friends too. Just keep being your friendly self." How many times could I say friend? Was my voice wobbling? What the hell?

"Speaking of being friendly..." Vander's hand was back, cupping my jaw and making my eyelashes flutter like I was a moth drawn to a flame. His head dropped just enough to graze his lips over mine, as if asking permission.

My body must have said yes because his sweater was now fisted in my hands and his head slanted for more. My eyelids gave up the fight and now all I saw was a pleasant darkness that left all my other senses on high alert. I breathed in his cologne. I felt his tongue push between my lips. I tasted the beer he drank in between songs. I felt the heat of him press against me like a space heater on a cold morning. And his hands. Holy shit, his hands were everywhere, skimming along my body and molding me to him.

If his kiss was hesitant at first, his touch was not. The man was memorizing every dip and valley of my body before sweeping back to touch me again. God help me, I kissed him back. I never meant to kiss Vander. Ever. But now that he'd broken that seal, I was all in. And so was he if that groan from the back of his throat was any indication.

My back hit something hard and cold. Much later I realized Vander had turned us and pressed me up against the side of his truck. His hands lifted my one leg and wrapped it around his hip. I ground against the hard length he now sported in those jeans. The darkness behind my eyeballs exploded into darts of light. I panted into his mouth and pulled him closer.

"Yeah, Bubbles, just like that. Use me." Vander plucked kisses from my lips that weren't nearly deep enough for my liking.

"Shut up." I let go of his sweater and grabbed his head, holding him while I deepened the kiss. He took over, undulating his hips and rubbing his erection right where I needed him. How the man knew the exact spot that would send me over the edge, I'd never know. Right then, in the moment, I didn't care. I just wanted him to never stop.

I felt it building. I knew it was just a matter of seconds before I embarrassed myself, but I couldn't stop it. Wouldn't stop it. Because dammit, Audrey was right. I missed the orgasms from an actual real live man.

When the wave hit in the next second, I threw my head back and whimpered my pleasure into the night sky. My whole body shook and Vander buried his face in my neck, giving me everything I needed until I was finally quiet and limp in his arms.

I blinked my eyes open as Vander sniffed my neck. What the fuck was he doing?

"Damn, Bubbles, you smell so good." He pulled back with the cockiest smirk I'd ever seen on a man. "I know I'm good, but damn, that might be a record."

I narrowed my eyes and tried to get my breathing under control. "Don't get full of yourself. It's not you, Annoying. I just orgasm easily."

Now Vander narrowed his eyes. "What do you mean?"

I shrugged and pulled my leg down from his hip, refusing to pay attention to the tent he was sporting in his pants. Not my problem. "I orgasm at the drop of a hat. It's a condition actually."

I'd looked it up freshman year of high school, but had never gone to see a doctor about it. Could you imagine trying to explain that? I'd gotten through school by learning to keep a perfectly straight face no matter what my body was doing. It's actually frowned upon to wiggle in your seat during an algebra final and have an orgasm in a class of thirty kids. Thankfully, no one had ever guessed my secret. My poker face was legendary.

Vander's mouth dropped open. He looked like a kid on Christmas morning. "That's fantastic!"

I put my hand on his chest and tried to push him back. He didn't budge, so I put my hand in my pocket and fingered the switchblade. I wasn't afraid to brandish it.

"No, it's not fantastic. I have accidental orgasms sometimes. It can actually be very inconvenient."

Vander put his hands in his hair, smiling like a loon. Did I just blow his mind? "Wait. So, like, what could cause an orgasm?"

I looked around, wondering how I'd gotten here to this conversation. Oh that's right. I'd kissed Vander when I promised myself that would only complicate things. Technically he kissed me, so maybe it wasn't so bad. Though I *had* orgasmed and told him my secret, so that was probably not the best idea. It was just that he'd been so open with his friend-making anxiety, I felt like I owed him a secret too. A secret exchange to keep the cosmos in balance.

"Anything, really. A shirt that rubs against my breasts. Sitting in a car that vibrates too much. Tickling."

Vander put his hands on my shoulders, leaning back in so that all I could see was him. His eyes were practically dancing inside his eye sockets. "This is fantastic, Bubbles. Can I do it again?"

My eyebrows pulled together. "What? Make out?"

He was nodding like a bobblehead. "Yes. Make out. Tickle. Play with your nipples. I want to find all the things that make you come."

My jaw dropped while my thighs violently clenched. Shit. Add dirty talking to the list of things that made me come. "Why?"

"Because, I don't know if you know this, but I find you super hot. And intriguing, which is just what my brain needs. I get bored easy and I have a feeling you would never be boring.

I want to make you do it again. I want to press your O-button."

My O-button. Jesus. What the hell was happening here?

"I don't want a relationship," I stated clearly. Not with him. He was not marrying potential. I wanted a long, happy, cohesive marriage like my parents. I didn't even like Vander.

"I don't either!" Vander answered like this was a good thing.

"I don't get it."

Vander cupped my face, which felt sweet and very relationship-y. "We both don't want a relationship. So, it's just sex. Just finding your orgasm buttons."

"Just sex?" I repeated in a daze. My mind was rolling that idea around and finding not one reason not to do it. "Please no. Oh, God, no. That would be terrible."

Vander froze, then grinned. "You're teasing again, aren't you? See? You're not boring!"

"I'll be sure to put that on my gravestone," I deadpanned.

"You should. It's the highest compliment." Vander leaned down and kissed me. "So, we're good? We're doing this?"

"Wait." I wasn't one to jump off cliffs without investigating all the ways it could go wrong. "Are there any rules?"

Vander shrugged, still cupping my face. "Just sex. I think that's the extent of my rules."

I rolled my eyes. Of course. What a man thing to say. "I have a few."

He nodded once. "Name them."

I held my hand in front of his face, counting the rules off on my fingers as they came to me. "One. It's just sex. Two. If you don't get me off in five minutes, it's not going to happen, so bring your A game. Three. Nothing in front of friends. Four. We keep this whole situation a secret. Five. This has nothing to do with that land we both want."

He barely blinked and I figured my rules had pissed him off. His jaw tightened into granite with each one I listed. "So I'm your dirty secret now, Marlo?"

I let my hand drop to my side. He could take it or leave it. Frankly, it would be far smarter to leave it. We were only playing with fire. "Yep."

Vander made a fist and pulled it back, letting out a celebratory whoop that startled me. "I've always wanted to be a dirty secret!"

For fuck's sake.

CHAPTER THIRTEEN

ander

TODAY WAS GOING to be a good day. I could feel it in my bones. Despite Marlo telling me to go home last night before I could explore this new agreement we'd made, I felt just as happy getting Marlo's phone number as I did when I saw the number of zeroes on the purchase deal for my company. When I'd asked for her number, she'd made a stink face, and I was pretty sure her hand was still on that switchblade.

But she gave it to me. Maybe the orgasm had softened her rough edges.

Maybe there was a time limit on the softening after an

orgasm. I, for one, couldn't wait to test that theory about textual orgasms.

> Me: Ooh. We'll have to try that later. Right now I'm late getting G-Mil to her appointment.

Marlo didn't respond, even though I stared at my phone for two whole minutes I couldn't afford, waiting for some kind of text. When nothing came through, I just chuckled and shoved my phone back in my pocket. Marlo was the most unique person I'd ever met. Apparently unique was my catnip.

I came to a halt in the hallway, seeing G-Mil using her walker to ever so slowly shuffle to the front door.

"Mildred Booth, what are you doing up on your own?"

She stood up straight and shot me a look over her shoulder that rivaled Marlo's anytime I tried to crack a joke. "I'm not an invalid, Vandy. I can do what I damn well please."

I opened the front door and then got my hand on her elbow, making sure she stayed steady on her feet. She was a tough broad, having given up the pain meds two days ago. Said she was just a little stiff and needed to move to get back on her feet and back in her house. Based on the snail's pace we were moving at, I knew she had at least a few weeks of recovery at my place.

"What the hell is all that shit?" she squawked, getting her first look at the chair lift I'd had added to the front of the house. Her bedroom was on the first floor, but if she wanted to leave the house, she had to deal with the ten steps from the front door. A chair lift was necessary. "Please tell me you didn't break your promise about spending a small fortune on stupid things!"

I rolled my eyes and helped her get into the chair before locking her in and hitting the start button. The thing actually moved pretty fast. I'd asked the guys to take the governor off the speed controls when they were here setting it up. G-Mil let out a whoop that made me smile. Her arms came up in the air like she was on a roller coaster. The chair glided smoothly to the bottom, and with a quick click, the electric motor turned off.

"I take it back, Vandy boy!" G-Mil called over her shoulder. "Let's do that again."

Her attitude had completely changed as I came down to get her out of the chair. "We will when we get back, but we're going to be late if we don't get going." Once I had her in the truck and belted in, I ran over to the driver's side and started the engine. "Where exactly are we going?"

G-Mil clutched her purse on her lap like she might have gold bars in there and I was a potential robber. "We're going to Blueball Endless Eternity."

I nearly ran us off my driveway and into the ditch. Honestly, I should have seen this coming. G-Mil was a notorious matchmaker and I'd given her way too much ammunition where Marlo was concerned.

"Like, to say hello? Or...?"

G-Mil wouldn't meet my gaze. "We have an official appointment. I think it's time we pick out my casket and plot, don't you?"

"Um, no, actually. You're going to live way past a hundred."

G-Mil chuckled. "Absolutely. But it doesn't hurt to have all the details squared away. Just in case."

I didn't like thinking of what "just in case" entailed, but I did like the idea of seeing Marlo so soon after last night. G-Mil leaned over and cranked the volume button, spilling big band music through the speakers. I frowned at the radio dials. When the hell had she changed all my presets to her music?

I quickly forgot about that when the funeral home came into view again and I pulled into a parking space right outside the front door. I could have walked over, obviously, but G-Mil wasn't up for that long of a walk quite yet. It took a few minutes to get her out of the truck and into the funeral home, but when we stepped inside, I looked around in awe. The place was charming. And homey. And exactly the kind of place you'd want to be when you were grieving. Soft music played from the speakers, fresh flowers dotted a few tables here and there, and even the carpet was cushy beneath our feet.

"Good morning," Marlo greeted us, coming around the corner and coming to an abrupt halt when she saw who was standing there. She quickly schooled her features and approached Grandma. "Oh, Milly, I didn't realize you were coming by. I have an appointment right now."

G-Mil patted Marlo's hand. "I know, dear. I'm Ms. Smith."

Marlo blinked while I bit back a laugh. Leave it to G-Mil to be sneaky about things just to add a spot of fun to her day. "Oh. Um, okay. Then come on back to my office. We have coffins so nice you'll die to have one."

Marlo turned away from our shocked laughter and walked slowly down the hallway to our right, looking darkly beautiful in a swishy skirt thing that was actually pants but so voluminous it looked like a skirt. She'd swapped out her kick-'em-in-the-ass boots for another pair that had a pointy heel. Her black blouse was see-through and feminine, making me want to peel it off of her to get to the tight camisole underneath. She came to a stop and held out her hand, pointing to two comfortable chairs.

"Would you like some coffee or water, Milly?" Marlo asked, so politely I found myself staring at her. She was never this nice to me.

"Coffee with plenty of cream would be delightful, dear."

"I'll be right back with your coffee." Marlo stepped out of the room, and once G-Mil was mostly settled in her chair, I followed Marlo, catching up to her in a little room toward the back that was a kitchenette.

"Hey."

Marlo jolted and almost dropped the coffee mug she had in her hand. Her dark eyes, lined with black eyeliner and crowned with long lashes, studied me from the tips of my shoes to the top of my hair. When she licked her lips, I went semi-hard. I'd always thought she was hot, even that first night in her ugly underwear, but now that I'd kissed her, I knew we had chemistry. The kind of chemistry that could cause another fire just as hot as the one that had burned her.

"Not now, Vander."

The smirk came naturally. I knew where her brain had gone. The same gutter mine was in.

I leaned in and traced my thumb across her bottom lip. I felt her suck in a gulp of air, which didn't help the situation in my pants. With more regret than I could ever express, I let myself get one whiff of her intoxicating scent and then pulled away.

"I, uh." I had to clear my throat to get the words out. "I wanted a cup of coffee too."

Now it was her turn to smirk. "Well, I guess we know touching my lip won't get the job done." She winked and I had to literally spin on my heel and wait in the hallway, begging my erection to go down before I had to sit next to my grandma and talk about her impending death.

Marlo kept up a steady string of conversation with G-Mil, smoothly going through a presentation she'd probably done a thousand times before without it sounding like she'd memorized it. G-Mil picked out a casket, but then slumped in her chair suddenly.

"Oh, I'm so tired," she wailed dramatically.

Marlo jumped to her feet, but I wasn't alarmed. I was impressed. Grandma made all the costumes for the kids in plays and musicals in town for one reason: she used to be an actor in the Blueball community theatre program years ago. The woman could act.

"I better take a snooze in the car while Vandy wraps things up for me," G-Mil finished.

"Of course. Can I get you anything? Water?" Marlo looked distressed. "A doctor?"

I helped G-Mil get to her feet and use the walker to exit the office. "She's fine. Just needs to rest. Give me one minute."

When I got G-Mil to the truck, I shot her an unamused smile. "I know what you're doing."

She didn't blink an eye. "I figured you would. Now don't let my efforts be in vain. Flirt with that woman!"

I snorted and made sure she was situated in the truck. "You're a character, G-Mil."

"Takes one to know one!" she shouted right before I slammed the door. She smiled innocently through the glass as I shot her the middle finger. But I was also a bit appreciative. Now I had a reason to spend time around the one woman who had ever caught my interest.

"Is she okay?" Marlo asked the second I came through the front door.

I put my hands on her shoulders, liking how she was almost as tall as me in those heels. "She's fine except for her nose."

Marlo's persistent frown got deeper. "Her nose?"

"She keeps sticking it in other people's business," I answered, lifting my hands and steering her back toward her office before she could ask more questions. "You have another appointment after us?"

"No. Not until after lunch." Marlo dug her heels in right at the door to her office. "What are you doing?"

I crowded her back against the doorjamb. My hands went to her hips and I knew she could feel my erection pressing into her belly. "You ever orgasm in your office, Bubbles?"

Her nose wrinkled. "Knowing at any given time there's usually a dead body just a room or two away?"

I shrugged. "Maybe not the perfect situation but I can deal if you can." I leaned down and kissed her neck, getting a lungful of her scent. She smelled like wildflowers, mystery, and formaldehyde.

Her shiver gave her away. "I can deal." The words came out on a moan.

I grinned against her skin and backed her into the office, kicking the door shut behind me. Stepping back, I gave her the once-over. So much landscape to cover, so little time before she kicked me out.

"Experiment number one. Let's start with your nipples, shall we?"

The color was back in her cheeks, making her absolutely stunning. She stood there, letting me look my fill, neither hiding nor flaunting. As if to say that this was what she had to offer, take it or leave it.

And I was most definitely not leaving it.

"Unbutton your blouse, Ms. Balmero."

One eyelid twitched. "I hate my last name."

That simply wouldn't do. A perfect woman couldn't hate her own name. "Why?"

Her shoulders delicately lifted and dropped. "Try being the undertaker's daughter with a last name so close to what we actually do every day: embalm bodies."

That sounded like a challenge to me. I lifted my hand and motioned to her chest region. "That shirt's not going to unbutton itself, Ms. Balmero." At her immediate frown, I explained. "When I get done with you, you're going to love your last name."

Her tongue darted out to lick her bottom lip. Her fingers shook but she got started on her buttons, pulling the blouse off her shoulders and letting it fall to the carpet. Her breasts weren't large, but her nipples must have known they were my target today. They strained against the thin black camisole, like they were trying to escape their confines and find my fingers.

"Back against the wall."

Marlo took two steps back and stopped with her back against the wall and her head next to a framed picture of a pasture. Her breathing was picking up and I was rock hard. I stood right in front of her, refusing to let any part of my body touch hers.

"Whatever you do, don't look away from me. Got it?"

"Lots of rules, Mr. Booth."

I grinned. "I only had the one actually."

Lifting my hands, I barely brushed my palms against her nipples. She gasped and her eyelids fluttered, but she didn't break our staring contest. I wanted to watch her fall apart and I had a feeling I wouldn't need anything but a finger or two to get it done.

Without warning, I pinched both nipples. Hard. Marlo let out a stuttered wail, but her breaths were coming in pants now. Toying with the tightening buds, her whole body began to shake. She looked at me like I held the keys that controlled her body. It was a heady feeling.

"You're stunning, Ms. Balmero," I said through a clenched jaw.

A few more tweaks and she was gasping, her eyes going wide. She came with a stifled scream and a whimper that was music to my ears. I didn't let go of her nipples until she slumped against the wall. Fuck, that was hot. Watching her fall apart while she stared into my eyes.

My dick didn't understand this wasn't about him. I hadn't taken matters into my own hands last night even though I wanted to. Badly. I wanted this ache in my balls. I wanted to be so hard I felt like I was losing my mind. Because when I finally sank into Marlo's heat, I intended to make us both come so hard we felt like those bodies on her table in the back room.

Marlo's hand came up to cup my balls suddenly and I jumped. She smirked. "Go take Milly home, Mr. Booth. I have work to do. In fact, people are dying to work with me."

My lips tugged at her dark joke. "So it's like that, huh?" I adjusted myself and she watched with avid attention. My undertaker goddess was a thirsty girl. "Get you off and off I go?"

Marlo shrugged and sat back down in her chair, blouse already over her arms and waiting to be buttoned back up. "Rule number one. Just sex."

I was harder than I'd ever been before, but not even the pain could make me stop smiling. Not when Marlo still sported a flush to her cheeks that I'd put there.

"I'll see you soon, Ms. Balmero."

And with that, I walked out, spending a good five minutes at the funeral home's front door, thinking of pickles in tuna and nails on chalkboards, trying to get myself under control before I drove G-Mil home. I heard Marlo moving about the funeral home as if that orgasm hadn't happened.

Which was fine by me.

I was playing the long game.

And I loved a good cat-and-mouse chase.

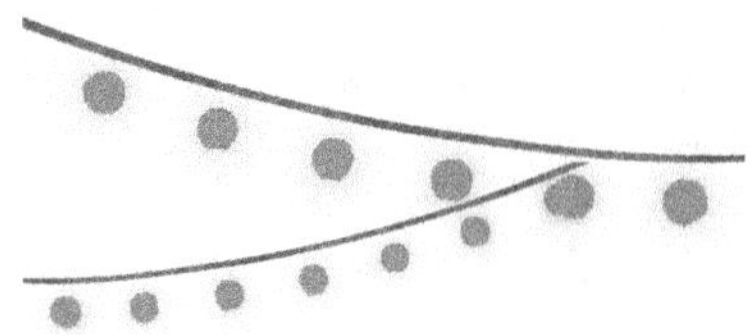

Gannon: Familiarize yourself with this top country hits list for next Friday.

Me: Only if you say please.

Gannon: Fuck off.

Lincoln: Let's not piss off our lead singer so early on in our band's formation, huh?

Boston: Yeah, what he said. I don't want to have to go back to being the singer. Audrey was wearing me out.

Gannon: Are you seriously complaining about getting too much sex?

Boston: Never thought I'd see the day, but yeah. Girls go crazy for the singer in the band, man. It's a known fact.

Me: So I can expect to get jumped after next week's jam session?

Lincoln: Can't guarantee it, but maybe if Marlo's there…

Me: Nothing's happening with Marlo.

Gannon: Pretty sure my Ring camera picked up a guy wearing a sweater making out with the duchess of darkness outside our house Friday night.

Me: Shit.

CHAPTER FOURTEEN

$\mathcal{M}$arlo

SUNNYSIDE HAD CALLED yesterday to inform me they were out of my pamphlets in the activity room. Personally, I thought it a bit insensitive to keep funeral home pamphlets in the activity room of a senior home, but they assured me their residents appreciated the easy access. When you used a walker or wheelchair to get around, you didn't want to have to go to some obscure office to get information about your final resting place.

So the senior home was first on my list this morning. Then I needed to go to the store and buy more snacks and bottles of water for the reception room. And then I had a meeting with the town council this afternoon to discuss what kind of plan we could put together to hopefully buy that piece of land from Milly Booth. Dad had suggested we start there as the city owned the cemetery land itself, but the operators and owners of the funeral home was the Balmero family trust. It was a major relief to find out I didn't have to come up with the money to pay for the plot of land, but I also knew the city wasn't going to be willing to pay top dollar for that piece of land either. If we got into a bidding war with Vander, we'd lose. I had to hope that Milly had a heart—unlike her grandson—and would sell it cheap to the city to benefit the whole town. Which meant my strategy had to change.

"Have a good day, Daddy," I said quietly, kissing him on the cheek while he sat in his recliner. It was eight o'clock and he hadn't even gotten dressed yet.

"I think a nap will perk me right up," he said, giving me the smile he didn't give anyone else. He and I had always been close, and I knew I only came second in his life to Mom.

He'd been tired since the new doctor changed his medications. Seeing him sitting more than ever made me realize Mom was right. I didn't want to burden him with talk about the business. I needed to handle things on my own. How soon before my own father came through that funeral home door horizontally? I simply couldn't let my mind wander into that territory or I'd fall apart and then the third-generation business would fail and then he'd really have something to stress about.

Instead, I hustled out to my car, determined to spend even more time making sure the business thrived. There was a small box on top of my car, a big red bow nearly eclipsing the box. I frowned, wondering if this was some new sex trafficking method of capturing young women. I looked around, but didn't see any bad characters. Didn't even see a white murder van with no windows. I reached up and flicked the box with my fingers. It jolted, but didn't explode.

With a sigh, I picked it up and lifted off the lid. My quick intake of air didn't do this piece of jewelry justice. The necklace wasn't dripping in diamonds. It was fucking better. A perfectly round and polished black obsidian ball dangled between a pair of intricately etched silver wings that fanned up to a chain. I pulled it out of the box, putting my purse and coffee mug on top of the car so I could wrap it around my neck and secure the clasp. I bent down to see myself in the side mirror of my car and gasped again. It was stunning.

My brain finally let go of shiny object syndrome and worked out where this gift must have come from. My spine snapped straight and I was cautiously confused. This had to be from Vander. Was he trying to buy his way into my pants? But I already gave him pants access, so what was his deal?

"Just sex, motherfucker," I muttered, now getting angry. You didn't give a girl a gorgeous, unique necklace that steals her breath when you weren't in a relationship. I liked this necklace. I'd probably dream about it for years to come, knowing I'd never have the money to buy it myself. And now I had to give it back.

I left everything where it was, marching across the front yard and through the line of trees. Climbing out of the ditch had my thighs screaming, but anger fueled me. As soon as I got to his driveway, I saw him standing on his veranda, a mug of coffee in his hand. He was half naked again, and while that made my mouth go dry, his physique on display did not calm my anger. If anything, it fanned the flames. He was a gorgeous asshole breaking every rule we'd made.

He smiled at me as I walked up to stand on the patch of perfectly mowed green grass and glare up at him on the second-story veranda. "Damn. That looks even better than I imagined against your pale skin."

I pointed my finger at him. "Don't you compliment me, you bastard."

He froze for a second, then tossed his head back and laughed. Which made his abs flex and I wanted to lick them right before I punched him in the gut. I waited him out, tapping my boot against the grass and hoping I was making a divot that would mar his pristine yard.

"You're welcome, Bubbles."

My face got all twisted up. "I didn't say thank you!"

He shrugged, looking down at me on the ground level, a little smirk still lingering. "I know you like it. The second I saw it, I thought of you and had to get it. The stone is shaped like a bubble. Get it?"

My hand came up to touch the obsidian lovingly. "Oh, I get it. I just can't accept it."

Now Vander was frowning and I considered it a win. Funny though, it didn't feel very good like wins were supposed to. "Why not?"

"Because you're breaking rule number one again!" I hissed, belatedly wondering if his grandma's room was near where I was standing. "I won't be swayed by gifts."

Vander sighed. "Wait right there." He put his coffee down on a white wooden table next to a set of chairs with festive pillows and disappeared from view. I kept working on that divot in the grass, mumbling under my breath about all the reasons I'd have to say goodbye to this necklace.

"What did my grass ever do to you?"

My head came up and there was Vander, tan and toned and grinning at me like I was adorable. I was never adorable. The man was seriously sick in the head.

"Take this thing off me and take it back." My fingers refused to do it.

He stepped up closer, his bare feet caging me in. Then his hand was in my hair and he dipped his head to sniff my neck. Why was he always doing that?

"No."

My eyelids fluttered shut and my hands found his bare chest. "Yes." It came out weak and I hated myself for it. I opened my mouth to say it like I meant it, but his lips came down on mine, stealing the words and my breath. His tongue flickered against my bottom lip but he didn't deepen the kiss.

"Keep it." He plucked another kiss from my lips. "I want to see you wear it and nothing else."

My eyes rolled back in my head and I cursed him for being so good with his words. Nothing came out, of course, because one kiss from Vander and I lost all ability to speak. He lingered there, just teasing me with one soft kiss after another. Then he pulled back and grinned as he scanned my face.

"Let's go walk the cemetery and pick out G-Mil's plot."

I gave a quick shake of my head, his fingers sliding through my hair. "Can't. Have a long day of stuff."

His thumb began to sweep up and down my neck, ending behind my ear and making my knees weak. "Then meet me there after work."

"Fine."

"Bring the bubble machine."

"Not a chance." Not even that magical thumb or those truth serum lips could get me to bring the bubble machine. Cemeteries were no place for fucking bubbles. Plus I'd been running the machine in my room and was flat out of the special soap that went in it.

Vander let go of my hair, but snuck another quick kiss before spinning around and marching away from me again. I blinked, trying to clear the fog. Somehow I'd come over here spitting nails and not only had I not given the necklace back, I'd agreed to meet with him tonight.

"Quit staring at my ass, Bubbles!" Vander called without turning around.

"I'm not, you narcissist, gift-giving bully!"

I totally was staring at his ass.

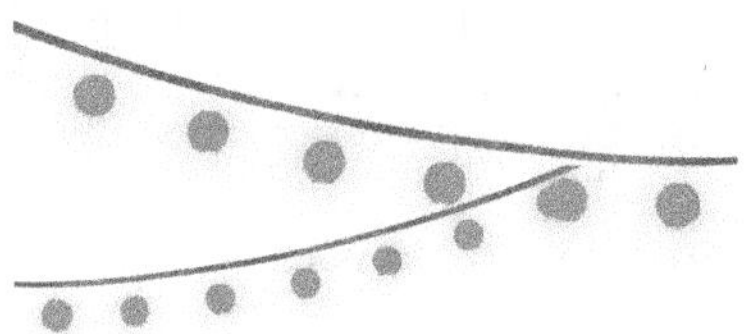

Me: How do we feel about a friends-with-benefits idea?

Audrey: OOOOHHHH

Paisley: That's Audrey language for "yes, girl, get it!"

Keva: It's complicated, but if anyone can do it, I feel it's you, Marlo.

Me: No, no. This question was hypothetical.

Audrey: Bahahaha! Sure…

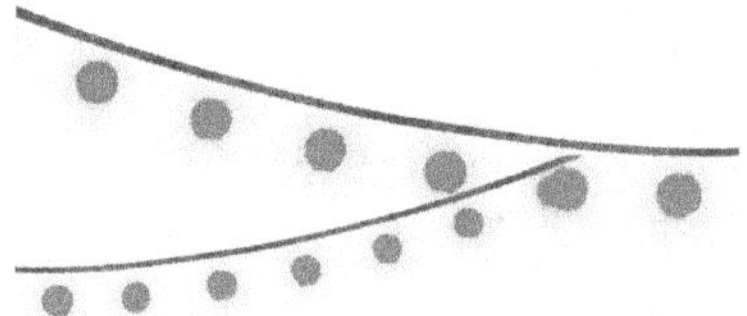

I spilled the stack of brochures all over Mr. Landerbury, who used his cane to reach the ones that went under the table, then tried to lift my skirt with said cane. I accidentally bought snacks that had tree nuts in them and had to take them back after I got home and realized my mistake. Business was good enough without resorting to killing our guests with deadly allergens. I probably looked like an idiot to the town council when I told them about the extra land that would work best and paused mid-sentence when I mentioned the Booth family owning it.

Damn Vander and his stupid perfect gift.

I waffled all day, convincing myself not to go to the cemetery that night to meet Vander. Then I'd slap myself with the truth that I wanted to meet him more than I wanted those new embalming drainage tubes that self-cleaned. I wouldn't go so far as to say that I liked Vander, but I did crave what he could do to my body, and in a weird way, I looked forward to our arguing. I'd never been with a man who didn't seem to treat me any differently because of my job. It was intriguing, that was all.

I didn't bother touching up my dark lip stain or changing clothes before I walked out the back door and traipsed across the cemetery. I wasn't trying to impress Vander. Though it seemed like he was trying to impress me.

He stood underneath a large oak tree in the back corner of the lot where the gravestones were over a hundred years old. As I approached, he held out a black, long-stemmed rose.

"What is this?"

He didn't look taken aback by my abrasive tone. "Your car was gone all day. Figured you were working hard and coming home to a pretty flower might be nice."

I took it, burying my nose in the bloom and trying not to let my heart race. "I've been asking our local flower shop to carry black roses for years and they've never done it."

Vander shrugged. "I have my sources."

I narrowed my eyes, but somehow my lips were tilting up at the corners.

No! Do not be charmed by him!

When he held out his hand for me to take, looking like a handsome prince in those stories I'd make up in my head as a child, I told my brain to shut up. For once, I didn't wish for a dragon to swoop down and burn everything to the ground. I wanted to see if the prince would kiss the princess and change her whole life.

CHAPTER FIFTEEN

ander

I HIT a button on my phone and slid it into my pocket. One slight tug on her hand and Marlo was in my arms. As the music played softly from the speaker currently sitting on Mr. Albert Blaggerty's gravestone, I swayed side to side, taking Marlo with me. She was stiff as a board, but the further my hands traveled, the more she relaxed. Her blouse covered her from neck to wrists but there was something enticing about knowing what those breasts felt like in my hands. Couldn't see 'em, but I remembered how they felt.

"What are we doing?" she asked, one hand gripping the shoulder of my shirt like it had personally offended her.

"We're dancing."

She snorted, making me smile. "I know that. But why?"

I shook my head, wrapping my arm tighter around her waist and pulling her fully into my body. Marlo wasn't like any woman I had ever dated. Not that we were dating. But I wanted to. Maybe. Sometimes.

"Why *not* dance?"

I placed her hand on my chest and left it there so I could grip her hip before sliding around back to squeeze her ass. I felt her shiver. My brain burst into a thousand excited thoughts about what other zones she had that would lead to an orgasm. Her body was truly a playground.

"Because we're in a cemetery?" Marlo's voice came out just above a whisper. Like her body wanted to give in to the romance, but her brain was the drill sergeant who would never bend.

"What better place than one that reminds us to live life to the fullest?" Her hips shifted and rubbed right against the erection I couldn't hide even if I wanted to. "There's beauty to life, you know."

"I know that." She tried to snap at me, but it came out too breathy to have teeth.

"Do you, Bubbles? Seems like maybe we should snatch up the moments of joy and embrace them with everything we've got before we all end up in this exact spot, except underground."

Marlo laid her head on my shoulder. "Impossible. This section is full."

I grinned into the darkness like a loon. What was it about her dark and deadpan humor that made me hornier than those old ladies at the clothing store today when I took G-Mil to get new pants that were easy to get on and off? They'd pinched my cheeks and one even copped a feel of my ass.

We swayed just like that through a whole song and into another. An owl hooted somewhere in the trees above us. The whistle of the occasional breeze through the pine trees was barely discernible above the music. It was peaceful here. Marlo relaxed enough to mold herself to me, her unique scent filling my nose and turning me on.

"Only one thing would make this better," I whispered.

"What?" Marlo's breath tickled the side of my neck.

"Bubbles."

She huffed and it sounded suspiciously like a laugh. "Shut up about the bubble machine already."

I stroked her back. "I don't know. Nothing says take a trip to orgasm-town like bubbles."

The music changed to some sappy country song my new friends had wanted me to learn the words to. Something about not being what a woman wanted but becoming what she needs. I hadn't really given the words much thought until I was pressed up against Marlo while the singer was crooning about it. Somehow it made more sense. I was definitely not what Marlo wanted. She'd made that abundantly clear. But maybe I could be what she needed right now. Just in this season of her life.

My hands shifted lower and I grabbed one cheek in each hand, lewdly spreading her apart and taking control of her hips. I rubbed her front against me and felt her breath hitch. Another rough squeeze and rub and she was letting out little mewling sounds in my ear.

I kept grinning, easing up on the grabbing but keeping my hard-on pressed right where she needed it. She let out a shiver and a long gust of air. When the only thing holding her up were my arms, I pulled back enough to peer down into her face. Damn. The woman had done it again.

"That's it. It's official. You have the coolest party trick I've ever seen. Can you do it again? This time with less clothing?"

Marlo's face was utterly relaxed as she kept her head on my shoulder, not one frown line flaring to life. A grin flickered and fizzled out all too soon.

"Give me a minute or two."

If it wouldn't have broken the mood, I would have whooped and thrown my fist in the air. Instead, my head swiveled around, looking for a place to accomplish my naked goals. I quickly realized my dilemma. "Um, well, we can't go to my place because G-Mil is up watching her dating shows."

Marlo's eyes popped open and her head came up. "Well, we can't go to my place. I live with my parents."

"Well, shit."

"Better think fast, Annoying." I looked down to see Marlo giving me a challenging grin, right before she grabbed my balls and squeezed.

I lurched back, but she clung on like the cholla cactus that was so abundant back in Arizona. Goose bumps lined every inch of my skin as panic and pleasure mixed together. Her tongue darted out to lick her bottom lip. One hand kept up the pressure on my balls while the other stroked my length through my pants.

"Oh fuck." My eyes rolled back in my head. I was either going to lose control of my appendages and slump over right here in the cemetery, or I needed to get us out of here as soon as possible. I chose door number two.

With the last bit of control I had left, I reached down and scooped up Marlo and the folded blanket on the ground next to us, leaving the speaker and the confines of the cemetery. Marlo let out a giggle as I ran, which made this mad dash worth it. I stopped right there in the tree line that separated our properties.

"Do that again."

"Do what?" she asked, clinging to my shoulders.

"Giggle."

One dark eyebrow lifted. "Earn it."

Fuck me. Why did she have to always say the exact thing that made me go stiffer than a porcupine quill? I started running again and she bounced in my arms, but never returned to the giggle. Maybe I was learning something new about myself. I'd always been a take-charge kind of guy, but maybe I liked a woman to talk back. And give orders. And be generally disagreeable.

I stopped by an oversized bush just over the property line. The ground looked flat and mostly soft given the overgrown grass and wildflowers. It wasn't the most comfortable spot, but more romantic than a cemetery.

"Right here?" Marlo asked.

I put her down slowly, feeling like maybe I needed to think

this through better. Every woman deserved more than a quick fuck in the middle of a pasture. "Yeah, sorry. Dumb idea. Maybe we can relocate this? I can see if there's a hotel—"

"It's actually kind of perfect," Marlo said, looking out at the property that we were currently fighting over. To be honest, with G-Mil's accident, I'd forgotten all about the land. Not that that was odd for me. I had a habit of bouncing from one thing to the next, never staying in one place for long.

"Yeah?"

Marlo spun toward me, looking like the queen of the night with that necklace sparkling in the moonlight. "Yeah."

I grinned at her and she grinned right back. It was as perfect of a moment as they came. Then she dropped the smile. Probably her smile muscles got tired from disuse.

"You still have to play by the rules."

I started unbuttoning my shirt. I'd play by any rules she wanted. As long as we were both naked. "Which ones?"

Marlo's gaze dropped to my hands, watching my every move. I slowed down, making sure I gave her a good show. When my shirt finally slid off my shoulders to the ground, her gaze snapped back up to mine.

"All of them, but especially the five-minute rule."

I held up my finger, then bent to spread out the blanket. I kicked my shoes off and did a forward fold. Then I straightened up and twisted left, then right. A couple of arm swings and I was ready.

Marlo had crossed her arms over her chest during my warmup, giving me a dry look that only made me want her more. I shot her a wink.

"Okay. Start your timer, m'lady."

CHAPTER SIXTEEN

$\mathcal{M}$arlo

"Hey," Vander whined, pulling off his pants and tossing them aside. "You said you'd get naked."

I wasn't hesitating because I felt self-conscious. I was hesitating because I was too busy watching this man disrobe. He was beautiful. Long, athletic limbs lined with sinewy muscle and a dusting of hair. Not one thing about him was awkward or misshapen. It was as if the gods had decided that a perfect male specimen needed to be born and there he was: Vander Booth in all his naked glory.

And I sure as hell wasn't going to tell him any of that. The man already had an ego that required a wheelbarrow to trail behind him to hold his big head.

"You first," I shot back, gaze dropping to the Calvin Kleins that covered the good stuff. I'd felt his erection too many times already to not be the tiniest bit excited about its unveiling.

Vander smiled smugly, as if he had a front-row seat to the thoughts running through my head. He hooked his thumbs in the waistband and shimmied his hips. There was no music, but this man didn't need any. I wanted to be unmoved by him, but my quivering thighs wouldn't lie. He finally shoved the underwear down around his ankles, his cock bobbing free and stealing the show.

I swallowed hard. *Fuck.* I was right. The man had not one imperfect thing about him. Acknowledging that made me doubt myself suddenly. He took a step toward me but I lurched back, finger extended.

"Ah, ah! Lie down, good sir."

Vander shot me a smile that did far more to liquify my insides than his naked body. "Yes, m'lady."

He knelt on the blanket, looking up at me like I was making all his dreams come true when the opposite was more likely. Doubt built in my chest until I couldn't breathe around it. Vander lay back on the blanket, leaning his upper body against the tree and stacking his hands behind his head in a lazy position that formed an idea in my head.

Sex had never intimidated me. I took what I wanted, made sure my partner had a good experience, and moved on. But the men I'd been with had been awkward. Quiet types with more gaming skills than social skills. Quite a bit like me actually. I'd never been intimidated by any of them because I understood them. Vander was like a different species altogether. He'd done nothing to make me feel uncomfortable...that was all in my own brain. I just needed to feel in control again.

I whipped my blouse over my head and stared down at Vander. "I have another rule."

He chuckled, hand coming down to skim along his chest. "Of course you do. Give it to me."

"I need you to not do anything to me unless I give you permission."

Vander's hand stilled. He lost the playful expression, muscles tightening like he intended to jump up and slay a dragon. "Did— did something happen?"

I shook my head. "No. Nothing like that. I just—I want to call the shots tonight."

He studied me, his eyes serious in the moonlight. "Okay. Fine by me. Whatever you need."

My breath whooshed out of my lungs. Relief made room for arousal again. I pulled the camisole off and tossed it aside to land on my blouse, somewhere in the tall grass. Vander's hand dipped lower, wrapping around his cock and squeezing.

"Can I say your tits are masterpieces?" Vander asked, voice raspy.

I put my hands on the waistband of my slacks. "You can say anything you like, just don't touch." I pushed down my pants and stepped out of them, toeing off my shoes also.

"I kind of miss the granny panties."

I shook my head at his joke. I was wearing a lacy black pair that were date-worthy. Thank God. I stripped them off too, finally naked. Vander looked his fill, not reaching for me like I'd asked. His cock leaped in his hand and grew impossibly larger. It was the encouragement I needed. I rolled my shoulders back and stepped closer to him, knowing he found me attractive.

Vander's gaze finally lifted to mine. "Use my body however you want, Marlo. Whatever you need, take it. Let's see how many orgasms I can give you without actually getting my hands on your skin."

His words were magic, exactly what I needed to let my inhibitions go. I needed to know I was in charge here. Stepping my foot over his legs, I walked up his body, getting closer and closer to his face.

"Put your hands under your legs." I didn't want him to be able to forget the rules and touch me accidentally. He complied and that first command obeyed made me feel a thousand times more confident.

With him restrained, I moved closer so that his face was even with the part of me that wanted him most. I looked down at him, his nostrils flaring as he gazed at me. His chest expanded as each breath got heavier. I teased him by pressing my hips against his face for just a quick second before dropping into a squat. My breast was in his face now.

"Suck."

I'd barely gotten the word out and he opened his mouth to obey. Within mere seconds I was coming, my whimpers fading out into the night.

"There's one," Vander rasped, popping my nipple out of his mouth.

I set my knees down on either side of him and shifted lower until my mouth was even with his dripping cock. My tongue darted out and licked the head of him. Vander hissed and I moved on, lifting my upper body and rocking my hips against his leg.

"Can your thigh get me off?" I asked, voice barely a whisper. My record was coming three times on one date. I had a feeling Vander could blast through that record like it was a joke.

"Try it and see." His eyes were hooded, his intense gaze trained on where I was rubbing against him.

My hips undulated, barely needing the friction to build up into another orgasm. We could both hear the slick rub of skin on skin. When I felt it approaching, I bent down and kissed the tip of his cock as I fell apart. His cock jumped and he cursed. I squeezed my eyes shut and rode out the waves before stilling.

"Two," Vander croaked.

My whole body felt lazy and sedated. I turned my head to the side to see his angry cock, purple red with blood flow denied release. I grinned at his cock and sat up. Fuck, this was fun. Vander had a bead of sweat dripping down his temple, clearly suffering, but still offering me a half smile.

"What next?" he asked, breathing hard. "Ride my shoulder? Do you have a toe fetish I can satisfy?"

I shook my head slowly, feeling like an absolute temptress as I crawled back up his body. I sat on his chest, grabbed him by the hair, and kissed him. Just when he began to get into the kiss, trying to dominate it with the thrust of his tongue, I pulled away.

"I was thinking I'd like to see what this mouth can do."

Vander squeezed his eyes shut as if in pain and then opened them. "Stand up, Bubbles. Spread yourself for me. Let me taste you."

I inhaled sharply, nearly coming at the mental image his words provided. My legs were shaking when I stood, but that didn't stop me from grabbing him by the hair and lining him up with my body. He inhaled, then buried his face between my legs like he wanted my scent all over him. My cry filtered up between the tree branches.

Taking back control, I moved away for just a moment to make sure he heard me. "Make me come and I'll put you out of your misery."

And then I reached down and spread myself open. Vander dove in without hesitation, his tongue spearing up inside me before coming around to my clit and giving it all his attention. His nose, his lips, dear God, his teeth, were all involved, teasing me mercilessly until I broke apart on a lightning-quick orgasm. My legs quaked and I had to let myself go to hold on to the tree trunk behind Vander's head. I could feel him smiling smugly between my legs.

He kissed my flesh right before smugly calling out, "Three!"

My legs finally gave out and I sat on his lap to catch my breath. His face was covered in my arousal. I reached over to grab his shirt and wipe his face. Like a good boy, his hands stayed under his legs. He was grinning at me like he wasn't dying to come himself.

"I think giving me three deserves a reward."

His smile grew and so did his erection poking me in the back. "Yes, please."

"Did you bring a condom?" I had not had the foresight to do so.

His head tilted. "Wallet. Back pocket of my pants."

I leaned back over to discard the shirt and fish out the condom.

"Am I still not allowed to touch?" he asked as I rolled it on his length, his voice hitching as I stroked him hard.

I shook my head with an evil grin. His jaw clenched but he dipped his head in consent. "You can come when I tell you to. Not before or this is over. Understand?"

"Fuck, Bubbles. You're going to kill me." He rested his head back against the tree trunk and groaned. "But if it keeps you smiling, I'll do it."

My evil grin turned decidedly less evil. If I wasn't careful, I'd actually start liking my new neighbor. He wasn't the rich, entitled jerk I'd thought he was. His constant joking around puzzled me still, but this perfect body and willingness to make me come multiple times was making up for it. Big-time.

I slid down his torso and notched him at my entrance. "Ready or not, here I come." I sank down his length all at once, shivering at the delicious tight fit. Vander shouted out a curse, his muscles taut and straining beneath me. "But not you. No coming yet."

His chest began to shine in the moonlight, sweat building as he tried to hold himself back. I rose up his length, thighs burning already. I slammed back down and nearly swallowed my tongue. Dammit, this wasn't going to last long.

"Marlo. Fuck. Shit. Don't—wait." Vander wasn't making any sense, so I stopped, feeling him twitch inside me.

"Don't you dare come yet," I growled.

The cords in his neck were on full display. He looked angry as he glared down at me, nostrils flaring and jaw locked tight. "You're evil, woman."

I grinned, wanting to keep moving so badly, but wanting to give him time to settle down first. "You agreed."

Vander swallowed and blew out a breath. "I know. But I didn't know it would be this hard."

"That's what she said," I drawled.

Vander looked at me and then tossed his head back and laughed. When I lifted off of him and slid back down again, he lost the laughter, but still had a tenderness in his eyes that I actively avoided. "You're something else, Bubbles."

Just a few more lifts of my hips and I was ready to come. The tenderness hadn't left his eyes, even as his jaw stayed clenched and the sweat began to drip down his other temple. I looked everywhere but in his eyes, feeling that familiar wave, knowing it might crush me.

"Come, Vander. Now," I whispered, feeling myself being drug under as he instantly roared his own release.

I trembled and shook, falling onto his torso and losing all track of time and consciousness. My eyes blinked open sometime later and I realized I was on my side while he cuddled me from behind. His big hand was stroking all the skin he could reach. And it felt good. Too good.

What did not feel good was the insect that was crawling across my thigh. I tried to swipe it away with a squeal. Vander jumped to his feet, the loss of his warmth an unwanted jolt back to reality.

"I'll slay the dragon, m'lady!" He made an exaggerated motion to swipe the insect from my leg and then flexed like a conquering knight in shining armor. Always joking. Always happy. Always so fucking hot.

I shook my head at his antics, but then snuggled up into his chest when he lay back down beside me. I ducked my head and blinked back sudden tears. I absolutely would not read anything into Vander's jokes. Nor would I fucking cry after sex. Good God, talk about a cliché.

Vander didn't live in an actual castle. He wasn't a prince. I was not his princess.

Those were just stories I made up in my head as a little girl. Before I knew that life always ended in death and real-life dragons could arrive at any time and snuff you out without a fair fight. I saw it all the time in my line of work. I saw the devastation. The grief. Who had time to joke around when you were up to your elbows in death?

Vander was right. I needed to embrace all the good I could find while I was still here. And sex with Vander was definitely good. But that was all it was: just sex.

After all, I'd been the one to make the rules.

CHAPTER SEVENTEEN

 ander

I SHOULD HAVE EXPECTED THIS. Should have known it from the first day I met Marlo. She'd never be what people would define as normal. Ordinary. I wouldn't even say she was quirky. Marlo Balmero was the quintessential person who walked to the beat of their own drum. They'd probably made up that phrase just to describe her.

I should have known sex with her would be not only incredible, but mind-blowingly different than anything I'd experienced before.

"Holy shit," I mumbled, still blinking up at the branches above my head. I could barely make out the leaves twisting in the breeze. It was late and I should probably let Marlo get home before our families came looking for us and got an eyeful.

"Holy shit good? Or holy shit bad?" came Marlo's reply somewhere against my ribs. I also had not expected her to be a snuggler, but the woman was positively plastered to my side. I was not complaining.

I began to laugh, my whole body shaking with it and disturbing her rest. Marlo lifted her head and shot me a glare. Was she serious?

Wrapping my arm tighter around her, I tried to allay her fears. "Sweetheart, I've slept with a lot of pretty women."

"This is not going well," she interrupted.

I pinched her side. "You didn't let me finish! I've never once said holy shit afterward."

She was still frowning. One day I was going to fuck the frown right off her face, but sadly, today was not the day. I reached over and pulled her on top of me. I cupped her face and made her look at me. She tried to jerk away, so I squished her face and forced the eye contact. She was pretty even all squished up.

"That was the most enjoyable sex I've ever had, so if you don't mind, I'd like to do that again. Preferably at least one hundred more times."

Her eyes relaxed slightly. I lifted my head and kissed her, taking my time and savoring the moment. I had a gorgeous naked woman on top of me in just the necklace I bought her and two more condoms in my wallet.

Marlo bit my bottom lip.

"Ow!" I whined, pulling away from the kiss. "What was that for?"

She shimmied her hips and I realized I was fully ready to go for round two. "You think I can't feel that thing? Down, boy."

I grinned at her, despite my stinging lip. "What? Four orgasms is all you got?"

She shrugged, the tips of her breasts rubbing up and down my chest with the movement. That was not helping. "I just don't want to break my vagina first go-round. She's been underused recently. Gotta break her back in."

The laugh was loud and long. She was talking about her pussy like it was a leather shoe. Fuck, I liked this girl. "Okay, fine. Lie down and let's recover together."

Marlo slid to one side of my body, still half on me, with her face on my chest. She tilted her head to meet my gaze as she twirled a finger along my abs. "Why do you have a hard time making friends? You seem friendly enough." She snorted. "Too friendly."

I drilled a finger in her side and she jerked. "Probably the same reasons you find it hard to make friends."

Her perfectly straight nose wrinkled. "I seriously doubt that. I'm majorly weird, which I count as a plus, by the way, so don't think I'm putting myself down. You're only partly weird."

This tree was going to leave a permanent indentation in my back, but I wasn't ready to break up snuggle time just yet. "I know you'll find this hard to believe, but I was the class clown growing up." Marlo sputtered out a laugh like I knew she would. "No one really understood me growing up. My parents, Larry and Mary, loved me, but they also looked at me like I was part green Martian. Larry's an accountant and Mary was a stay-at-home mom who didn't understand why I spent so much time on my computer programming as a teen."

"You call your parents by their first names?"

I squeezed her waist. "Focus on the important points in the story, Bubbles."

She rolled her eyes, but I continued, simply because she was easy to talk to. I knew that whatever I said, she wouldn't think less of me. She already thought very little. Beyond the orgasms. I was pretty sure she held me in high regard in that matter.

"Anyway, I was dating this girl junior year of high school and she was pretty popular. So, I'm on the basketball team, feeling like I'm the shit, right? Thing is, I wasn't very good. I didn't have the patience to put in the practice needed to be great at anything. But Coach put me in one game and my girlfriend was one of the cheerleaders on the sidelines. I get passed the ball but I was busy doing the running man to get laughs from the crowd. Instead of running backwards like a normal person, I tripped over my own feet and the other team stole the ball and scored.

Of course, I flailed spectacularly when I fell and fractured my ankle."

"Did your girlfriend rush to your side and provide aid?"

I shook my head, able to grin about it now, even though this particular memory stung for years afterward. "No. In fact, she pretty much ignored me for a few weeks. I'd try to catch up with her in the hallways, but couldn't because me and crutches didn't get along. Larry was on my ass because I was failing Algebra II and coach told me I was benched the rest of the season for my little stunt, even if I healed quickly. Shit hit the fan, so to speak, and I lost my sense of humor. I quit being the class clown for a bit and I noticed that no one paid me any attention. All those friends I thought I had turned out not to be friends. I provided them entertainment, but when life got hard, they weren't there for me."

Marlo's face gave nothing away. She just looked at me for long moments, absorbing my story. Or maybe she was falling asleep with her eyes open. I wasn't exactly sure.

"So, if you learned being the class clown doesn't get you friends, why do you keep doing it?"

It was one thing to be a dumbass in high school. It was another thing entirely to be reminded you were still a dumbass over ten years later. Somehow I couldn't hold her gaze while admitting it. Instead I looked out over the plot of land we were supposed to be fighting over.

"Well, Bubbles, sometimes we get stuck in ruts. Habits that aren't exactly good for us, but they're familiar. In my lizard brain, I'll always side with familiar over new and different. I embraced my ability to work a room and haven't stopped since."

Marlo pushed off my chest and stood. I figured my weaknesses weren't exactly attractive qualities and she was headed home. But I was also a guy and I couldn't help but let my gaze run down the length of her body, taking in the slight curves and silky white skin.

"Wanna play a game?"

I tilted my head to the side, sure I heard her wrong. I thought she'd simply say goodbye and goodnight. "Come again?"

Marlo cracked a smile. "I'm hoping you will. Are you in or out?"

"In." Without hesitation.

"What was her name?"

Now I was really confused. "Whose name?"

Marlo huffed, like conversing with me was taxing. "Your ex-girlfriend. The smag from high school."

"Jackie."

"Okay, so here's the setup. You're seventeen-year-old Vander. You have one last night with Jackie and you're pissed she ignored you when you needed her most. How are you going to use her body?"

"Uhh..." My brain went blank. I cared about consent with my partners and I normally didn't think about how I could use a woman's body. That seemed wrong.

Marlo stepped closer, holding her hand out. I took it and stood. She put her hand on my chest. "You have my permission to use my body. Pretend I'm her. It's not humiliation if I'm telling you I want it."

My eyeballs nearly fell out of my head. My dick told me he was on board with this plan before my brain wrapped itself around what the hell I wanted to do.

"Ticktock, Vander." Marlo stepped back. "Need me to do some annoying cheer to get you started?"

I shook my head. I was having so much fun with Marlo, I was practically giddy. "Get on your knees."

Marlo's grin was devious. "There you go."

"Don't speak," I snapped.

Marlo's eyes heated, but she immediately dropped to her knees and looked up at me. Suddenly I couldn't even remember why the girl from high school had hurt me. She hadn't meant anything to me. I wasn't in love with her. She wasn't even pretty compared to the woman who was on her knees for me just so I could exorcise the demons from my past.

I brushed a lock of hair away from Marlo's face, tracing her smooth skin down to the jewelry around her neck. "I know this is going to be hard for you, but I don't want you to come. Understand?"

Marlo nodded, but her breathing had picked up.

"Hands behind your back. You're not allowed to touch me."

Marlo complied, the new position jutting her breasts between us. I tweaked a nipple between my thumb and finger and she whimpered. Her eyelashes fluttered and I knew she could come at any second.

"Don't come," I reminded her.

She swallowed hard and looked up at me again.

"Now wrap those red-stained lips around my dick and don't stop until I'm coming down your throat."

Marlo didn't hesitate. She bent her head and dashed her tongue across the tip of my cock. Then she opened her mouth wide and bobbed down my length. I hit the back of her throat and she came back up, swirling her tongue over the head. Fuck, that felt like heaven. My fingers dove into her hair, fisting at the back of her head and putting me in complete control of her movements.

"Again," I barked. I put pressure on her head and she took me into the back of her throat, making a choking noise before I let her pull back.

Rapid breaths huffed in and out of her nose, her eyes watering above. My balls pulled up tight and I could have blown right then and there. I needed this heaven to last just a bit longer, so I closed my eyes and blocked Marlo from my view. The vision of those ruby-red lips on my dick would be burned into my memory forever, but for now I had to block it out.

I tugged on her hair again, not letting her take me quite as deep but increasing the pace. Her mouth was hot and tight and wet. Utter perfection. My thighs began to shake and I knew I didn't have long. I locked my jaw tight and thrust into her mouth, using her to get off when I knew I should be more gentle, but was unable to stop now that she'd given me permission.

She hummed like she was enjoying being used and the vibration set me off. I yanked on her head one last time, burying myself deep in her throat as everything exploded along my spine. My dick jerked and I knew I was flooding her mouth. It went on and on, the waves of pleasure more intense than ever before.

I wasn't sure how I kept on my feet, but I do remember forcing my fists to let go of her hair before I suffocated her. The devil-woman pulled back but licked me clean with little swipes of her tongue while I shook and jolted. Twin tracks of tears ran down her cheeks and I felt like I'd taken a blow to the chest. I opened my mouth to apologize, but couldn't seem to form words yet. Marlo let me pop out of her mouth with a satisfied smile that erased my fears of hurting her.

"Feel better?" she said from her knees.

Words were still too hard. I reached down and picked her up under the armpits like she weighed nothing. Her legs came around my waist and I backed her into the tree trunk with a kiss that told her exactly how much better I was feeling.

After two more orgasms—for her, not me...I'm not actually a superhero, I just look like one—I folded up the blanket, we got dressed, and I walked her back to her house. We both silently agreed I shouldn't meet her parents, so I slipped back into the shadows and waited until she was safely in the house before turning and walking up the hill to my house.

G-Mil took one look at me from her recliner in front of the television and hooted like she knew exactly what I'd been up to. I rolled my eyes and headed for the shower before helping her to bed.

$\mathcal{M}$arlo

I HAD another meeting with the city council later today after they'd had a chance to see the plot of land I suggested for the expanded cemetery. Considering being able to speak intelligently was important to my cause, I should have been in bed by ten, getting my beauty sleep. I snorted as I layered more concealer under my eyes. I'd never be what most people would call a beautiful woman. The most I could hope for was fascinating. At least Vander seemed to think I was interesting. I smiled at my tired reflection in the bathroom mirror, thinking back on last night under the tree. Sex with Vander had not only been fun, it had been...deep. For a guy who laughed a lot and claimed not to make real friends, he'd somehow struck a chord with me that seemed deeper than two people just messing around.

Movement out my window caught my eye and I snuck over to the side of the drapes to see Vander's truck leaving his property. I tapped the concealer against my palm, debating the thought that had occurred to me this morning when I woke up and stretched out my tired legs. Vander would be pissed. Somehow, knowing that made my decision for me.

I was going to have a little girl-to-girl chat with Milly while Vander was practicing with his new friends.

I hurried through the rest of my morning routine, kissing Dad on the cheek before running out the back door and jogging across the cemetery. When I reached the tree line, I slowed down, mostly because I was out of breath already. I really needed to exercise more, but the idea of joining a gym was abhorrent. All the women in tight leggings and perky asses. Overgrown men flexing in the mirror to catch the attention of the women with the assets. I'd be over in the corner glaring at all of them until the manager kicked me out for making people uncomfortable. Best I just let myself become a decrepit, flat-assed old lady.

The doorbell clanged through the whole house when I pressed the ornate button, a gentle roll of bells that sounded stately and foreign to me. Our doorbell was literally a buzzer straight out of the seventies.

"I'm coming! Keep your shorts on!" Milly's shaky voice came through the huge doors, along with the squeak of her walker on the tile.

"Take your time, Milly. It's just me, Marlo," I called back.

The door opened a minute later, revealing Vander's grandma with a big smile on her face. Her track suit was bedazzled at the shoulders and she wore a stack of rings on each of her ten fingers. Milly Booth did not do casual, even with a bruised hip. "Well, what a lovely surprise this is! Come in, dear, come in."

I stepped into Vander's house, feeling a lot more comfortable now than when I'd first been here in my damn underwear. Milly led me into the parlor room and had a seat, looking like she was moving pretty good already.

"What brings you by, dear?" she asked, folding her hands in her lap.

"Well, first I wanted to see how you were doing."

Milly's eyes twinkled with repressed laughter. "I'm doing just fine. If the therapist gives me the green light later today, I'm going to switch to a cane. Even if he doesn't give me approval, I'm switching, but shh. We won't tell Vandy that."

I made the motion of zipping my lips. "I'm glad to hear it."

"So what's the *real* reason you're here?" Milly's eyes sharpened, not unkindly, but intelligently. The woman was old, but her mind was sharp as a tack.

I leaned forward, putting my elbows on my knees. "The cemetery is running out of room."

Milly's mouth dropped open. "Oh no! Are you saying I can't be buried there?"

"No, no!" I was quick to jump in. "There's space for your plot, but what I meant was that if we don't expand, we're going to run out of space within the next couple of years. Now that Dad's handed the business over to me, I've started to look at our long-term projections and we have a problem on our hands."

Milly was already shaking her head, clearly not happy about this situation. "Well, that doesn't sound good. What can we do?"

"Well, we can ship people to a nearby town for burial, but we'd hate to break up families with loved ones already buried here in Blueball. Or..." I let the word hang there for a moment. Just until Milly leaned forward like I was about to impart a juicy secret. "We could buy more land right here in Blueball. Specifically, the land right behind the cemetery."

Milly's mouth snapped shut with a snap of her teeth. She sat back in her chair and eyed me like she was at a poker table and she either had the worst hand in the world or she was about to lay down a full flush and take every chip I had on the table.

"The land behind us, did you say?"

I nodded, heart beating out of control. "I won't insult your intelligence, Milly. I know you own it, and I'm here to offer you a deal."

Milly clapped her hands together, all those rings clinking on contact. "Oh goodie. I do love a negotiation."

I suddenly felt like I'd voluntarily jumped into shark-infested waters. "If you're inclined to part with the land—the city will pay you a fair rate for it, of course—but I can sweeten the deal. I can allot an entire area just for your plot. A statue? A sitting area? A marble tomb? A freaking disco ball? Sky's the limit, Milly."

Her growing smile reminded me of Vander so much I shifted in my seat. He'd kill me for going around him directly to his grandma, but the future of Blueball's cemetery hung in the balance. I had to fight dirty.

"I will certainly keep that in mind, Marlo. You have intrigued me." Milly suddenly shifted forward, inching her hips closer to the edge of the chair before grabbing her walker and pushing up to standing. "But for now, let's have some fun."

"Fun?" I stared up at her.

Her smile reminded me of that shark again. "Yes, my dear. Fun."

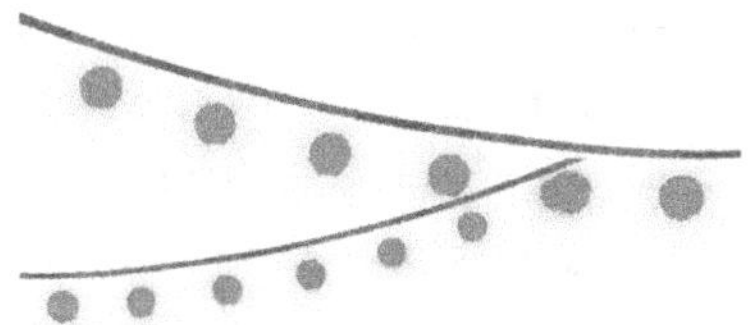

"I know it's in there somewhere," Milly muttered, hovering behind me while I was bent over with the upper half of my body inside a large moving box. "Vandy said he'd get it for me this weekend so I could sunbathe nude on the veranda."

Note to self: do not look outside my window this weekend.

"What do you and your parents like to do for fun, dear?"

"For fun?" I muttered, sifting through what seemed to be the box for trash. A turquoise feather from a feather boa at the bottom of the box stuck to my face. I huffed and it floated away.

"Yes, for fun." Milly was sounding a bit grumpy. "Why do you keep repeating the word like you've never heard of it before?"

My hand grazed something solid amidst all the junk drawer items of random slips of paper, keys to mystery locks, and broken remotes. "Aha! I've got it!"

I waved the portable speaker in front of Milly and placed it on the kitchen island. She pulled a cell phone out of her track suit and shoved it across the granite toward me.

"If you can connect my phone with the tooth thing, I have the perfect playlist."

My lips wobbled. I was starting to see why Vander liked his grandma so much. She was a hoot.

"Did I ever tell you I used to work for a lawyer in San Francisco?"

I looked up from the phone, seeing a soft smile on her face as she reminisced. Apparently, my response was not needed as she kept right on talking.

"He used to be such an ass. Making me work long past my stated hours and then not paying me for the extra time. This was back in the sixties and workers didn't have the same rights they have today, especially women. One day I got so fed up, I pushed away from my desk at five o'clock on the nose and lit a joint."

I choked on my spit and forgot about the phone entirely.

Milly looked positively gleeful. "Oh, he came roaring out of his office, yelling this way and that. I waited him out, taking deep inhales, calm as only weed can make a gal. When he finally wound down, I told him that life was short, the pay was shit, and if he wanted me to work past five, then he either needed to pay me, or I was going to have fun working." Milly winked at me and nudged the phone in my hands. "I never had to work past five again."

"That's quite the story, Milly." After updating all her apps, I finally got the Bluetooth on her phone to connect to the speaker and handed the device back to her.

"I know your father handed the business off to you, dear, but you can't forget to have some fun mixed in with all the work. You keep stressing yourself out and you'll be as boring as Paige Pearse."

I nearly choked again, this time on laughter. Paige was Paisley's mom, and while my friend Paisley was well aware how prim and proper her mother was, I didn't know that Milly didn't care for the woman either.

"Well, we're only here for a short time, Milly, so I want to make sure the business doesn't fail. I'll have fun later."

Milly's head popped up and she pursed her lips. "That's the thing, my sweet girl. We're actually here for years and years. You gotta enjoy it. You start being too serious now, and before you know it, you're old and lonely and just as crotchety, wishing you would have lightened up when you were younger."

Then she dropped her head and scrolled on her phone for a while, muttering under her breath, but otherwise blessedly silent. I wasn't sure I could handle any more stories or life advice. Eventually music came through the speaker. At full, ear-piercing volume.

Milly grinned from ear to ear. "Dance with me!" She lifted her hands off the walker and did an impressive shimmy.

I tried for a smile, but it was probably more like a grimace. "I'm good, thanks though!" I shouted over the music.

Milly wasn't having it. She ditched her walker, which made me highly uncomfortable. If she fell on my watch, Vander was going to be even more pissed at me. But then she grabbed my hips and gave them a good shake. Quite impressive for the over-eighty set, actually. Maybe Milly wore tight leggings and went to the gym. Either way, my hips were moving and Milly's antics were making giggles find their way out of my mouth. Before long, she didn't have to jiggle me. I was doing it all on my own, both of us with our hands in the air and the bass thumping through the kitchen.

The song switched and Milly limped her way over to the moving box to pull out the feather boa. With the most hilarious conga line dance move, she came back to me, tossing the boa over my head. She also found a black pirate-style eye patch in the box, and while I wasn't going to ask why that was even in there, she put it on and it did make me laugh. We danced some more and I was embarrassed to admit that Milly had more moves than I did.

By the time sweat started to bead on my forehead, something magical happened. The more uninhibited Milly was with her dancing, the more I was too. Being around someone like her, totally confident in who she was, had given me permission to be fully me too.

I was mid performance of Sandra Bullock's fireside dance scene in *The Proposal*, ass shaking and singing the song at the top of my lungs when fiction came to life. I backed my ass right into a solid, warm lump of human flesh.

Specifically, Vander.

I squealed and jumped, turning around with my hands up to fight off my attacker. My attacker, however, had his arms crossed over his chest, fighting a smile, not me. Milly turned off the music and all you could hear was our heavy breathing in the quiet kitchen.

"Hey," I said lamely. I stared at his chin. His chin was fascinating.

"Hey," he said right back. Then he ducked and somehow I was looking into his eyes. "Impressive moves."

I scoffed. "You should see your grandma."

Vander's expression shifted, thunder in those gorgeous eyes of his. "Oh, I saw her moves. Interesting moves for a lady supposed to be using a walker."

"Oh, would you look at the time? I'm late for my nap. Thanks for visiting, dear." Milly squeaked out of the room at a snail's pace when not twenty minutes ago she'd been teaching me how to twerk, based off a YouTube video she'd watched with her best friend, Gertie, before her accident.

Vander stared me down the whole time she hobbled out of the room and down the hallway. I focused back on his chin and willed the sweat to dry up. Once the squeak of her walker was gone, he opened his mouth. Probably to let me have it, but I cut him off.

"I told her to use the walker."

Vander slashed his hand through the air and then ran his hand through his hair, looking exasperated. "It's not your job to make sure she stays safe. That's mine. I'll be talking to her later."

I looked him in the eye then. "So, you're not mad?"

I noticed he actually looked hot. Temperature-wise, I meant. His T-shirt clung to his biceps, his jeans were well worn, and he sported sweat along his hairline. He looked like a regular guy who shopped in regular stores.

His eyebrow lifted and the tug on his lips was back. "Oh, I'm mad alright, but not over Milly dancing."

I licked my lips. Why did I want to climb him like a tree and beg him to take me right here on this huge island? Hadn't I gotten enough last night? "What, then?"

He took a step forward, putting his hands on my hips and dropping his voice so low it made me shiver. "I'm pissed you danced with my grandma and not me."

CHAPTER NINETEEN

ander

I'D NEVER WALKED into something more ridiculous than seeing Marlo shaking her uninhibited, gorgeous ass with a feather boa around her neck and an all-black outfit with combat boots while my grandma tried out the moves to "Renegade" with a stiff hip. I never should have installed TikTok on her phone.

I should never have left her alone either, knowing Marlo might come over to see me after last night. Not that I expected a lively dance-off. Marlo dancing in my kitchen was the last thing I would expect, yet it made my insides heat to the point I was about to sweat just as much as Marlo.

Lord have mercy on my soul, getting a hard-on while my grandma was in the room. She was leaving, thankfully, one squeaky revolution of her walker wheels at a time. When the last squeak faded down the hallway, I pulled Marlo close.

"So you're not mad?" she asked, looking like she'd stolen my silverware while she was doing the macarena. Then it dawned on me that G-Mil shouldn't have been shaking her booty when she was just days out of the hospital because of a fall. Maybe I should be mad about that, but I'd learned a long time ago there was no stopping Mildred Booth. Better to just let her do her thing and deal with the consequences afterward.

"Oh, I'm mad alright, but not over Milly dancing."

Marlo licked her lips and I was jealous of her tongue. My God, what was wrong with me? "What, then?"

I dipped my head and buried my nose in her neck, inhaling her scent deep into my lungs. "I'm pissed you danced with my grandma and not me."

I felt Marlo's shiver and it made me feel ten feet tall. My dick must have felt the same way too, based on how he was trying to escape my jeans. "I wasn't planning on dancing."

The woman was hot, in a dark and mysterious way, but it was clear she didn't see herself that way. She only saw the weird darkness and missed the way everything else about her shined bright. Even the darkest of night skies has a moon that illuminates the whole world. Marlo was that for me: a darkness so deep and vast, split in two by a bright shining light.

I grinned against her skin, plucking a kiss. "I know. That's why it was so hot to see you do it."

I felt her melt into my body, letting me slide my arms around her and cop a feel of her ass. And then she giggled, rubbing her hips against my erection.

"While I'd love to stay and *dance* some more, I have to get to work."

I pulled my head up, pouting shamelessly. "But my version of dancing leads to so. Much. Fun."

Marlo's cheeks sprouted two little dots of red that pleased me endlessly. She shook her head. "You and Milly, I swear."

I frowned, still trying to block her path to my front door. "Just one more kiss."

Marlo lifted her nose in the air. "No. Our deal was orgasms, not kisses."

I slid my hands up from her hips to cup her breasts. "But what if kissing leads to an orgasm?"

Marlo swatted my hands away before I could attend to the nipples that were already beaded and begging for my touch. "Your grandma is in the next room. Unhand me, sir."

I whined like a little kid denied sugary cereal in favor of plain old, lumpy oatmeal. "Fine. But let's plan for some alone time soon."

Marlo rocked up on her toes to press a quick kiss to my cheek before practically running to the front door. "We'll see. My schedule is kind of packed."

I shook my head, watching her leave as I tried to tell my body to slow the fuck down. Playtime was officially over, before it even started. The woman was playing hard to get, even though we'd already had sex.

And I fucking loved it.

"Milly?" I hollered over my shoulder.

"What?" she hollered back.

"You're in trouble!"

"No, I'm not." I heard her giggle all the way at the front of the house. "I *am* trouble."

I rolled my eyes, shut the front door, and walked to her room at the back of the house, on the first floor. She was folding clean clothes on her bed, the walker neglected at the doorway, like she couldn't wait to get rid of it the second she entered her bedroom.

I gave it a gentle shove with my tennis shoe. "Did the PT clear you already?"

G-Mil started humming, like she couldn't hear me, when I knew for a fact she could hear a mouse fart a mile away. "That Marlo gal is my kind of woman."

I walked over, heaving a sigh. Might as well get this conversation over now before G-Mil did something so over the top I might be embarrassed. "Yep, I saw that. You two dancing was something I'll never be able to get out of my brain."

"Mhm." Grandma handed me the pair of jeans I'd worn last night, a grass stain still marring one leg. "Rolling in the hay might leave less stains."

"Milly!" I snapped, grabbing the jeans and folding them to hide the stain.

"Vandy!" she snapped right back. "What? I may be old, but I'm not dead. I know what it's like to get a little frisky outside."

I squeezed my eyes shut. Did I say my grandma was my best friend? I was mistaken.

"Please don't ever say frisky again."

"Pfft. I've been saying for years you need a girlfriend and here you are...finally taking my advice."

"Marlo's not my girlfriend." I opened my eyes to see disappointment on G-Mil's face.

"Oh, I see. Netflix and chill?"

I shook my head, needing a subject change fast. Or a lobotomy. "So, I've come up with a business plan."

"Oh?" G-Mil's head popped up, hope restored.

"Yeah. Even sent it off to one of the guys on the board of my old company and he said it checks out."

G-Mil's face squished up. "Another app to lower a person's self-esteem in comparison to a perfection that doesn't actually exist?"

I dropped my chin to my chest. Grandma didn't pull any punches. My first company had been built around an app I'd created that would alter photographs. Specifically, it would let a user alter their body and face in their endless selfies. It had taken off, earning me millions of dollars and destroying the self-confidence of a whole generation of young girls and boys. That's why I'd sold the company. I could no longer go to work and feel good about what I was doing. Sometimes brilliance leads to downstream consequences we never could have imagined.

"I want to create a place where families and friends can leave their screens behind and play. Have fun. Talk. Compete. Share in an experience."

"Sounds good so far."

"I want to buy a plot of land and build a paintball course."

G-Mil froze, as if waiting for the punchline to a joke. When I didn't give her one, because this wasn't a joke, she finally broke the awkward silence.

"What the fuck is a paintball course?"

"Language…" I feigned offense. When she waved me away with a huff, I explained. "You run around with these paint guns with your team and try to take out the other team first. It's friendship, trust in teammates, exercise, and most importantly, no cell phones or time for selfies. Good, clean, wholesome fun. Well, dirty fun, I guess."

G-Mil stared at me, studying my face. When she finally spoke, a brick took up residence in my gut. "You know I'd never lie to you, right?" I nodded. "It's not a good idea, Vandy."

I was shocked, honestly. The buddy I'd spoken with had done the market research and these kinds of courses had low overhead with a high return. There wasn't another course in a fifty-mile radius. We'd own the market. Why was G-Mil dismissing the idea outright? She was usually my biggest supporter.

"What do you mean?"

She ticked off the reasons. "It's violent, and this world has enough of that already. It requires a lot of land, I presume, which could be used for something far more useful. If you really want families to come, you don't hand a five-year-old a play gun and tell him to take out his sister." She lifted her hand and patted my cheek. "Back to the drawing board, Vandy."

"But—"

"Ah!" G-Mil cut me off. "I know you have your fancy numbers and business plan and all that shit, but once you settle down and really think about it, you'll know I'm right."

I shook my head, unwilling to accept her opinion. "I need chocolate," I muttered, spinning around and heading for the kitchen once again.

The squeak of her walker trailing behind me echoed off the

stone floors. She just kept going on and on about why my idea was shit, which really pissed me off. I thought she'd be proud that I was doing something that would provide pure fun, not vanity this time around. I reached into the highest cabinet over the refrigerator, where G-Mil couldn't reach, and pulled out the package of gourmet dark chocolate I kept for emergencies. I kept my diet pretty clean otherwise, but a guy had to have a vice. Chocolate, of the finest quality, was mine.

"Fuck me," I muttered, seeing that there was only one tiny square left. I had to order this stuff all the way from Switzerland. It cost more than I would ever admit, but I had to have it.

"Are you even listening to me?" G-Mil asked, interrupting my moment with the chocolate.

"No." I talked around the chocolate melting against my tongue. "Hey, can I borrow a few bucks?"

"What? How are you out of money already? Your allowance amount is double what mine is!"

I shrugged, not wanting to get into it with her. How I spent my money was my business. This whole allowance thing was bullshit anyway. What grown man needed his grandma to put him on an allowance? Pretty sure anyone could just google my name and discover I'd sold my company for an insane amount of zeroes. I didn't actually need to limit my spending like this to fit in around Blueball. Sadly, I'd probably never fit in.

G-Mil squeaked back down the hallway, muttering under her breath about how much chocolate a man could eat before he was diagnosed with diabetes. I didn't appreciate the guilt trip, especially after she'd crapped on my paintball idea. I'd simply have to show her the plans. Maybe take her to the paintball place I'd found a few hours away. She'd see firsthand how fun they were the second she nailed me in the chest with a round of paintballs. Then I could talk her into letting me use a portion of my savings to buy that land behind my house. I'd even give her a pass to use the course anytime she wanted. For free.

My phone dinged in my pocket and I slid it out, thinking I'd order my chocolates online now. By the time they arrived in the mail, I'd have another allotment of allowance money and G-Mil would have no reason to lecture me about my spending habits.

> Gannon: Dudes, we sound incredible!

> Lincoln: We're so getting lucky Friday night...

> Boston: Okay, that's my sister you're talking about. Can we keep it PG?

> Lincoln: Like Audrey won't be begging for it the second you take her back to your little cabin.

> Gannon: Wait. Maybe we should hire someone for Vander so he doesn't feel left out.

> Me: What the fuck? I don't need a fake girlfriend, thank you very much.

> Lincoln: Oh, that's right. I heard something about you and Marlo and the great outdoors...

> Boston: Marlo, huh? Is that a real thing?

> Gannon: Ohhh...she's twisty...bet the sex is top notch. If you like that kind of dark kink.

I groaned up at the ceiling. Gossip spread fast in this small town. Even though the boys were entirely correct, and even though I was unhealthily obsessed with the town undertaker, everything was too new and fragile to be making the gossip rounds. If Marlo caught wind of the rumor, she'd shut me out and bury our tentative agreement six feet under.

Only one person knew I'd rolled in the grass with Marlo last night. Only one person could have started that rumor.

"Milly!" I shouted.

"What?" she shouted back.

"You're in trouble!"

Her cackle of laughter didn't help my bad mood.

CHAPTER TWENTY

$\mathcal{M}$arlo

I SHOWED up late to Friday night's jam session at Glamper's Paradise and had to park halfway into town and hike in. It was like the universe was trying to tell me I needed my exercise. Milly had brought her friend, Gertie, over to the funeral home to discuss their urn selections. The two of them had cracked me up with their off-the-wall suggestions. I'd found myself combing the internet for a bejeweled urn in the shape of a cowboy boot as a hat tip to her favorite country artist, Morgana Mavis. Wouldn't you know it? I actually found one.

"I knew she'd show up!" Audrey hollered, lifting her beer bottle in the air and pulling me into the huddle of bodies around a picnic table. The boys were already on stage and I forced my neck not to turn and stare at the man who had not left my brain, no matter how hard I tried to push him out.

"Don't I always come to these torture sessions?" I deadpanned.

"Hey, Marlo."

My neck did swivel that time. Zeke Burns sat to my left, looking as uncomfortable as I usually did in any social situation. "Hey, Zeke. What brings you here?"

He shrugged and his thumb fiddled with the label on his beer. "Not sure. Gannon and Paisley basically threatened me if I didn't come."

I swung a leg over the bench and had a seat next to him, figuring I might be the only one who understood not liking these types of social gatherings. Audrey sat next to me, shoving me into Zeke. It was hard to fit all us girls, plus babies, at one picnic table. My shoulder collided with his and we both apologized at the same time.

"You're just in time. They were mostly just warming up, but now that you're here, they'll get going." Paisley waggled her eyebrows, bouncing the baby in a carrier strapped to her chest.

I frowned, unclear why my attendance had anything to do with their timeline of singing. Turning to Zeke, I tried to rope a fellow wallflower into conversation. "I have to be honest, I'm not sure why I'm here either. It's mostly these friends of mine. They force me to be social every week. It's quite annoying."

Zeke's lips tipped up into a ghost of a smile. "Good to have friends, I suppose."

"I suppose," I muttered, not sounding at all certain.

Then I wanted to smack my forehead. Or at least pull my foot out of my mouth. I remembered now that Zeke had had a best friend back in high school. Rainey something. I wasn't friends with her, but everyone knew those two. They were tighter than coach seats on a full flight. Zeke and Rainey did everything together growing up. We all expected them to get married despite their protestations of being just friends, but right after graduation, Rainey ran away with some guy who came through town and was far too old for her. Zeke had been crushed. He'd mostly turned into a hermit since then.

Zeke nudged me with his elbow. "It's been twelve years. I'm not still crying in my cereal."

I winced. "I need to work on my poker face."

He smiled, but there wasn't a lot of happiness behind it. "Nah. Your face is pretty perfect."

Well, that was nice of him to say, considering I'd just made him uncomfortable. The song ended and the steady beat of conversation and the snap of the fire pit not far away were the only sounds filling the night.

"Zeke Burns. Are you flirting with Marlo?" Keva piped up, the set of lungs on her only outclassed by her newborn baby.

The microphone let out a squeal that made everyone in the vicinity gasp. Vander's voice came out of the speakers loud and clear. "Sorry to interrupt." I swiveled on the bench to see him glaring at Zeke. "Thank you to everyone who came out tonight to drink our beer and hear us play a few tunes."

Audrey sounded like she was either choking or smothering laughter. I pounded her back until she reached over and pinched my thigh.

"We have a few practiced songs and then we'll take requests, which we'll play at your own risk. But first, I want to play this one for Miss Marlo Balmero."

I would have gasped as all heads swiveled in my direction if I hadn't been frozen solid at being the center of attention at a local shindig. I could lead a funeral in front of the entire town, but don't shine a spotlight on me in a social situation where I was already feeling out of my depth. Zeke shrank away from me as he realized Vander's look of death was meant for him.

"Shit, sorry, Marlo. Had no idea about you two," he said out of the side of his mouth.

"We're not—"

But then the band struck up a familiar song. The same one that had been playing in the cemetery when I'd been dancing with Vander under that pine tree and he'd made good on his orgasm promise. My cheeks flamed hot and the denial died on my lips. A weird mix of emotions flooded my body, leaving me without words to properly express what I was feeling.

I was hornier than ever listening to Vander sing that particular song while staring at me with fire in his eyes in front of everyone. I was embarrassed about all the people who were still looking at me and speculating what Vander was to me. Add in a healthy dose of guilt that I'd gone behind his back to get that land from his grandma, and I was one mixed-up girl.

When the last note of the song faded into the night and the crowd clapped, Vander put a stop to the question on everyone's lips. He pointed right at me and spoke into the microphone.

"That's now our song, Bubbles."

My friends erupted, shoving my shoulders and adding to the general mayhem of women sighing over how romantic that was. My eyes narrowed. Motherfucker. I was going to kill him for that stunt. He'd clearly broken several of our rules all in one very public show of stupidity. All because I was talking to Zeke.

Men. Such idiots.

I spun on the bench so fast I'd be picking out splinters from intimate places for days to come. I did not want to see Vander's face again tonight or I might just make good on my original murdering suggestions. "We're just friends, so quit your swooning. You're embarrassing yourselves."

Keva's mouth dropped open. Paisley looked ready to pummel me. And Audrey had had enough beer to just slap the table with her hand and burst into uproarious laughter. I pointed my finger at all three of them.

"You're all on my shit list."

Keva rolled her eyes. "We're always on your shit list. Tell us something we don't know."

I leaned forward, hissing loud enough only they could hear. Well, plus Zeke, but since he was sitting at the girls' table, he had to deal with it. "We're just friends. In fact, that's one of our rules. The other was keeping things quiet, which clearly, asshat over there doesn't remember."

"Keeping what quiet?" Paisley challenged, wanting me to spit out what they both suspected and had heard via the gossip grapevine.

"Yes, alright. We're sleeping together. Casually fucking."

Zeke choked on his beer, but I was on a roll. "This is all supposed to be on a friends-with-benefits level. So quit trying to set us up. Or get us together. We're already together. But not. Okay?"

Audrey burst out giggling again. I really wanted to pull her beautiful long hair sometimes.

"Sure. Okay. Keep telling yourself that, babe, but I think there's a lot more there than just casual fucking." Keva reached over and grabbed my hand. I dug my nails into her skin, but she held on. "Definitely on Vander's end. You might want to quit denying things so hard and just explore if something more is what you want."

"At any rate, you can't storm off now without making another scene, so sit and chat with us while you stew, huh?" Paisley, ever the levelheaded one, was right. I was stuck. At least until everyone forgot about Vander's little stunt up there.

I did just that, my arms folded over my chest while I let conversation flow around me. Zeke piped up occasionally, but we were both like bumps on a log, refusing to actively participate. I didn't know what his deal was, but I was good and pissed. Mostly because I was confused and I didn't like being confused. Things in life should be cut and dry. Good versus bad. Life versus death. I didn't like those gray shades in between because they didn't have defined limits and rules so I avoided them like the plague.

The band shifted into another country tune I liked, but refused to get into, just out of spite. A tap on my shoulder had me spinning around. Vander stood behind me, his palm up. His hair was wild and there was a sheen of sweat on his forehead. One dimple winked at me in a half smile. He looked fucking good.

"Will you dance with me, Marlo?"

I'd meant to leave toward the end of their set but before they were done so Vander couldn't follow me. The tricky bastard had left the band up there playing without their lead singer.

"No." I spun back around, but he tapped on my shoulder again.

"People are looking…" Keva whispered.

"Argh," I muttered, turning back around. "If I dance one song with you, will you please leave me alone afterward?"

Vander's expression faltered, but he nodded. "As you wish, m'lady."

I rolled my eyes and put my hand in his. He tugged me off the bench and into his body, moving us gracefully to the edge of the dance floor. His arm slid around my waist and my body began to melt under the assault of his body heat and the scent of his cologne. I held on to the mad and stepped on his toes on purpose with my clunky boots. He winced, but held on tight. I could feel the weight of people's stares as we began to sway to the music.

"Beats dancing in the cemetery, huh?"

"I'm not talking to you right now." I trained my gaze on his shoulder.

He dipped his head and did that thing where he sniffed my neck. I jerked away but not before my body betrayed me with the shiver only Vander could induce. "Why not?"

I scoffed, stepping on his foot yet again. His eyes shuttered but he didn't make a peep. "Because you broke all the rules in our rulebook and now our agreement is off, which pisses me off because the orgasms were really good while they lasted." I darted a glance at his handsome face. The fucker was smiling.

"Really good, huh?"

I stepped on him again and this time he grunted. "Focus on the point, Vander. We're done."

"Done with our agreement?" he asked like the words just weren't soaking into his brain.

"Yes. Done. Over. Dead and buried."

"Mind if I cut in?" came a masculine voice just to my left.

Vander and I both looked over to see a nice gentleman who was closer to my father's age than mine. He wore a cowboy hat and a friendly smile. He shot me a greasy wink and Vander expanded like an angry pufferfish.

"I do mind," Vander snapped, snatching my hand in his and tugging me off the dance floor and away from the gathering.

He didn't stop until we found ourselves in a campsite that wasn't currently being rented. We could still hear the music, but it was definitely more private. He spun around right there in the dirt and put his hands on my shoulders while I tried to catch my breath. That had almost been a straight run and my lungs were not ready for that quite yet. Maybe never.

"I'm so glad we're on the same page."

"Huh?" Maybe the lack of oxygen had affected me more than I thought. The least he could do was act like he was heartbroken over cutting off our arrangement.

Vander grinned and my body responded. I swayed toward him and he looped his arms around my waist, plastering me to his impressive physique.

"No more agreement," he confirmed.

"Right."

"No more rules."

"Exactly."

"Now we're dating."

"Yes—no! Huh?" I jerked away from him. "What are you talking about?"

He pulled me back in. "I want to date you, Marlo."

"No."

He chuckled. "Yes. I do."

"Well, you can't."

"Why not? You just said the orgasms were really good."

I sputtered. "Sure. But so are the orgasms from my vibrator."

"Ouch." Vander winced.

"I want a husband and babies. Probably more than two."

Vander blinked, but didn't run off screaming. "I'm not on

board with two or more husbands, but I like your idea of kids. Like a whole Addams family."

Ignoring his usual humor, I kept going, needing him to understand. "Yes, exactly. I want a husband, kids, and a black picket fence. And you don't want any of that." I reached down and unlooped his arms from my waist. I couldn't have this conversation while he was touching me. His hugs felt too good. They were distracting me.

Without me to hang on to, he folded his arms across his chest. "So these men you were dating before? The date you had the night we met. They wanted marriage and babies and an ostentation crypt?"

My lips wobbled before I could tell them that nothing was funny about this conversation. "Well, not exactly."

"Exactly," Vander parroted. "So go out with me. On a real date. We can discuss all the details of our five-year plans. What do you say, maybe on our fifth date?" When I didn't answer right away, he got his hands on my hips. "You know you want to."

"No, I really don't."

I really did.

I wanted Vander to be the guy who could give me the happy marriage and the house full of kids, but this was all just a joke to him. He said it himself: he got bored easily. It was all fun and games right now between us, but before long, I'd develop feelings and he'd get bored. This spelled disaster all over it.

Vander dropped his chin to his chest and I studied the crown of his head. When his head finally came up again, there wasn't a single trace of humor on his face. If I had to bet on it, I'd say he was tired. Defeated. Beat down.

"I just need one person to believe in me, Marlo. Someone who sees beyond the jokes and thinks I can do more in life."

I remembered the panic on his face at the hospital when he couldn't find Milly. The way he'd carried his grandma to the house so she wouldn't hurt herself. How he'd picked out a necklace that was unconventional yet exactly what suited me. It scared me to death to admit how I felt, but I couldn't lie.

"I believe in you, Vander."

He leaned down and kissed my cheek. When he pulled back, he stared into my eyes for so long I couldn't breathe. Couldn't look away. I felt like I was standing on the edge of a growing chasm in the earth, being asked to jump to one side or the other. Knowing the wrong choice would lead to utter destruction.

"Here's the thing, Bubbles. Your face says you don't want to date me, which is what everyone else looks at. They see that sour expression and dark cloud hanging over your head and they assume things about you. But I'm looking in your eyes and they're practically begging me to take you out on a date."

And there it was. My truth on display for Vander to read like a book.

"Fine," I said on a heavy exhale. There wasn't really a choice after all. Not really.

Vander didn't wait for clarification. His mouth was on mine, a punishing kiss of tongues and teeth just to prove his point.

And I let him.

ander

I STARED into the fridge and skimmed my gaze over the yogurts stacked up on the top shelf, colorful fruit overflowing the drawers, and skim milk in the door. All G-Mil's groceries. What even was skim milk? Water with white dye added? Gross.

Ten days she'd been living with me and she'd already taken over my house. With a heavy sigh, I opened the freezer and found my frozen waffles under a box of assorted fruit-flavored sugar-free popsicles. Double gross.

"Vandy? Is that you?" G-Mil hollered from the parlor.

"Yeah. Just making some breakfast," I yelled back, popping two waffles into the toaster.

"It's almost noon," G-Mil admonished. She said something else, but I couldn't make it out.

I'd been out late again with Marlo the night before, making her see stars up against a pine tree where no one at the Friday night jam session could see us. The woman had me tied in knots and more confused than ever. She'd agreed to date me, but it had felt like calling a cease fire where the opponent hated your guts even as they waved the white flag. The victory wasn't very sweet.

When my waffles popped up, I didn't bother with a plate. I wrapped them in a paper towel so I didn't burn myself and headed for the parlor, taking a huge bite of the waffly goodness.

G-Mil was on the couch with another old lady. This one was taller and thinner than Grandma, her hair more silvery than white. Her clothes, however, looked like they came straight out of G-Mil's closet. I almost doubled back for sunglasses to protect my eyes from the neon track suit, but didn't want to be rude.

"Oh good, Vandy, you're here. Meet my bestie, Gertrude. Gertie, this is my darling Vandy."

I transferred the waffles to my left hand and shook Gertie's liver-spotted hand. She held on with the grip of an old lady keeping one foot out of the grave at all costs.

"I've heard so much about you, Vander."

And I've heard nothing about you. I didn't think that would go over well either, so I gave her the smile that always worked on G-Mil. "Same, Gertie, same. Although, I am a bit hurt to hear I'm not G-Mil's bestie." I gave Grandma the puppy dog eyes while trying, unsuccessfully, to get my hand back.

"Ohh," G-Mil groused, waving away my antics. "You're my best male bestie. Everyone needs a male and a female bestie. Some things I can't talk to you about, Vandy."

I frowned, deciding maybe my hand was now going to be Gertie's. "Like what?"

G-Mil's eyebrows went up into her hairline. "Like vaginal dryness, for one."

I reared my head back involuntarily. "Please don't ever say those two words again."

G-Mil smiled smugly. "You've made my point."

"Are you single, Vander?" Gertie interjected, her eyes taking on a gleam I didn't like. Probably because she started petting the back of my hand, right when G-Mil talked about vag—nope. Not even going to think about those two words.

"Actually," I preened. "I'm not single. I'm officially dating Marlo."

"Oh, that's wonderful!" G-Mil clapped her hands and Gertie momentarily let go to catch the waffle that fell out of my free hand. I used the distraction to move myself three feet away. Unless ol' Gertie had unusually long arms, that ought to be enough to stay out of the grabbing zone. I did miss the waffle though, but sacrifices had to be made.

"It is wonderful. In fact, I'm taking her out on a date shortly, so I need to run and get things set up. You going to be okay here by yourself this afternoon, G-Mil?"

Grandma watched Gertie as she sniffed the dropped waffle and then popped it in her mouth with a shrug. "I should be fine. Gertie will be staying over tonight while the cleaners are working on her place. Like a sleepover!"

I frowned. *Two* old ladies in my house? I might have to buy a second fridge and keep it in my bedroom. "That sounds like a pretty deep clean."

Gertie smacked her lips and swallowed my waffle. "Oh, it is. I had a cat, you see. Died last month, may she rest in peace."

Gertie sniffed and I reached over to the end table to grab her a tissue. I had to practically throw it at her as I didn't want to get close enough to get ensnared again. The tissue just floated in the air and sank to her white-tennis-shoe-clad feet. Grandma shot me a dirty look, but I ignored her. I didn't have time to play hand-holdsies with Gertie. I had an epic date to plan out.

"Gertie's granddaughter is coming to town and staying with her for a few days, but she's horribly allergic to cats."

Gertie gave us a sour look. "She's allergic to staying in one place too. That girl has moved to all the major cities in America and left a trail of broken hearts everywhere she goes. Rainey is stunning, but she's also trouble with a capital T. I'm going to try my best to be a good influence."

"Can't wait to see how that works out. I remember Rainey from when she grew up here. She's quite a pistol." G-Mil nodded her head effusively.

I shoved the last bite of waffle in my mouth and brushed my hands off with the paper towel. "Okay, well, I have to get going."

Gertie waved her hand in the air. "I'll be out of your hair in just a few days, my boy!"

That stopped me in my tracks. I turned to G-Mil with a lifted brow. "A few days?"

She turned her head in my direction, but trained her gaze over my left ear. "Don't you want your grandmother to be happy?"

I sighed. We both knew the answer to that. And quite frankly, I had the room in this big old house. How would a houseguest for a few days do any harm?

"Don't wait up for me tonight," I tossed over my shoulder as I left the parlor.

"I wouldn't dream of it, Vandy!" G-Mil called back.

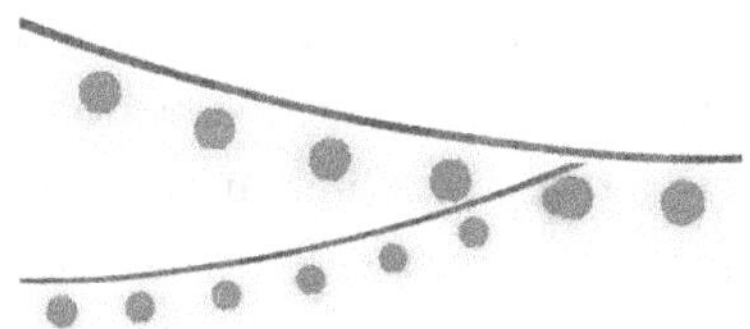

"What the hell is this?" Marlo gestured to the unmarked barn that looked like it had seen better days. Maybe even better centuries. She looked adorable in tight black jeans, her signature Doc Martens, and a black-and-white flannel that was unbuttoned enough to have me stealing side glances at her cleavage.

I grabbed Marlo's hand and tugged her along to the side door I'd been instructed to enter. "You look good, Bubbles. Like open-casket good." When she groaned, I kept going. "Do you trust me?"

"No."

I smirked at her. "Yes, you do."

She sighed and then snuggled into my side. "Okay, fine. I do. Just don't tell anyone I've gone soft."

"I wouldn't dare." I pulled open the door and gestured for her to walk in before me. It took a few seconds for our eyes to adjust. When they did, Marlo gasped.

Rows of glassed-in lanes spread out before us. All the lanes had bullseyes at the far end. Just inside each lane's door was an array of weapons, all the way from hatchets to pocket knives to ninja stars to bows and arrows.

"Can I help you?" a man said from our right.

We turned, seeing a man with a hefty beard lined with gray. He wore flannel like he'd just come from felling a tree out in the forest.

"Hi, you must be Joel. I'm Vander and this is Marlo. I called earlier today and requested a lane for the afternoon?"

"Ah, yes. Nice to meet you both. I have you down at the far end in the luxury lane. Every type of weapon we have on the premises is at your disposal. Your instructor will be with you the first hour, showing you how to safely use each weapon. From there, you can practice as much as you'd like. We also have a food and drink menu, so just let us know when you're ready for a break." Joel spoke over his shoulder as he walked us to the far end of the barn.

He introduced us to the instructor and then left us alone. While the instructor got the place set up for us, Marlo turned to me, her mouth dropped open still.

"What is all this?"

I shrugged, acting nonchalant when I actually felt pretty good about my date idea. No other woman would appreciate this kind of date, but I had a feeling it was exactly what would impress Marlo.

"You told me you knew ten ways to murder a man. I figured that number was a little low. Let's find at least ten more, shall we?"

Her mouth snapped shut and then the corners tipped up. I waited her out, like watching the full moon rise in a midnight sky, knowing it'll be spectacular. Pretty soon, the grin was amplified to a straight up smile, and then I nearly had to shield my eyes from the blinding beam. Marlo's eyes, creasing in the corners, made me think she was actually thinking of ten new ways to please a man. Specifically, me.

I growled, pulling her into my chest and dipping my head to whisper in her ear. "I love the smile, Bubbles, but if you keep looking at me like that, I'll have to kick out the instructor, clear that table of weapons, and take you right here where everyone walking by will see."

Marlo pulled her head back, eyes only heating further. "Hmm."

I squeezed my eyes shut and touched my forehead to hers. "Shit, Marlo. You're killing me."

Marlo shimmied her hips, rubbing up on the weapon in my pants, the little devil. "I can't help it. You brought me weapons and it turns me on."

"Okay, everyone ready?" the instructor called, clapping his hands as he entered our lane.

We startled and broke away, but not before Marlo's cheeks took on a pink tinge, giving us away. The instructor cleared his throat and admirably went on with this instruction, showing us each weapon and how it worked. By the time he left, Marlo was so hot and bothered, I wasn't sure she was still listening to the poor guy. The second he walked out the door, leaving us alone in the lane, she picked up a ninja star and twirled it around her finger once, making me a bit nervous.

"I had no idea..." she whispered, shaking her head slowly, like this date had awakened something inside of her. Then she twirled and threw the weapon toward the target, actually hitting the outer ring, lodging the blade in the wood backing. She tossed her arms up and cheered.

I shook my head, grinning like a fool at my girl. "I probably won't be able to recreate that, but I'll try." I grabbed my own star and tossed it like the instructor had shown us. It wedged into the wood alright.

About three feet south of the target.

Marlo burst out laughing, snuggling into me and saying I'd do better next time. It would have been more convincing if she wasn't choking on laughter. And so it went for another hour. Marlo tried out a weapon and rocked at it. I tried the same weapon and made a fool of myself. I finally gave up and ordered a round of beer and wings while Marlo kept herself entertained. It was far more fun for me to watch her in her element.

When she'd finally depleted her energy and plopped down on the couch next to me to swig her room-temperature beer, she looked happy. Happier than I'd ever seen her.

"You know, fun looks good on you," I murmured, handing her a plate of wings.

She plunked her beer down on the table and bit into a wing. "I'm not opposed to having fun. I guess the problem is that what most people consider fun, I don't. I always thought there was something wrong with me for not liking all the things my friends like. I've always been kind of a weirdo."

I put my arm around her shoulder and tucked her into me. "There's not a damn thing wrong with you, Bubbles. You're just misunderstood."

She snorted. "Now I sound like some kind of temperamental artist."

The door to our lane opened and the woman who'd taken our food order stuck her head in. "Ready for another round or the bill?"

I looked over at Marlo. She gave me a small smile, that

heated look back in her eyes. I looked at the server. "Bill, please."

Marlo giggled as the woman left and the lighthearted sound did something to me. I wanted to find more ways to make her giggle. Find every last activity on this planet that was fun to her. To make sure she always understood that she wasn't weird. Different didn't mean weird.

Marlo made a move for her wallet, but I stilled her hand.

"The date's on me, Bubbles."

Her smile turned sharp. "You may be a bajillionaire, but if I let you buy our date, you'll start to think I owe you. You'll make me pay you back in twisted sexual favors."

"God, I hope so," I muttered, earning myself a sputtered laugh from Marlo before those smoldering eyes were back on me.

"I might find it fun to really owe you. I'd like you to buy me one of those ninja stars, then."

"Your wish is my command." I did the math in my head. I'd need to borrow money again from G-Mil. My allowance wasn't going to keep covering my groceries plus all the things I wanted to buy Marlo.

But the look Marlo gave me when I placed a shiny new murder star in her hand made the groveling for money worth it.

The enthusiastic blow job she gave me in my truck—which, thank fuck, didn't include any actual weapons—just a mile down the road from the barn made it worth it too.

CHAPTER TWENTY-TWO

$\mathcal{M}$arlo

THERE WAS a rhythm to funeral homes. People seemed to leave this earthly plane all at the same time, as if to have some friends along to make the journey to the afterlife. Holidays were a tough time, mostly because loss was felt so acutely then when all should be warm and fuzzy. Thankfully, I'd gotten through the holiday rush of funerals and I had much more free time on my hands now that spring was upon us. Even for a dark girl, one could only take so much death and darkness.

This meant I had all kinds of time on my hands to think of Vander. And boy, did I think of Vander. I'd watched my friends turn to simpering giggles and blushes when they got obsessed with a guy, but I'd never experienced it myself.

It was horrible.

I'd purposely kept a bit of distance between us the last few days. There was something growing between us that had my lungs constricting in a panic. The pull had only gotten stronger, which mystified me. I actually found my chin in hand, staring out the back window of my office today, replaying all the things Vander could do with his hands and body in the cramped space of his truck. A cawing black bird had flown across the window so abruptly I had no choice but to blink back to the present. When I realized I'd gone all moony again, I'd slapped myself across the cheek. Gently, of course. If there was to be any significant slapping, I wanted it across my butt cheeks and done by Vander.

Shit. See? There I went again, thinking about Vander.

I shoved away from my desk and called it a day. I wasn't getting anything done anyway. Once all the lights were turned off and the trash was collected, I headed upstairs to see if I could help with dinner.

"Hey, Marlo, you're done early," Mom called from the kitchen, her back to me. My thick boots weren't exactly quiet going up the stairs.

"These old goats in Blueball refuse to die, I guess," I drawled, knowing she'd shake her head at me but secretly find me a tiny bit funny.

"Just means you have more time to hang out with your parents and we know how much you love that."

I wasn't the only one who spoke in varying shades of sarcasm in this family. I came up behind Mom at the stove and gave her a quick hug. "What's for dinner? Can I help?"

"What? No date tonight?"

I reared back and got busy washing my hands. "Why would I have a date?" Normal women would have already told their parents about a guy they were officially dating, but I'd never had a boyfriend, so the rules of etiquette were vague and easily overlooked.

"Marlo," Mom muttered, handing me a head of lettuce from the fridge and pointing to the chopping block. "I may be busy with your dad's doctor appointments, but don't think I don't notice you sneaking out and staying out late. There must be a boy."

I took the lettuce from her and used the largest knife we

owned to massacre it. "First of all, I'm twenty-six years old, so if I were dating someone, he'd be a man, not a boy."

"So are you saying you *are* dating someone?" Mom handed me an onion and a tomato, a mama on a mission to uncover the truth.

"Valeria?" Dad's voice carried up the stairs. "We have a guest for dinner!"

We both spun around, Mom with a massive phallic cucumber in hand, and me with a giant knife poised for attack. Dad came around the corner of the kitchen with his hand on Vander's back, both of them grinning. Probably for different reasons.

"Here are my girls," Dad murmured, oblivious to how awkward we looked. Awkward was just normal for us.

"Yep, there's Marlo. Deadly, just like I like her," Vander quipped.

I slapped the knife down on the counter and Mom did the same with her vegetable, wiping her hands on a towel before shaking hands with Vander.

"I'm Valeria, Marlo's mother."

Vander shot her a smile that made my knees weak. Damn, the man could turn on the charm like a spigot of water. "I'm Vander Booth, your new next-door neighbor. I can see where Marlo gets her good looks."

Mom smiled like the king of fucking England had graced us with his presence.

"I found him skulking around the house," Dad said dryly.

Vander's ears went red. "Thought I saw an opossum go under your back porch."

Dad clapped him on the back. "Sure you did."

Vander looked over at me in alarm. I shot him a look back that said, *hey, you got yourself into this, don't look at me to save you.*

"Would you like to join us for dinner? I made eggplant lasagna and Marlo is fixing up the salad. We eat pretty healthy around here, so you'll have to pardon the fat-free dressing."

Vander, bless the liar, smiled like eggplant and fat-free salad dressing was his catnip. "I'd love to. Thank you so much. Can I help set the table?"

Mom was smitten and Dad was eyeing the two of us like he was trying to solve a complicated math equation. As for me, I hid my flaming face by chopping up the rest of the salad. When we had a seat at the table, Vander directly across from me, Mom gave him a pointed look.

"Are you the reason our daughter is rarely around these days?"

Vander looked at me, almost as if he was asking for permission to speak freely. I lifted a shoulder and let it fall. The cat was out of the bag.

"Yes, ma'am, I believe that I am. I can't seem to stay away."

Dad grunted while Mom swooned. I straightened my spine and did what I should have done last week.

"Vander and I are dating."

The silence around the table pressed on my skin. Vander's foot nudged mine under the table. I glanced at him and he had a twinkle in his eye that made the uncomfortable announcement easier. Dad's chair let out a creak as he leaned forward, elbows on the table, eggplant forgotten.

"Our girl has always been the blessing we never saw coming."

"Dad," I said softly, begging him over the invisible airwaves to quit whatever he was about to say. I didn't feel like being so embarrassed I'd have to go dig a hole and fall into it.

"No, no. He should hear this. We didn't think we could have children, so when Marlo arrived, we felt like we'd been blessed beyond measure. For whatever reason, she was unlike other children. She started reading at three. Helped me with the business before she started kindergarten. And then there was bedtime."

Mom let out a laugh, wiping her mouth with a napkin and taking over the story. "Most kids want to be read to, but not our Marlo. She wanted to tell *us* a story. So each night, she'd make up a long tale centered around castles and princesses and dragons. The princess and the dragon always fell in love and lived happily ever after in the castle. We tried to tell her that's not how fairy tales ended, but she wouldn't change her mind."

Vander's gaze was like a heavy weight on my skin. "I think the fairy tales must have gotten it wrong, then."

I didn't want his words to seep into my soul and bolster the self-esteem that had always taken a hit around "normal" people, but damn, did they soothe something that had stung for so long, I'd forgotten it was still there.

"She got a dollhouse one year for Christmas," Dad said, voice somber. I cringed inside, knowing what was coming. "She loved that thing so much I couldn't get her to leave her room to go play with friends."

Vander smiled at me, unaware of the ending. "Did she buy miniature furniture for it?"

Dad nodded. "Saved every penny for each piece. Cut cloth to make drapes. Painted the porch rails navy blue when we told her she couldn't use black. Even made one of the rooms a funeral parlor like her dear old dad."

"Do you still have it?" Vander asked me, leaning his elbows on the table.

I shook my head and dropped his gaze. "Nah. Some girl in third grade came over for a playdate and kicked it. Her foot went right through the dang thing, splinters flying everywhere. Said I scared her when I showed her the miniature coffin."

Vander's mouth dropped open in outrage. The table went silent. I brushed away the old hurt with a practiced shrug. "Then I found Paisley, Keva, and Audrey. We became friends and lived happily ever after."

Vander's foot found mine under the table. "I got a dog for Christmas one year when I was eight. Larry was allergic though and we had to get rid of it two days later."

Mom's fork clanked to her plate. "I guess life doesn't come without disappointments, does it?"

Conversation flowed freely after that, though it didn't take long before Mom and Dad were talking over us, leaving us out.

Vander's head darted side to side like he was at a ping-pong match. He finally gave up following when it was clear our participation in the conversation wasn't necessary. His foot began to rub up my leg, an evil grin tugging at his lips. He looked just like the dragon in my memory, sweet-talking the princess into turning her back on the prince and choosing a different kind of life.

Suddenly, I wanted to be free of this house as soon as possible. I scraped my chair back and collected the dishes. Vander leaped to his feet and helped me, earning himself a pleasantly surprised look from my mother. When we were at the sink and blessedly alone, Vander snuck a sniff, burying his nose in my neck and inhaling.

"Fuck, I've been wanting to do that all night."

I chuckled, even as I shivered. "You're very weird."

"High praise, my dear." He pulled back and helped rinse the dishes before putting them haphazardly in the dishwasher. I didn't have the heart to tell him that Mom would go behind us and rearrange everything. "Do they always do that?"

I looked down at him, bent over the dishwasher. "Do what?"

"Talk around you like that?"

I grabbed another plate and handed it to him. "Pretty much. Hence the reason for two point five children at the very least. I want them to have built-in friends so they never feel alone."

Vander didn't have a chance to respond to that when my parents walked into the kitchen. Mom went straight to the stovetop while Dad cornered Vander.

"Let's box up some of these leftovers. You kids can take some next door to Milly."

I glanced up sharply. "How'd you know Milly was next door?"

Mom just sighed. "I do have eyes, Marlo. Why else would Vander have installed a chair lift on his front stairs?"

I opened my mouth but closed it again when I heard Dad's question to Vander.

"I hear you're jobless. Have plans to remedy that?"

"He's not jobless, Dad. He's retired," I interjected, quick to stand up for Vander. He was a millionaire, not an adult still living with his grandma. I mean, he was, but for honorable reasons.

Dad put his hands up in peace. "Just wondering what kind of man retires at twenty-eight." He narrowed his eyes at Vander. "Thirty? How old are you, son?"

"I'm thirty-two, sir. I actually sold my first company and I'm taking care of my grandmother while I figure out what my next business will be."

I snapped the lid on the Tupperware and shoved it into Vander's gut before he could start talking about the land behind our properties and the various reasons why Blueball needed a paintball course. I didn't want to ruin a perfectly good night with an argument about land. The city council had already made contact with Milly about purchasing it from her, so it was best to just keep our noses out of it.

"Gotta get these leftovers to Milly before they get cold!" I pulled Vander across the kitchen.

"Thank you so much for dinner. It was lovely finally meeting you!" Vander barely got the words out before I was pulling him down the stairs. "Jeez, Marlo. What's the hurry? To be honest, Milly probably won't eat this once she hears it has eggplant."

"I know," I hissed back. "I was just trying to get out of there before they roped us into a game of Monopoly."

Vander tossed me a funny look. "You guys do that often? Play board games?"

The cool evening air hit my overheated skin as we pushed outside and began to walk over to Vander's house. "Sadly, yes."

"Hmm."

I looked over at him, looping my arm through his. "What?"

He looked up at the tall pine trees between our two properties. "I don't think I can recount even one time Larry and Mary played a board game with me."

I winced, forgetting just how lucky I was in a lot of ways I tended to overlook. It wasn't the worst thing to be an only child to parents who were embarrassingly in love.

"I'll play a board game with you, Annoying."

Vander's grin was quick. "Yes! Have you ever played strip Chutes and Ladders?"

Vander's front door opened before we climbed his porch steps. An old man stood there with a frown on his wrinkled face. He was also missing a shoe. "What's all the racket out here?"

I looked at Vander, who looked just as confused as me.

"Who are you?"

"I'm Jerry. Who the fuck are you?"

Vander looked ready to dump eggplant lasagna over the man's head. "I'm Vander. The owner of this house."

The old guy sniffed and did a cursory glance over us both before he moved away from the door. "I guess you can come in, then."

"Why, thank you so much." Vander replied, using all the sarcasm I usually toted around in case of a social emergency like this, and handed me the Tupperware. "Where's Milly?"

"In the parlor with Gertie," the man said gruffly. "Gotta warn you though. We're five hands into strip poker and you might see things you've never seen before."

Vander stopped on a dime. He shut his eyes, his fingers gripping the bridge of his nose. "My house is being overrun by old people."

I hooked a thumb over my shoulder in the direction of my cemetery. "Welcome to my life."

That got his eyes open again, snapping with anger, but also a resigned kind of mirth. "Jerry!"

"Yeah?"

Vander's gaze didn't leave mine while he barked out directions. "Share that lasagna, don't spill on my couch, and for fuck's sake, don't come near my bedroom for the rest of the night. We clear?"

Jerry cackled. "I have a feeling your night might be more fun."

"Jerry!" Vander snapped.

"Alright, alright, I'm going." Jerry shuffled away.

Vander didn't move, his gaze burning me all the way down to where my scuffed boots were melting into his pristine floors. "You still want to stay?"

I scoffed. Wild dragons couldn't drag me away. "Old people in residence are a step up from dead people. Of course I'm staying."

Vander's grin was everything. Then he was a blur of motion, bending down to pick me up and toss me over his shoulder. I squeaked but he ignored me, running us down the hallway to the stairs that led to his bedroom. I hadn't seen it before, but I had a feeling I wasn't going to get much of a tour this time either.

CHAPTER TWENTY-THREE

 ander

EARLY MORNING LIGHT filtered in through the windows I had yet to buy curtains or blinds for. My bedroom was at the back of the house with a view of the cemetery and the parcel of empty land behind it. For privacy's sake—I didn't need the spirits of generations past looking up and seeing me naked, inspiring a haunting by some thirsty ghost-wench—I should get window coverings, but I didn't want to disrupt my view. Every morning I would wake up and stare out at the greenery and take it all in. The stillness outside was what I needed to inspire calm inside my brain. I enjoyed the way nature didn't need jokes and brash voices to continue on with its rhythm. Little birds and insects marched along, doing their jobs, all in organized chaos. It was a big ecosystem where everyone fit in and everyone had a purpose.

"You have a line between your eyebrows when you're broody," came Marlo's sleepy voice.

I glanced down at her, tucked against me, her black hair spread out like ink on the white pillowcase. She wore only the necklace I'd given her, a sight that never failed to turn me on. I'd kept her up most of the night, or rather, she'd kept *me* up. The woman was insatiable.

"Did my heavy breathing wake you?" I leaned down and kissed her, wanting to capture that first waking moment from her. It was a gift to wake up with her in my bed.

Marlo wrapped her hand around the back of my neck and held me still. "Don't do that," she whispered.

"Do what?"

"Joke right out of the gate. Not with me." She held my gaze, not accusatorially, but with a knowing that made my skin itch. "You don't need to."

I skimmed my nose along her cheek. I'd wanted someone to see the real me for so long, now that someone was here, it was unnerving. "It's a habit now."

Marlo kicked my shin under the covers. "Good thing you're not an old dog."

"Ouch, woman. I'm more of a horndog than an old dog." She snorted and I nipped at her earlobe with my teeth. Soon we were tussling under the covers, naked body parts brushing and squeezing and, in my case, growing.

"Good morning!" G-Mil trilled, knocking loudly on my door before whipping it open.

Marlo yelped and yanked on the covers to cower. I felt a breeze on my backside that spelled trouble for G-Mil's viewpoint, but it served her right for barging in.

"Jeez, G-Mil," I groaned, grabbing a pillow to cover my torso and sitting up. "How about some warning?"

"I knocked!" she snapped back, like the millisecond of warning was plenty. "Besides, I don't have my glasses on yet, so I can't see a damn thing. Is that lump Marlo?"

"Morning, Milly," Marlo deadpanned from somewhere under the sheets.

"Good morning, dear! Hope we didn't keep you two up with

our rousing game of strip poker. That dirtbag Jerry cheated. He had on three pairs of underwear!"

I ran a hand over my face, desire from just a moment ago dead and buried. "I don't want to know about Jerry's underwear-wearing habits, G-Mil. Was there a point in barging in here so early?"

Grandma came closer, her glasses dangling on her chest from the bejeweled string she kept them on. "Yes, actually. I invited a few people over to a barbecue tonight. Don't worry, I already called in an order from Grass. You won't have to lift a finger." G-Mil chuckled. "Unless ol' Darcy tries to table dance again. It took two grown men at the senior home to get her down."

I groaned. "More old people?" My house was being overrun by the geriatric set. Every time I turned around there was another one. They were multiplying like bunnies.

"It's your fault!" G-Mil trilled.

"How do you figure?"

"You installed that chair lift and everyone wants to give it a try."

"Is Blueball really that starved for entertainment?"

"Yep," Marlo answered from under the sheets. "One Christmas break we bought blocks of ice and held races down the hill out by the highway. Would have been a fine way to pass the day except one of the guys I went to high school with convinced some girl to get on a block with him. He got a certain part of himself stuck to the ice block trying to get frisky and had to be taken to the ER. Pretty sure he moved away not long after that. You don't really get over having your balls stuck to a sheet of ice in front of the whole town."

I gaped at the mound of sheets, moving my hand to shield my own balls, shrinking back inside my body in sympathy. And fear.

G-Mil snickered. "I remember that kid."

"Is that when they named the town Blueball?" I asked. Marlo snorted and the sheets began to shake. "What?"

G-Mil shook her head and spun around to leave. An idea hit that would save me from the geriatric barbecue tonight. And save my brain from thinking about that poor kid's balls. There was only one problem. I scrambled out of bed, the pillow glued to my hips. "Hey, G-Mil?"

I caught her by the door, lowering my voice so hopefully Marlo wouldn't hear. "I plan to take Marlo out somewhere nice tonight. Any chance I can borrow a few bucks?"

G-Mil reached up and patted my cheek. "This allowance thing isn't really working out, is it? How about we forget about it? I can't be keeping track of the money you borrow, and frankly, I like Marlo. I want to see you spoil her."

I pulled the strong but tiny woman into a hug, which was a bit awkward with a pillow between us, but would have been more awkward without it. "Thanks, Grandma."

She left with a wink and I ran back to pounce on the bed. Marlo yelped and tossed the sheets back to finally reveal herself. Her dark hair was a tangled mess around her face and her cheeks were pink from being stuffed under the covers for so long. Her eyes snapped with intelligence. Hell, even the flutter of her eyelashes was intoxicating. She was fucking gorgeous.

I climbed over her like I was going to tickle her, my dick already back in action with my balls having forgotten the ice-block story. They had a one-track mind, thank God.

"Allowance?"

My gaze snapped back to Marlo's face. Shit. She wasn't supposed to have heard that part. "Yeah, we had a deal when I moved back to town. I was supposed to be living on a fixed income."

Marlo's fingers crept along the line of her necklace, feeling each dark stone I'd given her. "Why?"

I shrugged, wanting to hurry and peel back the layers of sheets until I got to her naked body. "G-Mil wanted me to act like a normal person, not some millionaire playboy with money to burn."

"But you bought me a necklace. And paid for our date. And bought me the ninja star."

I was starting to feel uncomfortable again. I searched my brain for a joke but came up empty. The truth would have to do. "I wanted to buy you those things. It wiped out my monthly allowance but seeing your face was worth it." I sighed, a smile tugging on my mouth. "I kind of see why G-Mil wanted me to save. I'd gotten to a point where I didn't appreciate the little things money could do."

Marlo stared up at me, her dark eyes burning into my skin.

I squeezed my knees against her sides. "Say something."

Her head began to shake side to side. And then she lifted off the pillow and opened her mouth, flicking her tongue against the tip of me like I'd presented her with an ice cream cone. Every muscle in my body tightened all at once. When she began to work me over in earnest, the hot cave of her mouth making my brain shutter to a stop, I gripped the headboard behind her and tried not to fall completely in love with the dark-haired woman who'd lit something inside me with every frown and dirty look.

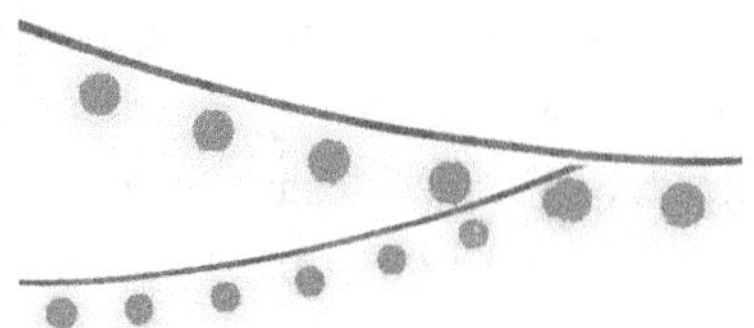

"What is all this?" Marlo spun in a circle, taking in the hotel room I'd booked for this evening quite a few miles outside of Blueball.

Marlo had gone to work for a few hours while I planned

our date. It was appalling how far one had to drive to find a decent five-star hotel. After watching Marlo's parents at dinner, I'd gotten a much better insight into the inner workings of her brain. Surprisingly, it wasn't a dark and stormy place. Marlo wanted what most people wanted: acceptance and love. She wanted the tight marriage her parents had, and she needed to be someone's first priority. I didn't know if I had what it took to be good at marriage, but I sure as hell had no problem making her my priority and this date was part of showing her.

There was something soul-satisfying in making Marlo forget to scowl.

"This," I answered, flipping on the lights and shutting the door behind me, "is our date."

A table had been set up by the broad window, silver domes keeping our dinner warm. A bottle of champagne sat in a bucket of ice and a plate of chocolate-dipped strawberries kept the whole presentation festive.

Marlo didn't answer. She looked all around the room in a daze, as if someone would soon jump out from behind the ottoman and tell her she'd been punked. I shook my head, wondering what the hell was wrong with the men in Blueball for not taking this woman out on the regular. Did they really only see the black combat boots, a heavy scowl, and dark flashing eyes? Did she intimidate them? Whatever it was, I was grateful for it. I could swoop in here like some dashing prince from her youth and sweep her off her booted feet.

I held out a hand, palm up. "Madam?" Marlo slid her palm in mine and let me tug her over to the table where I handed her a single long-stemmed black rose. "How about dinner, then dancing? Or we can buck tradition and dance first, then eat?"

The first smile hit me like a cashmere sweater sliding over my head. I wanted to burrow in and never let go. "Dinner, dancing, and..." She let her voice trail off, sexy as hell when she cleared her throat suggestively.

"Fucking? Please say fucking," I suggested with a bit-back smile.

She shook her head and licked her bottom lip. Suddenly dinner and dancing sounded like a very stupid idea when there were far better things to do all alone in a hotel room. "I need alliteration."

I swallowed hard, Adam's apple bobbing. I'd give her alliteration every fucking day if she just kept looking at me like that. "Dinner, dancing, dicking?"

The snort was inelegant, but the sparkle in her eyes was enough to make my night. I slid out her chair and gestured for her to sit. She did, tucking her long dark skirt beneath her while I pushed in her chair. I whipped the black cloth napkin off the table in a flourish and placed it across her lap.

"I contemplated showing up in a full suit of armor to pick you up like a proper prince, but the breastplate chafed horribly." I snatched the dome off her plate and watched her eyes sparkle with laughter.

"I don't really want a dragon to snatch me away at the end of the night, so perhaps it's better you left the suit of armor at home."

I sat across from her and we both dug into our meal, though I couldn't have recounted what the food actually was. I watched the way Marlo tasted everything as if eating for the first time. She ate most of what was on her plate, but she also savored every bite of it. I'd never thought of eating as sensual, but Marlo managed it with her full lips, straight spine, a flash of her tongue, and hooded eyes.

When she placed her fork next to her empty plate, I was harder than a steel pipe. I reached over to hold her hand, my thumb stroking her pale skin. "You deserve to be treated like that princess you imagined, Marlo."

She lifted a shoulder and let it drop. "Princesses and dragons. It's all just a storytime myth perpetuated on children to keep them reaching for the unachievable."

I rolled my eyes. "That's dark, even for you. And I'll prove you wrong. Time for the dancing portion of this evening, m'lady." I stood, scraping my chair back and holding my hand out for hers. I needed to touch more than just her hand or I was going to lose my mind.

She stood, letting me pull her further into the tiny living room area. I grabbed the remote the hotel staff had put out on the side table just as instructed, hitting play. Music floated across the room from hidden speakers, a '90s ballad heavy on the guitar. I'd seen her embalming playlists and knew the electric guitar was the most important component. I didn't care what we played, I just wanted Marlo in my arms.

I pulled her in close, each familiar curve pressed against my body. This time, she relaxed immediately in my embrace, as if my touch was no longer foreign. No hesitation. I considered it a huge win.

"I came up with a new slogan for the funeral home," I said conversationally as we swayed to the music.

Marlo lifted her head from my shoulder, surprise stamped across her face. "Oh yeah?"

I grinned. "We put the fun in funeral."

Her grin matched mine, and try as she might to fight it, I felt the rumble of laughter in her chest. "That's so Vander. I'll keep that in mind. In case I don't run the funeral home into the ground in the next few years."

I tightened my arm around her waist, suddenly serious. "Marlo."

I'd been thinking about everything and what she'd said about using the land for the expanded cemetery made a lot of sense. I could make my business dreams come true anywhere. I didn't want a fight over land to come between us. It was insignificant.

"It's fine, really," Marlo interrupted. "I'm not going to argue about the land. My friends actually came across a website today and sent me the link. Want to take the quiz with me?"

"Is it one of those magazine quizzes? Like, what kind of sex god am I?"

Marlo shook her head, giving me the stink eye. "No need for a quiz. I already know what kind of sex god you are."

I let go of her waist to grab my chest. "A compliment, dear Marlo?"

She drilled me right in the gut with her finger. "I'm serious! It's a career quiz. Let's find out what profession you're best suited for. Mine said I'd be a good politician or a spin instructor." I reared my head back while she shrugged. "I think the quiz got a sense for my rays of darkness."

I put my hand out. "Hand me this quiz. I will prove it's bullshit and you can rest easy you'll never be mayor of Blueball."

Marlo grinned up at me and then sat on the loveseat, pulling her phone out of her pocket. "Let's find you a career, Mr. Booth."

I sat next to her, inhaling her scent while she asked me the questions. I wasn't sure what I answered. All I wanted was to keep the smile on Marlo's face. It struck me that this was not normal behavior. I'd never, not once, worried about the expression on a woman's face. That was her business, not mine. So why did Marlo's happiness mean so much to me? The answer was obvious. I didn't even need G-Mil to smack me upside the head to figure it out.

"Did you hear me?" Marlo's voice broke me out of my thoughts.

"Huh?"

She snuggled into my side, flashing her phone in my face. "It says you should own a bed and breakfast! Isn't that perfect? The ol' Skinner house would be an amazing B and B!"

I blinked, shaking my head already. "No, no, no. Absolutely not. That test is rubbish."

Marlo scoffed. "No way. You'd be so good at it."

A warm glow filled my chest at her belief in me, as crazy as the idea was. "Thank you, but no. You just want me to give up the paintball idea."

Marlo stilled, and I wanted to punch myself in the face for killing her good mood.

"Well, you're not wrong." Marlo's voice was soft and slow. Like she was speaking her mind and measuring her words at the same time. "How is it that we can be fighting over this land and I still want you this much?"

I opened my mouth to tell her I didn't even care about the land anymore, but she lifted a leg and crawled over me, straddling my lap and setting my brain cells on fire. Her hands smoothed up my chest and gripped my hair. My heartbeat galloped away and I lost the thread of the conversation.

"You must really, really like me," she whispered in between kisses.

Fuck yes, I did.

CHAPTER TWENTY-FOUR

$\mathcal{M}$arlo

THE SECOND MY lips touched Vander's, he was tucking and rolling me. I found myself wedged between two couch cushions and his heavy body. He made me feel loved and protected, even if his designer clothing made me roll my eyes. It was something about the way he took such care with me. He genuinely wanted to get to know me beyond the undertaker role that everyone else fixated on. To be honest, he looked at me like my father looked at my mother. And that made me both scared and so hopeful my ribs ached from trying to hold in all the emotion.

"I do like you a lot, Bubbles," Vander said, his lips still so close they were brushing mine as he spoke. "But it's way more than that. I love you, Marlo."

I blinked, the wind rushing out of my lungs. He said he loved me. Just said it right there in the open like it wasn't the most amazing thing someone had ever said to me before. His gaze held mine, steady and unblinking. He wasn't searching me for a response. It was more that his gaze was caressing my skin, tracing over every detail and committing it to memory.

Before I could formulate a sentence, my traitorous eyes started burning. Then Vander's widened.

"Oh shit. Don't get all scared and freak out on me. You don't need to say it back." Vander's arms flexed, and for a terrible moment, I thought he might be getting off me.

I slammed my thighs around his waist and held on for dear life. If he was going to death-roll me to get out of this embrace that I'd made awkward by freezing up, I was going to cling to him the whole way. I squeezed my thighs and he wheezed, his face turning red.

"I'm not scared," I said on a rush. It was so obvious what was happening here and yet I'd blindly ignored it, thinking something so wonderful was certainly just a fairy tale. But if Vander could be brave, I could too. "I'm in love with you too."

Vander froze for far less time than me. He grinned and it was like watching the first ray of light come up over a dark, frozen tundra. "Of course you are. I'm irresistible."

I rolled my eyes but didn't get a chance to address his overinflated ego before he was pulling my blouse up and over my head. His hands trailed over my torso, leaving a trail of goose bumps in their wake. His breath was hot on my skin as he kissed each inch his hands had already discovered.

"How is it that you're this fucking hot and you love me?" he whispered to himself, so low I almost didn't catch it.

My head tossed back when his lips latched on to my nipple through my lacy bra. Then his words hit home and I struggled to pull my head back up, my fingers tightening in his hair again. I gave the strands a good yank and he looked up, his eyes glassy and mouth wet. Vander talked a big talk, so much so I sometimes forgot the truth: his ego was not nearly as big as his mouth. I was the lucky one who got to see beneath the shiny, confident veneer he showed the world.

"Your best friend is your grandma and you buy me gifts with all of your allowance. I'd say I'm the lucky one, Vander."

His eyes heated and the smile wasn't cocky this time. The smile was mine, the one he only gave me. For a girl who never valued smiles before, I was finding Vander's to be priceless.

"I've got rose petals strewn all over the bed in there." Vander cocked his head behind him to the left where a door was closed.

I reached down and pulled the cups of my bra below my breasts, baring myself to him. That bedroom looked too far away. "We can get there eventually, but let's start here."

I didn't even catch his grin this time. He dove in face-first to my breasts, wrenching a quick orgasm out of me before any further articles of clothing had come off. When I was chanting his name, he released my nipple from his mouth with a pop, shifting further south to kneel on the ground. The couch groaned, and when he tapped my thigh to get me to lift my hips, I slid halfway off the couch along with my skirt and shoes.

Vander knocked my knees outward, his broad shoulders taking up residence in the space between, staring hungrily between my legs as I perched on the edge of the couch. "Just like I like you."

He didn't bother removing my panties. He simply moved the soaked fabric to the side and used that talented tongue to taste the desire only he could put there. A single finger slid inside and then he focused on that bundle of nerves that was a sure thing. Stars exploded behind my eyelids and orgasm number two slammed into me without warning. My legs trembled, and when I blinked my eyes back open, I was half on the floor, my neck bent at an odd angle.

"Thinking that bed sounds good right about now," I said dryly, ignoring the way my voice shook. I could act unaffected, but the fact of the matter was that Vander knew all my buttons. He could work my body better than any man I'd ever been with.

Vander kissed the inside of each of my thighs, then stood up, offering me a helping hand. I took it, standing on wobbly legs and realizing he was still fully dressed. He must have realized it too because he looked down at himself. Only his hair was a disheveled mess. When his head came up again, his eyes sparkled with mischief.

"How about you lie down on the bed and get comfy?" He tugged me toward the bedroom, opening the door.

I gasped when I saw the huge bouquet of red and black roses next to the bed in a glass vase, along with matching petals strewn across the floor and on the bed. The place smelled heavenly.

"And what are *you* going to do?"

Vander waited until he'd brought me to the side of the bed and I climbed up, getting situated. "I figure you dress and undress lots of people in your line of work. Figured maybe it would be nice to watch someone else strip for you."

I barked out a laugh. It was true. I'd dressed a lot of dead people over the years. I loved how that information wasn't off-putting to Vander. He simply took it all in stride. I snuggled into the pillows behind me and lifted a hand in the air. "Proceed, stripper boy."

His hand went to his chest as he backed away from the bed. "Oh, no, m'lady. It's Stripper *Man*."

My cheeks literally hurt from smiling so much. "Pardon me. Proceed, Stripper Man."

Vander gripped his shirt behind his head, pausing dramatically before winking. "It's actually Stripper Man With the Giant Cock, but I'll let the shortened name slide." And then he was a blur of motion, his polo shirt flying over his head to land in a heap on the floor. The laughter dried in my throat, taking in his defined pec muscles and the stack of abs below. He shimmied left and then right, just a subtle shake of his hips that had me sitting up straight. My man could dance.

"Why didn't you join in when Milly and I had our dance-off?"

Vander's hands slid down his torso like he'd been practicing his moves while watching *Magic Mike*. They settled on his belt buckle while he slowly turned and gave me his backside which was just as impressive as the front.

"For shame, Marlo. You wanted me to strip for my grandma?"

I barked out another laugh. "No! I just meant I didn't know you had such impressive dance moves."

He bent at the waist and gave his impressive ass a shake. I squealed like the girly-girl I never knew I could be, which only egged him on more. Suddenly his arms were flexing and his belt was slapping through the air as he pulled it through the loops in one abrupt motion. I squirmed, squeezing my thighs together. Holy hell, that was hot.

Vander looked over his shoulder at me. "Did you like that, Bubbles?"

I bit my bottom lip and told him what he needed to know with my hungry eyes.

He spun back around and stalked toward the bed, still in his pants and shoes. By the time he got to the side of the bed, he'd toed off the shoes and had the pants unzipped and unbuttoned. He climbed onto the bed, careful to not touch me as he hovered above, like he was about to do pushups. His hands gripped the headboard and then he was undulating his body over me, *Magic Mike*-style, the pants slowly inching down his hips. My tongue darted out to lick my lips as my mouth went dry.

"Like what you see?" he huffed, his skin taking on a sweaty sheen. Stripping was hard work, a fact I never considered until just now.

I nodded enthusiastically.

"Then take me out and show me how much." His voice was nothing but a scrape of sound over gravel.

I jolted into action, dipping my hand into the band of his underwear and pulling out his fully erect cock. His skin was hot and velvety and straining against my palm. Vander let out a groan but didn't lower his body. Using just my tongue, I swiped across the tip and spread out the moisture that had beaded there. The bed began to quiver. I looked up at Vander and took in the vein in his forehead, the locked set of his granite jaw, and the way his arms trembled as he held himself over me.

Sliding my lips down his length, I took him all the way into my mouth until I was choking on him. Vander cursed and I pulled back, looking up at him coyly. His gaze was positively burning, watching me swallow him down.

"You like what you see?" I parroted.

"Yes, I really fucking do," he managed to say between clenched teeth.

I slid back down his length again, humming approval when he hit the back of my throat. His answering gasp would have made me grin if my stretched lips could have managed it. As it was, I came back up with a twist of my hand on his cock and immediately went back down for more. When he was panting above me a couple of strokes later, I cupped his balls, loving the power I held over his body in this moment.

"Fucking hell," he bit out, pulling his hips away from me and sliding out of my mouth. His body weight crushed me all at once as his arms gave out. He grunted and wedged between my legs, throwing them over his arms and thrusting inside of me in one desperate, inelegant move. We both gasped and he stilled, laying his forehead down between my breasts. His pants were still twisted around his ankles, but neither of us cared to stop.

"Needed."

My body pulsed, adjusting to his invasion, already lighting up and preparing for another orgasm. "Huh?"

"To." Vander sucked in a huge breath. "Be."

I poked his side, wanting him to move. "Are you stroking out or what?"

His head lifted, his chin still leaning on my breastbone. "Trying to talk here, Bubbles."

I grinned, squeezing my inner muscles and making him groan. "So say it already."

Vander let out an uncharacteristic growl and pushed up onto his elbows as if it took all the energy he had left in him to do so.

Nerve endings shot off and I tried to lift my hips to get him to move already. "I needed to be inside you." He pulled back and slid back inside, making my eyes cross. "Needed to be inside you when I tell you I love you." His rhythm increased and soon I was panting short choppy breaths.

Our bodies slid together, no room for air between us. It was like we both needed to be touching every inch of the other person. The second the wave crashed over me and my muscles squeezed him tight, Vander tipped over with me, his gaze locked on mine. "I love you."

His body shook and his skin immediately broke out in goose bumps, but he held my gaze like a life raft. Then he pulled out abruptly, hot ropes of liquid splashing on my stomach. He slumped against me, making an absolute mess between us. As we both came down, I ran my nails over his scalp, feeling like I was happier than I'd ever been.

"I love you too, Vander," I whispered, meaning it with every molecule of my dark little soul.

We didn't end up leaving bed until the next day. And only because we ran out of food and needed sustenance other than sex to survive.

And only when I finally agreed that he'd earned the name Stripper Man With the Giant Cock.

CHAPTER TWENTY-FIVE

ander

I COULDN'T RECALL a time when I'd been happier, yet also insanely calm. Normally happiness came from a fleeting moment at a good party or on an adventure, the high of something new never lasting long enough to become a deep-seated sense of joy. I was left to chase high after high, the aftertaste of boredom always quick to follow. It was exhausting.

But this thing with Marlo was all the highs strung together without the inevitable slide into boredom at the end. I woke up holding my breath until I saw her grumpy frown for the first time. When I lay down at night, it was either with her curled up next to me or on the phone retelling one of her dragons-and-princesses stories until I fell asleep. When she was working, I sent her juicy sexts just to see her deadpan responses.

"I think we need to institute a sock policy," G-Mil announced, adjusting her fake breasts before tossing an apron over her head.

I turned from the stove where I'd been stirring the pot of

noodles. I searched my brain but couldn't remember what we'd been talking about. I'd been daydreaming about Marlo again.

"Sock policy?"

G-Mil tied the apron behind her waist before slathering the French bread with butter and garlic. "Yeah. If you're getting frisky, you need to put a sock on your doorknob. Isn't that what they do at the colleges?"

I grimaced. "How about you just don't come in my room?"

G-Mil looked up at me with indignation alive and well on her face. "Well, what if I have a gentlemanly caller? I need a signal so you don't barge in on *me*!"

I grimaced harder. I did not need to be thinking of my grandma sleeping with some old guy. Especially not when she was dressed in a '20s flapper dress with fake breasts and a wig with long blonde hair. Smoothing my hands down my red-and-black velvet jacket, I considered putting actual tobacco in the pipe I held as a prop.

We were having Marlo over for a dinner party, and as we liked to do a couple times over the years when we saw each other, G-Mil and I had come up with a theme. Tonight's was Playboy. I was Hugh Hefner and G-Mil and Marlo had agreed to be Bunnies. Of course we'd have to take a picture all together. It might be my holiday photo instead of the Addams family one we'd done in the cemetery.

"How about you wait on the gentlemanly callers until you've moved back home?" I asked, concentrating on the noodles while the pasta sauce bubbled in a pot on the back of the stove.

"About that," G-Mil said slowly. "What if I don't go back?"

I quit stirring to whirl around. She had her hands on her hips, intelligent eyes examining my reaction from behind her glasses.

"As in, stay here?" I pointed at the floor to make sure we were talking about the same thing. G-Mil...staying here with me...at the Skinner house?

G-Mil shrugged dramatically and one gel cutlet escaped her dress and hit the tile floor with a splat. We both ignored it.

"Sure. I mean, it would be helpful for me. And for you. You wouldn't have to drive over every day to check on me. You sure as shit have the room." She cackled. "You got room for me and ten more just like me."

I rolled my eyes heavenward at the idea. "Lord help me."

The whirl and click of the chair lift out front interrupted our conversation. Which was fine by me. I needed to really think through this decision. Before Marlo, I would have jumped at the chance to have G-Mil live here with me, but given the Jerrys and Gerties that had arrived in her wake, I was reconsidering just how much privacy meant to me.

"Hold that thought." I turned down the heat on the noodles and hustled to the front door, throwing it open to see Marlo rising up the stairs like a queen upon her throne.

My jaw dropped open and I found myself drooling. Marlo wore a black patent leather bustier with all of her beautiful assets plumped up and served on a platter for my eyeballs. Her hair was utter perfection, a cascade of spiky layers that framed her gorgeous face. Eyes the color of midnight looked up at me from behind thick lashes and a smoky eye that made my pulse do a weird fluttering thing. When she reached the top of the stairs, she stood, her tall lanky frame encased in black leather pants that left absolutely nothing to the imagination. Marlo sauntered over on fuck-me heels, her fingers walking up my torso and closing my mouth for me.

"Like what you see, Hugh?" Even her voice was pure sex.

I nodded, unable to find the words. Any words. My hands landed on her hips and my dick forgot my grandma was right behind me. I pulled Marlo close and got my lips on hers, not giving a damn that her deep red lipstick was probably going to be all over my mouth. I just needed to consume this woman.

"We shoulda made Vandy a bunny. He's already too big for his britches without us pretending he's Hugh Hefner." G-Mil's voice from behind me broke us apart.

I was breathing heavy and so was Marlo. Probably more

because that bustier left zero room for inhalation. She smirked, swiping her fingers across my lips. I had to blink a few times before I cleared the sex fog from my brain.

"I'm too big for my britches because you keep putting my pants in the dryer, G-Mil," I tossed over my shoulder, voice rough. "I keep telling you they're dry-clean only."

"Pfft." G-Mil flapped her lips. "What kind of man wears dry-clean-only pants?"

I shook my head and grabbed Marlo's hand, threading our fingers together. G-Mil's comments had worked their magic, getting the situation in my pants under control enough to turn around and face the geriatric squad.

"How about we institute a sock policy and a laundry policy?"

G-Mil eyed me wearily. "Fine, but don't blame me when your laundry piles up and you have nothing clean to wear." Then her gaze snapped to Marlo. "Wait. What are you dressed up as?"

"My dream girl," I muttered under my breath. Marlo squeezed my fingers.

"I'm a Playboy bunny, but the dark version. I always wondered why Hugh only chose blondes."

G-Mil seemed to mull this over as we walked back inside the house. "I'm wondering that too, now that I've seen you. Holy smokes, Marlo. After eighty-three years, I might actually be a lesbian."

I put my arm around Marlo and steered her toward the kitchen. "Hey. Get your own dark angel. This one is taken."

G-Mil followed behind us, cackling the whole way. "You never were good at sharing, Vandy boy! Only-child syndrome and all that."

Marlo opened her mouth to protest, probably because she was also an only child and didn't appreciate the slight, but I silenced her with a kiss. "Ignore her. Easier that way," I whispered against her lips.

"For Pete's sake. Are you two just going to make out all

night? If I'd known this was an orgy party, I would have invited some friends."

Marlo and I broke apart on a shocked chuckle. Letting Marlo go, I put my arm around G-Mil and kissed the top of her head. "You're one of a kind, G-Mil."

She patted me on the chest. "Same to you, Vandy boy."

Dinner was as easy as it always was. Marlo blended right into our conversation as if it had always been the three of us. G-Mil got more smiles out of Marlo than most people, a fact that made me happy. The two most important people in my life got along famously.

It was at the very end of dinner, when Marlo and I took the plates into the kitchen to rinse and place in the dishwasher, when she leaned on my shoulder and looked up at me.

"I'm happy here, Vander. With you and Milly."

I searched her face, seeing how surprised she was by that realization. "Happy looks good on you, Bubbles." My lips found hers and we forgot about the dirty plates until G-Mil walked in and wedged herself between us.

"Let me in on that group hug!"

Marlo's cheeks heated a pretty pink but she was smiling ear to ear as we held G-Mil between us.

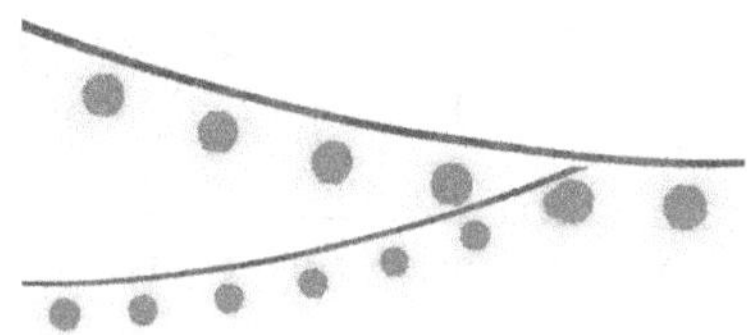

Marlo spent the night, which meant neither of us got much

sleep. Which was probably why I was still asleep even as the mid-morning sun shone brightly through my windows. I awoke with a start, instantly feeling for Marlo and finding the bed empty.

Letting out a groan, I rolled out of bed and found a pair of shorts to slip on. The best part of my day was waking up with Marlo and I wasn't about to start this day without her. In fact, I was thinking about starting every day with her gorgeous frown. I knew I could be impulsive, but nothing about asking Marlo to marry me was about impulse. It was about a deep need to share a life with this woman. To be the man she told me she wanted. I'd give her the black picket fence and the two point five children, along with anything else she wanted. Hell, I already had a fence around most of my property. I'd call today and get a painter to come out and make it black.

I followed the voices, getting closer to the kitchen on bare feet. G-Mil laughed, the sound music to my ears.

"Oh, I don't think Bill Johnson will lowball me. He's a good guy. Never did marry though, and that's suspicious, but otherwise, good people."

"Well, I just want to make sure you feel good about parting with the land. It's been yours for decades now."

"It's just been sitting there. I almost forgot about it. I'm happy to have it become the new cemetery. Especially if it means I can lay claim to the plot that leads to the little pond in the back."

"I promised you I'd make you whatever type of crypt you want, after all."

"Well, you don't need to do that, but I'll take you up on the offer just the same. I'm thinking of a granite slide that dumps you into the pond. Wouldn't that be something?"

I stopped walking, one hand on the wall, listening to a conversation that didn't make any sense. Marlo hadn't told me she'd found a new plot of land for the cemetery expansion. And I didn't know anything about G-Mil owning property here in Blueball. Far as I knew, she only owned her house, which I'd paid off for her years ago.

Feeling like I was missing the most important part of the conversation, I cleared my throat and walked into the kitchen. I made a beeline for the coffee pot, filling a cup and splashing in some milk before turning to the two ladies.

"Did I interrupt?"

Marlo's thumb tapped against the granite island, but she didn't come over to say good morning. If I had to guess, she looked nervous.

G-Mil waved my comment away from the barstool where she nursed a cup of coffee. She was in her robe and slippers, the newspaper laid out in front of her. She was the only person I knew who still wanted the actual paper delivered every morning. Said the news couldn't be trusted unless it got black ink all over your fingers.

"Marlo was just making sure Bill offered me a fair deal on that land behind you. The city council is known to drive a hard bargain, but I felt like his offer was reasonable."

The coffee turned to acid in my stomach. "The land behind me?" My gaze hopped over to Marlo, who was looking down at her hands, chipping at her nail polish. Dread filled my gut. Something was very wrong here. "You own that land?"

G-Mil nodded and took a sip. "Yep. Have since my father gave it to me before he died. Just had no use for it until Marlo here came to see me."

My head snapped up and so did Marlo's. She looked as sick to her stomach as I felt.

"You knew?" My voice sounded like I'd taken up smoking. "You knew G-Mil owned that land and you didn't tell me? You went behind my back?"

G-Mil's head swiveled back and forth between us, finally feeling the tension in the air.

Marlo licked her lips and then gave a quick nod of her head. G-Mil scrambled off the barstool and held her hand out to me.

"I think we got some wires crossed here. Let's talk it out over waffles."

I stepped around her and stood towering over Marlo. Or at least that's how it felt to me. I was pissed. Livid. Shaking with embarrassment. Dumb little Vander. Underestimated once again.

"Let's speak outside."

Marlo's eyes went wide, but she nodded again. I turned and marched straight out the front door, only realizing she was behind me when I spun around on the porch, hands in my hair.

"Vander," she started. "I've been so stressed about my dad, the business. You know this—"

I cut her off with a slash of my arm through the air. "No! There is nothing you can say right now that will make this right. Why didn't you tell me G-Mil owned it? Why did you go behind my back?" I shook my head, hurt slashing at my pride. "I would have supported you, by the way. I agree that using the land for the cemetery expansion makes more sense. You should have just talked to me about it."

A throat clearing had me whirling around. Marlo's dad stood at the base of the stairs, a cookie tin in his hands.

"Sorry to interrupt, but Valeria sent me over with muffins. Is this a bad time?"

I shook my head. I needed to be alone. Needed to figure out what the fuck had just happened. "No, it's a great time. Marlo was just leaving."

And with that parting shot, I walked right back into my house and slammed the door, refusing to look at her. I couldn't look at her. Couldn't see the guilt stamped across her face and know that while I'd been planning how to make her mine forever, she'd been focused on making that land hers. While I'd been willing to give her everything, she'd been busy making plans to take my business dreams away from me.

This was exactly why I didn't do deep relationships.

CHAPTER TWENTY-SIX

*M*arlo

MY STOMACH BOTTOMED out and the world dialed down to a dim shade of gray. If not for Dad's hand on my back, steering me down the front stairs, I would have stood on Vander's doorstep for hours, my gaze trained on the last spot I saw him before the door slammed in my face.

"Marlo?"

I blinked and we were in our backyard, the familiar shrub that was supposed to be a citrus tree but never actually bore fruit in all the years we'd lived here standing tall next to me. My feet halted in the grass and Dad stopped too, his forehead puckered in a frown. He watched me, as if he was afraid to say anything. Like I might break or explode or simply cease to exist if we talked about what had just happened. Dad knew how to portray a somber face like nobody's business, but this was more. He wasn't masking any emotion this time. It was stamped across his face in the form of wrinkled, aged skin.

"Did that...?" I tilted my head, wondering if perhaps I was

just stuck in a really bad dream. Reaching over with fingers I barely felt, I pinched the inside of my forearm. An immediate pain like a wasp sting informed me that this was not a dream. "Oh shit."

Dad nodded and my gaze flew to his face. Our eyes locked and I didn't dare to blink. I'd quit tilting my head, but the landscape kept twisting.

"Breathe, Marlo. Come on." Dad's big hand rubbed my back and that's when I realized I'd been holding my breath.

I sucked in a lungful of air and immediately felt like I wouldn't pass out. Damn. I put both hands to my head and squeezed, begging myself to use my brain. I'd never had a moment like this before. A time when emotions were so huge and overwhelming I forgot how to function. With each breath in and out, I began to feel a bit better. The world quit spinning, and when I dropped my hands, I was able to stand up straight and face my father. His expression was anything but somber. His bushy eyebrows, so like mine, were drawn together. If I had to guess, Dad was angry.

"I think we better start with why you've been so stressed out."

I shook my head to deny it, but he glared at me, so unlike the usual calm smile aimed my way I swallowed the rest of the lie.

"Try again."

I licked my lips and wondered why my mouth had grown cotton balls. "I, um, have been worried about the land expansion for the cemetery."

"Why? Didn't we talk about alerting the town council and letting them figure it out?"

I shrugged, picking a leaf off the imposter tree. "Yes. But I had my heart set on that land behind us and Milly Booth owned it."

Dad crossed his arms over his chest. "What did you do, Marlo Balmero?"

I gaped up at him. He hadn't used my full name since that

one time in first grade when I'd gotten into the funeral home's makeup stash and decided to give Mrs. Dellover a makeover before her showing. I still held firm she looked better after I'd gotten done with her. In my seven-year-old mind, all women should go out of this life with blue eyeshadow and bright red lipstick.

"I just had a little chat with Milly!" My arms flew in the air and I almost got hit in the face with a citrus branch in exchange for my confession. "I shouldn't have done it. I know. I just—well, I just didn't know what else to do! Vander wanted that land too, but I knew it made the most sense for the cemetery to expand in that direction and I didn't want to bother you with my stress because I didn't want you to have another heart attack and I certainly didn't intend to fall in love with the annoying man!"

I snapped my mouth shut and watched the various emotions cross my father's face. When his eyes finally softened and his arms dropped away from his chest and he held them out to me, I felt like crying. Instead of leaking out my eyeballs, I fell into him, wrapping my arms around his barrel chest. His big hands smoothed up and down my back for long minutes, reminding me of when I was little and he'd sit in his chair and stroke my back before bedtime to get me to wind down for the evening. I didn't like touch in general, unless it was someone I loved and trusted. For me, Dad was the ultimate safe place.

He kissed the top of my head and I wished to go back in time. Adulting was complicated and exhausting. Add in my social awkwardness and it was downright painful.

"I'm not so fragile that I can't have a conversation and offer advice, girlie." Dad put his hands on my shoulders and pushed me away so he could meet my gaze. "Your mother worries enough for both of us, but her fears are unfounded. I'm okay."

I sucked in a deep breath, but nothing felt okay. "What if you have another heart attack?"

Dad chuckled. "I've been eating nothing but vegetables and

fiber unfit for humans the last six months. My arteries are slick as a whistle."

I wanted to smile, but I couldn't. Dad dipped his head, his eyes earnest. "Seriously, Marlo. None of us are guaranteed tomorrow, but even if something happened to me, you'd be alright."

"How do you know?" I asked, the words small and fragile.

His smile left no room for argument. "Because the princess always tames the dragon in the end, remember? You'll conquer whatever comes your way, girlie. I've known that since you were a child." He wrapped his arm around me and steered me toward the house. "Now how about we talk about this situation with Vander? He was spitting a lot of fire back there, so we need a plan."

I didn't miss the way he used the collective "we," which had my eyes burning. I rested my head on Dad's shoulder and I didn't even protest when he made me sit down on the couch with him. I spent my whole life not asking for help, and yet, when I needed it most, Dad gave it so freely. Mom ran in with a half-folded bath towel in her hands and concern on her face.

"Who died?" she asked, which helped to stop the threat of tears, and for that I was grateful.

"My relationship," I muttered.

Mom gasped and had a seat on the other side of me, making a lovely Marlo-parent sandwich of concern. She handed me the towel, as if I was supposed to use it as a tissue, but I pushed it away with an attempt at a grateful smile.

"What happened?" Mom asked gently.

I looked over at Dad, who took pity on me and retold my morning in a nutshell. Mom immediately pursed her lips.

"Oh, Marlo."

"I know! I shouldn't have gone behind his back!" I felt like my skin was too tight. If I could have actually grown long enough fingernails, I would have scratched at it until it bled. Anything to stop the creeping shame that filled me with panic.

"You need to apologize," Mom said instantly.

I buried my face in my hands. Vander did not look like a man who wanted to hear a flimsy apology. Unlike the night I met him, when I had a baseless accusation, now he looked like he actually did want to murder me.

"I think we may need to think of something a bit more," Dad answered gently.

I groaned. Even Dad knew an apology wasn't going to be enough and he was oblivious to most interpersonal communication. Other than with Mom. I lifted my head and stared at him with a new idea.

"You're great with Mom."

Dad smiled. "Thanks."

"No, I'm serious. You're kind of closed off with other people, but you communicate great with Mom. Maybe you can tell me how to apologize in a way that will get Vander to listen."

Dad's mouth opened, then closed. He glanced at Mom and then sighed. "I can't tell you what will work. That's for you to figure out. It's different with each couple. Whatever you decide to do, I'll help you with it, but you have to decide what it is first."

My shoulders slumped. So much for asking for help. "Okay, well, thanks."

I spent the rest of the day helping around the house. Okay, not really. I moped like it was my new obsession, getting in Mom's way and driving Dad crazy. They finally kicked me out after dinner and told me to take a walk. I didn't think walking would do any good. Exercise was overrated in general, but it did get my legs burning and my lungs heaving. By the time I got back home, I collapsed in bed and didn't even peek out my curtains to look up at Vander's house. Sleep caught me before I'd come up with a solution or a way to talk to Vander. How does one apologize for being an asshole?

Voices woke me from a bad dream where the dragon actually burned off the princess's hair when they got in a fight. I blinked several times, disoriented. The voices came again, louder this time. I rolled out of bed and ran down the hallway, nearly tripping over my own feet when I saw EMTs coming out of Mom and Dad's room.

"Dad? Mom?" I cried, jolting forward and clipping the shoulder of a firefighter. Panic had my breath coming in pants.

Dad came out of his room on a stretcher, pushed by an EMT. He grimaced as he lay there, his face gray. Mom raced behind him, a robe tied around her waist and keys in her hand, which she handed off to me. I froze, heart pounding so loudly I wasn't sure if I was the one having a heart issue.

"Lock up the house after us and meet me at the hospital, Marlo," she snapped over her shoulder and disappeared down the stairs to the first floor with the EMTs.

I watched them all leave my house, frozen to the spot. Guilt and shame slammed into me, doubling me over and sending me to the floor right there in the hallway. The familiar blue and red lights flashed through our windows and then all was dark again.

The exact same scenario had played out months ago. Dad had a heart attack, the EMTs wheeled him out, and my life changed forever. A sob escaped my throat. I pressed my hand to my lips so hard I tasted blood. I wasn't sure how long I sat there, but eventually my brain came back online and I forced myself to my feet. Racing back to my room on unsteady legs, I put on the first T-shirt I found and slid into jeans. I forgot shoes, but found a pair of flip-flops under the seat in Mom's car. I wasn't sure how I even got to the hospital, but before I knew it, I was parking and racing through the double doors at the entrance to the emergency room.

There were only a few people in the waiting room, the benefits of living in a small town. Mom was one of them, her head in her hands as her shoulders shook. I stood there staring at her, knowing I'd done this. I'd unloaded my troubles on Dad and his heart couldn't take it.

I'd screwed over the two most important men in my life today.

I'd failed them both.

Like a dam breaking, the tears finally flowed down my cheeks.

CHAPTER TWENTY-SEVEN

ander

"What just happened?" G-Mil attached herself to my side the second I stormed back into the house. Her wide eyes stared up at me through her glasses like she could see straight to my soul. If I hadn't been so pissed off—with a healthy dose of hurt underneath—I would have laughed at her earnest expression.

While I wanted to stomp my feet and storm back to my room like a child, I knew Grandma wouldn't be able to keep up, especially since she'd followed me to the door without her damn walker. I slowed my pace and tried to breathe through the ache in my chest.

"I didn't do anything. That was all Marlo," I answered.

"Please tell me you didn't make that girl cry."

I spun and glared down at G-Mil. "Make *her* cry? She was the one who went behind my back to my own grandmother."

G-Mil batted her hand through the air like my accusation was absurd. "Oh, come on, Vandy. You were never going to use that land anyway."

Her words were like pouring salt on a wound. The hurt festered and became pure anger. I pointed my finger at her and she reared back. I wasn't one to ever speak a harsh word to this woman, but I felt righteous anger like never before.

"See? That right there? I told you I wanted to start a paint-ball course and you immediately dismissed it. Dismissed me. And so did Marlo. She just ran right over my ideas and went to you to get that land for herself. Do you not see how hurtful that is?"

G-Mil's face instantly softened. She reached up and grabbed my finger, petting the back of my hand. "Oh, Vandy. You love her, don't you?"

My throat closed and I pulled my hand away. "That doesn't really pertain to this discussion."

And then I turned on my heel and stalked down the hallway to the stairs. G-Mil called my name, but I refused to turn around. I just needed some goddamn space to breathe. To think. To figure out how the hell I'd let someone in so deep for the first fucking time and had a knife in the back to prove how stupid that move was in the first place.

My phone chimed from the nightstand in my room where I'd left it charging. I stormed over to shut it off, thinking it would be Marlo, but it wasn't.

> Gannon: Everybody still on for a short jam session tomorrow morning?

I cursed and glared up at the ceiling. I'd forgotten we had that on the schedule. I wasn't exactly in the mood to be around other people. Or to sing stupid love songs. But I also couldn't wreck the newly formed friendships I'd made here in Blueball. It might be awkward as hell to be up there on that stage with all of Marlo's friends, but there was a fire growing in my belly. I had a right to have friends too. I might have chosen to go after the wrong woman, but I felt like these guys might be what true friendships were made of. And I didn't want to give them up too. So I texted back I'd be there.

The rest of the day was spent moping, stewing in my hurt and anger until I couldn't stand myself. I ran around like a crazy man shutting all the blinds so I couldn't see Marlo's house. Then I ran downstairs and grabbed a frozen dinner before eating it in my room and falling into a fitful sleep. When morning came, I was no less cranky.

I got dressed, jammed a frozen waffle in the toaster, and headed to Glamper's Paradise once I'd forced myself to eat. I didn't see G-Mil as I went through the house, which was probably better for us both. I couldn't be trusted to say something I wouldn't regret later.

The boys were all there when I walked over to the wooden stage under the huge oak tree. Gannon saw me first, his face lighting up as I approached. The others shouted their hellos and I knew I'd made the right decision to show up. I grabbed the microphone and turned to view the guys.

"Only breakup songs and head bangers today, gents."

Lincoln was the first to react. He banged the drums and gave me a head nod. "Awesome."

Boston studied me quietly but didn't say a word as he strummed his banjo.

Gannon did the same, but after a few seconds, he just shrugged his big shoulders. "Done. We can talk later. Let's go."

We spent the better part of an hour playing exactly the kind of songs that both poked and prodded the ache in my chest and yet somehow soothed it. Not to toot our own horns, but we were getting good. Better than garage-band-level good. When Gannon finally called it, we ambled over to the cooler for some water bottles and had a seat on a picnic table to cool down. I knew a questioning was coming, based on the way all three of them eyed me like they thought I wouldn't notice.

"So," Gannon began. "What's with the breakup songs? Trouble in undertaker paradise?"

I took another long swig of water, just to give myself time to formulate the right words. I had to be careful here. These guys were Marlo's friends first.

"Well, we kind of had a fight. Or a falling out, I guess."

Boston snorted and slapped his hand down on the tabletop. "Happens just about every other day with Audrey and me. Give us the details."

I kept my gaze trained on the bottle of water, picking at the corner of the label and wishing it was beer, even if it was only ten in the morning. "I wanted to start a paintball course on that plot of land behind my house."

Lincoln nodded. "Yeah, I remember you saying that. But Marlo wanted it for the cemetery, right?"

"Yeah, which I agreed with."

"So what's the fuckin' problem, man?" Gannon said, clearly agitated and moving around on the bench. He was rocking the whole damn thing.

"I didn't tell her that yet! And then yesterday, I find out she'd already gone behind my back to my grandma and offered her a deal for the land. Fuck, I didn't even know Grandma owned that land!" Now I was agitated.

Boston put his beefy hand up in the air. "Hold on. Let me get this straight. You both wanted the land. Marlo outmaneuvered you while also warming your bed and now you're butthurt. Did I get it right?"

If looks could kill, Boston wouldn't have even been born. Lincoln jumped up from the bench and held both hands out in the air like we were going to come to blows. Thankfully, I wasn't that stupid, even in my current state. Boston was huge and I was coming from a decade of working in an office for a living. Not even close to a fair fight. Plus, I had a pretty face. I didn't want to mess it up.

"Guys! Have some compassion. The guy is clearly head over ass for Marlo and then she stabbed him in the back. We'd all be pissed. Am I right?" He looked pointedly at the two guys and they both reluctantly nodded their heads. Then Lincoln nodded at me, as if I should continue.

"That's the gist of it. I told the woman I loved her while she was plotting behind my back." I looked over at Boston. "And yes, I'm butthurt over it."

Gannon clapped me on the back. "That sucks, man. We need beer."

"It's ten o'clock in the morning," I reminded him with a half smile.

Gannon smirked. "Never stopped me before. And it's classic lovesick nutrition. Nothing works like a nice cold beer to soften the blow. Trust me."

"Cowboy!" Paisley's voice cut through the conversation, the edges of it bouncing off the tree trunks that surrounded the stage.

Gannon stood immediately, already striding quickly to her side. She was walking as quickly as she could with Aster strapped to her chest in one of those carrier things.

"What is it?" Gannon barked, his hands running over her and the baby.

Paisley put her hand on his chest and tried to catch her breath. "It's Marlo." Then she glanced around him at me.

I didn't even remember standing up, but suddenly I was gripping Paisley's arm. "What happened to her?"

Her eyes held an apology that made panic flood my veins. "Her dad was rushed to the hospital early this morning by ambulance. She just called me."

I was already running toward my truck, keys in hand.

"She's at her house, not the hospital!" Paisley called after me.

I gave her a thumbs up over my head and didn't break stride. I may be mad at Marlo right now, but I still loved the woman. No way was she going through something like that alone. I knew all too well how much her father meant to her.

Her house looked the same as it always did as I drove up the driveway and parked haphazardly, but I could feel something in the air. As if the panic of the early morning hours still clung to the place. I slid out of the truck and raced to the front door, pressing the doorbell several times before wincing. I didn't know if Mr. Balmero was back home already and my buzzing was waking him from a much-needed nap. No one came to the door though and I wondered if maybe Paisley had gotten it wrong. Maybe Marlo was still at the hospital.

In a last-ditch effort, I went around to the side of the house and found a few small pebbles on the ground. I looked over at my house and tried to figure out which window on the second story of this house would be most likely Marlo's, given that she told me she'd looked out at the Skinner house when she was a kid. I pulled my arm back and let the first pebble fly. It hit the window and fell, rolling down the first-story roofline. I waited a few seconds and then threw the next pebble. My arm was cocked with the third pebble when the window flew open and Marlo's head came out, anger pulsing from her like a fire-breathing dragon.

She saw me standing on the grass, her jaw going slack. "Vander?"

Something in me softened seeing her. I pointed to her front door. "Let me in, Bubbles."

She stared at me for a moment, then her head disappeared. I ran around to the front, and the second she opened the door, I pulled her into a hug without waiting for her to say a word. Her arms came around my waist and her face burrowed into my chest. She didn't fight the physical touch, despite the way we'd parted yesterday and that told me everything I needed to know. Her hands fisted in the back of my shirt, while her body shook. My heart, the one that was already hurting, broke.

"Come here, love," I whispered in her ear, bending down to pick her up.

She kept her face buried in my neck while I carried her upstairs. I could feel the cool wetness of her tears on my skin. I made two wrong turns before I found her bedroom. I knew it was hers from the various shades of gray that made up the bedspread and curtains. Nothing girlie about Marlo's room. From the silence—other than the suppressed sobs and occasional sniffle from Marlo—told me we were the only ones home.

My mind spun with the possibilities. Was her father still alive? Had he had another heart attack? Was he going to be okay? But I pushed all that aside and took care of Marlo. I sat on the chair across the room from her bed, smashing the pile of clothing that was carelessly laid there. I rocked her gently on my lap while she cried, wishing I could lessen her anguish somehow. Sure, she'd hurt my feelings, but no one deserved to see their parent whisked away in an ambulance.

Marlo had a single shelf next to her bed. On it were various books, a picture frame of her and her friends, a couple trinkets, and a four-inch-tall princess doll standing next to a fire-breathing dragon. Marlo put up a tough front, but she was still just a girl, wanting her dragon to fight for her. She was still a daughter who loved her father and wanted to see him live a long time. She wasn't a terrible person and I owed her at least a conversation. I'd walked away angry yesterday, but today I just wanted to hear her voice.

I realized she'd stilled, her sobs subsiding and the sniffling down to a bare minimum. I looked down at her and she lifted her head, peering up at me with red-rimmed eyes, messy hair, and a wet face. She'd never looked more beautiful. Only because she was finally letting me fully behind the tough-girl image she portrayed.

"Hey," I whispered.

She licked her lips and blinked her swollen eyes. "You came."

I shot her a small smile. "Of course I did."

She buried her head back on my shoulder, but this time her arms came around my neck and held on tight. My own arms squeezed her back. I realized two things in that moment: I still loved Marlo, even knowing she might not be capable of loving me back the way I needed. And things were sure a lot easier when I didn't get close to anyone.

I never had to worry over strained friendships. Or remember someone's birthday. Or care if my words hurt someone's feelings. Or nurse a broken heart. Things were simpler back then. Lonelier, but much, much simpler.

And now that I was here, heart a vulnerable painful mess, I wasn't sure I could go back to that old version of Vander Booth.

CHAPTER TWENTY-EIGHT

$\mathcal{M}$arlo

MY IMAGE in the bathroom mirror was a jumpscare worthy of a Halloween-horror-night attraction. My hair lay in a tangled mess, flattened on one side of my head. My eyes were bloodshot and the skin around them was red and swollen. No wonder Vander had left without saying much of anything except that I was to call him if I needed absolutely anything. I groaned and dropped my head.

Vander.

He'd been so sweet. He'd held me and let me cry it out for as long as I needed. Even after, he'd just held me, somehow imbuing me with his strength, something I badly needed at the moment. The sound of a door slamming downstairs had my head lifting. Mom and Dad must be home. She'd texted me a few hours ago saying they were discharging him and everything was going to be fine. I didn't know what that meant, but I hoped she'd say more now that they were home. I ran downstairs and nearly fell off our porch seeing Dad walk into the house without Mom's assistance at all.

"Dad?" It was barely a whisper, but he heard me, his face breaking into a broad smile. He held his arms out and I approached, hugging him back carefully.

"None of that, girlie. I'm fine. Hug me like you mean it."

I tightened my grip slightly, but I would never, ever make the same mistake again. Dad wasn't in perfect health and I didn't want to be the cause of more harm. I'd treat him with kid gloves, which was one hell of a weird phrase, but now was not the time to go off on a tangent.

We turned toward the front door and went in, arm in arm, Mom following behind us. When we were settled in the living room upstairs, Dad in his favorite chair and Mom and me on the couch, they explained what happened.

"Your father simply had heartburn," Mom said dryly.

Dad shrugged, a sly little grin on his face. "I may have gotten into the stash of flaming hot chips we stock in the downstairs reception room last night."

"Dad!" I didn't even eat those things. Not unless I wanted to sweat and not feel my tongue for a few hours.

"Apparently I'm not the only one who eats when emotional," Mom said, chuckling. "Anyway, nothing to be concerned about. In fact, the ER doctor said he's impressed with how Dad's responded to the new medication."

I ran my gaze up and down my father, assessing. He looked tired, but that was to be expected with an ambulance ride in the middle of the night. His color was good and his eyes were sparkling.

"So...you're okay?" I asked, feeling like a little girl who just wanted to be told a lie so she could rest easy.

Dad leaned forward and nearly knocked me over with his intense gaze. "I'm more than okay, Marlo. No need to worry. However, you do need to explain what you were doing home alone with a boy in this house."

My jaw dropped. Mom laughed next to me.

"While at the hospital, we got a notification on our phone that the front door camera went off. We could see that it was Vander," she explained, patting my hand quickly before I moved it away. "He looked panicked, actually."

"Still shouldn't be home alone with him," Dad groused, sounding exactly like his old self.

"I'm twenty-six years old, Dad." I managed to defend myself. "And Vander was worried about me when he heard about what happened to you."

Mom sighed like she was fainting right there on the couch. "That's so swoony."

I grimaced.

"You need to make things right with that man, girlie. He's good for you. Any man who puts aside his hard feelings to comfort you when you need it is a-okay in my book."

I rubbed my forehead. "I know. I just don't know how to be there for him in a way that shows him how sorry I am. And how much I love him. Words don't seem enough."

Mom wrapped her arm around me, and for once, I didn't mind all the touching. "You'll figure it out. You've always been a smart girl."

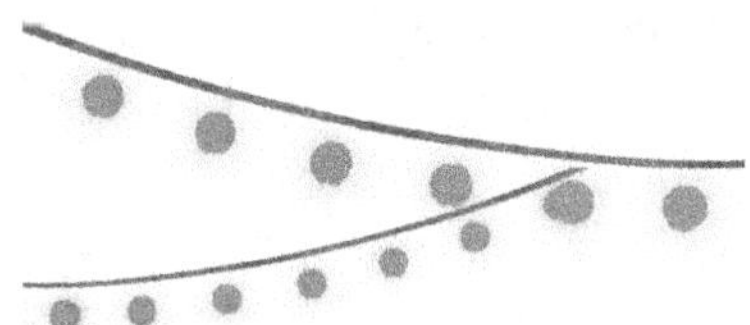

A day later, I found myself leaving work and glancing up at

the Skinner house. I hadn't seen Vander at all since he left my house yesterday. I'd even texted him a thank-you for comforting me. He hadn't texted back. With a sigh, I climbed in my purple car and headed for Glamper's Paradise. The girls had rallied the instant I texted them an SOS. Girls' night was officially on and I had my customary pan of brownies on the seat next to me.

Audrey and Keva were already there, considering they lived just down the street. What surprised me though was the door-bell ringing after I'd come inside and we were all seated in Pais-ley's living room. Paisley hopped up to get the door, and I remained confused on who else could be coming until I heard a familiar voice from the doorway.

"Did you know Uber drivers will just pick you up right from your doorstep? It's the coolest thing since sliced bread and I actually remember when sliced bread became the norm at the grocery store!"

I swiveled my head to see Milly prance her way into the living room with a bedazzled cane. "Milly!"

"Hey, honey. I heard the girls were getting together to discuss you getting Vandy back. I've come to offer support and perhaps an inside secret or two."

I hopped up to give her my seat on the couch, then settled on the floor, closer to the brownies. "Well, I love having you here, but I'm not sure about the inside secrets. I already did that once and it backfired. Badly."

Milly waved her hand through the air. "Pish-posh. That was for beating Vander. This is for giving him everything he's ever wanted. There's a difference, you know." Her face lit up when Keva handed her one of her blended margaritas with sugar around the rim.

Audrey clapped her hands to get everyone's attention. "Okay, so let's get this brainstorming session started! The goal: get Vander back in Marlo's good graces so she can get back to getting good dick."

My cheeks flamed hot. "Sorry, Milly," I muttered.

Milly only giggled like a young girl. "My grandson better use his appendage well or I'll kill him myself. We have an epidemic of sub-par dick in America and I won't let my progeny be part of that legacy."

I nearly choked on my brownie. Paisley had to beat on my back to keep me breathing. "Okay, well. Awesome. This is going great."

"You need to think about what matters most to Vander," Keva said, pulling us back on track. "Show up for him in the areas that mean the most and he'll know you truly see him. Really put yourself out there and face your fears."

Paisley snapped her fingers and pointed at Keva. "She's brilliant. Do all of that."

I opened my mouth to say I wasn't sure how to open a paintball course for him without burying myself in debt, but Milly beat me to it.

"Did I ever tell you why I knit him that sweater he loves so much?"

We all turned to look at her, probably wondering if we were going to get anything done tonight with the oldest member of our girls' night going off on storytelling tangents.

"I'm still halfway convinced the hospital switched out my newborn baby with someone else's."

Paisley and Keva, the two moms of the group, reared back in horror, but Milly kept going.

"Larry, Vander's father, was just cut from a different cloth. That boy is still half robot. I honestly think the only thing that gets a true emotional reaction out of him is a complicated math equation. I was positively elated when he married Mary right out of college. Sadly, she was just like him, always nodding politely, but never really connecting, you know?" Milly paused to take a long slurp of her margarita. I was still wondering what this story had to do with anything.

"Anyway, when they had Vander, I was expecting a little robot baby, a clone of his mother and father. Imagine my joy when I discovered he was anything but. Vandy was always so full of life. He entered a room and could work the pants off everyone in it. Even as a child. But Larry and Mary treated him so coldly, it broke my heart. I stepped in as much as I could, which is probably why we're so close today. Anyway, for every birthday and Christmas, they would get him one gift card. That's it! A single fucking gift card under the tree when all his friends had fun presents to unwrap and play with!" Milly shook her head and sat back on the couch.

It took a few moments for us to realize that was the end of storytime. I frowned, thinking of little Vander.

"Wait a minute. So you make him homemade gifts to make up for the cold and unfeeling gifts of his youth?"

Milly grinned at me. "I always knew you were smart, my girl."

My brain took off in a million directions combining her story and Keva's advice. Conversation flowed around me, but I didn't hear any of it. Long minutes later, I lurched to the side and gripped Milly's knee, grabbing her attention.

"Can you teach me to knit?"

"Sure, dear."

"No, like right now. I have a pair of apology pants to make Vander and very little time to do it."

Milly's eyes went wide, but her head was nodding. "Sure. I have my needles and some yarn in my bag. I take them every-where. Never know when the conversation will be boring." She looked over at Paisley. "Can you grab my bag, honey?"

"Wait, so that's the plan?" Audrey asked. "Knit him some pants? Can you even knit pants? I've never seen a pair of knitted pants."

"You can knit anything," Keva answered, shrugging. "Potholders, blankets, sweaters, toys for little kids. I've even seen knitted penis holders."

Audrey busted up laughing.

"Why would a penis need to be held by yarn?" I was horrified, but also oddly curious about this topic.

Keva shrugged. "Don't they get cold too? Maybe it's like a little slipper for his ding dong."

Audrey wheezed. "Don't call it a ding dong."

"Maybe we should keep the project smaller and do the penis holder, honey," Milly suggested. "But we can call it a cock sleeve. Everybody loves chickens. We could even knit a little red wattle that hangs down from the underside."

Audrey was just a pile of shaking laughter on the floor at this point. I shook my head violently, imagining knitting a cock sleeve with Vander's grandma. "Thanks for that suggestion, but I'm going to stick with the pants."

"I vote for pants too." Paisley handed over a huge bag to Milly. "But maybe we should add to this knitting plan in case things go south?"

I jumped up, too energized to sit still. "Oh, I have a plan. Vander said he had a work friend of his do some market research on his paintball idea. Audrey, will you run a search for five-acre properties in a fifty-mile radius of Blueball that would work for a paintball course? Paisley, will you have Gannon question Vander and get this work friend's name and contact info?"

Keva sat upright. "What about me?" I grinned down at my friend, her smile fading. "Oh shit, you scare me when you're this happy."

"I need you to make me a costume."

"Done."

I looked down at all the faces looking up at me. It felt good to know I had true friends who wouldn't hesitate to help me with anything when I asked. Sometimes when I didn't ask. I schooled my face into a severe frown, thinking of one last thing.

"I love you like sisters, but if you breathe a word of this to your men who then tell Vander and spoil my big moment, you're dead to me. Remember: bitches get ditches."

Paisley put her arm around my shoulders and squeezed.

"Proud of you, Marlo. Look at you asking for help and shit. And you only threatened us once."

My lips wobbled, and instead of fighting it, I let the smile take over my face. It felt pretty damn good.

CHAPTER TWENTY-NINE

ander

LEAVING Marlo that day had physically pained me, but even that was more palatable than the hurt in my heart. I'd been moping ever since. Not even her polite text of thanks made me feel any better. It fixed nothing. I was simply in love with a woman who didn't truly love me back.

"You look like someone spit in your tacos," G-Mil said the second I stepped into the kitchen.

I grimaced and got busy finding where she hid my frozen waffles. The happiness in her voice was irritating. "Good morning to you too, Grandma."

"Ohh," G-Mil said on a pout. "Don't tell me you're lovesick yet again today."

I swirled around, anger and low blood sugar making me feel ten shades above cranky. "You don't just get over someone you love in a matter of days, G-Mil."

She squinted at me, even though she had her glasses on her face. "You know I heard a quote once from a sideshow girl in the

1800s. Ella Harper, I think her name was. It was something about someone breaking your heart yet you can keep right on loving them with just the pieces."

I paused, a box of waffles in hand. "That's...well, that's pretty damn accurate."

G-Mil got off the stool and shuffled around the island, putting her arm around my waist and laying her head on my bicep. "I've never not believed in you, Vandy. I believe in you sometimes more than you believe in yourself. You can do great things in life, but shooting people with paint isn't it. Nothing wrong with a little entertainment, of course, but you have the potential to change *lives*, my dear boy." She lifted her head and looked up at me, love shining in her eyes. "Don't be afraid to be great."

I swallowed hard. My emotions seemed to be all over the place these days. If I wasn't so certain about my body parts, I'd wonder if I was pregnant.

"Thanks, G-Mil." I hugged her back, waffles forgotten. Her little face buried in the sweater she'd knitted me. When she poked me in the ribs, I finally let her go. I put my hands on her shoulders and tried to be great. "What would you say if I turned this old house into a senior living facility?"

Her face lit up. "I'd say you're on the right track."

We spent the next ten minutes sitting at the kitchen island talking through the idea and how to set up the house to ensure privacy for everyone while also designating areas for socializing. I warned her I hadn't even looked into the legalities of everything, so I wasn't sure if it could happen. She wasn't deterred though.

"You'll figure it out, just like you always do." She patted my hand and eyed my last waffle. I shoved the plate toward her and chuckled as her eyes lit up. She had a huge bite shoved in her mouth when she spoke again. "Have you figured out how to fix things with Marlo?"

That made the waffles turn to bricks in my stomach. I hung

my head between my hands. "I don't know what to do, G-Mil. She hurt me. She clearly doesn't trust me or she would have talked to me about that land before coming to you. How can I give my heart to a woman who doesn't even trust me?"

Grandma put the fork down, forgetting about the last bite of the waffle. "Have you looked at it from her perspective? Maybe it was less a matter of trusting you and more a matter of a massive amount of stress making her choose a path she was on long before you got here. Imagine three generations of a business all riding on you. Would you do whatever you could to save the business and not cause your loved one a heart attack? She was dealing with a life-or-death situation while you wanted to play with balls of paint. It's hardly the same stakes. Stress like that makes people do funny things."

I nodded, seeing what she was saying. Yet it didn't lessen the ache.

G-Mil spun on her barstool and grabbed my face between her wrinkled hands. She squeezed and I felt like I was six years old again, my lips squished up too much to form words.

"You love the girl, so don't give up without a fight. Talk to her. Let her explain herself. Give her a chance to make things right. I know you fell in deep and fast, but maybe you can back up and just get to know each other properly? Trust can be rebuilt, Vandy."

My heart grasped at her suggestion, wanting to talk to Marlo more than I could express. G-Mil wasn't done, but at least she let go of my face.

"Did I ever tell you about the time your grandfather almost cheated on me?"

My jaw dropped. I hadn't known my grandfather well, seeing as how he'd passed away when I was five, but from all the stories, I surmised he and Grandma had a happy marriage.

Grandma was smiling, which was weird given the bombshell she just dropped. "He came home the day before Thanksgiving one year with lipstick on his collar. I came unglued, as you can imagine. He swore on all his ancestors' graves that his secretary had tried to make a move on him and he'd pushed her away. Even showed me the letter in his briefcase he'd typed up afterward, firing her. I didn't believe a word he said until the following Monday when he returned to the office and I called in to give that secretary an ass whooping. Turns out, she was already gone. Your grandfather hadn't lied after all." Grandma paused, biting her lip. "Almost made me feel bad about packing his lunch that morning."

I groaned. "What did you do?"

She cackled, eyes sparkling. "While most men had leftover turkey sandwiches with all the fixin's from their Thanksgiving feasts, I sent him off with canned sardines between stale bread and a piece of pecan pie. He was allergic to pecans."

"Jesus," I muttered. Note to self: never make Grandma mad.

Grandma continued to cackle as I rose from the barstool, kissed her on the top of her head, and headed back to my room. I didn't think a sardine sandwich would fix this, but maybe some open communication would. I slid my phone out of my pocket and went to our text thread, seeing her last text of thanks.

> Me: What's your favorite food? And what's your most hated food?

I hit send before I could overanalyze it. G-Mil was right. I'd jumped in quick with Marlo and maybe we just needed to get to know each other better. Build a firm foundation before me and my overeager dick tried to find all her orgasm buttons. My phone pinged back almost immediately.

> Duchess of Darkness: Favorite is definitely licorice. Most hated might be cotton candy. It's like eating a sugary cloud of happiness. How about you?

I barked out a laugh. That response was so Marlo.

Me: Favorite: fine chocolate. Hated: licorice.

Duchess of Darkness: Sweet. More for me.

Duchess of Darkness: How are you?

Me: Okay.

Me: I miss you.

Duchess of Darkness: I miss you too. Terribly.

Me: Can we try this again? Slower this time?

Duchess of Darkness: Absolutely!! And you know I don't use exclamation points willy-nilly.

Me: lol I do know that. There is nothing willy or nilly about you.

Duchess of Darkness: Will you be at the jam session on Friday? I have something for you.

Me: I'll be there. Save a dance for me?

Duchess of Darkness: All of them are saved for you.

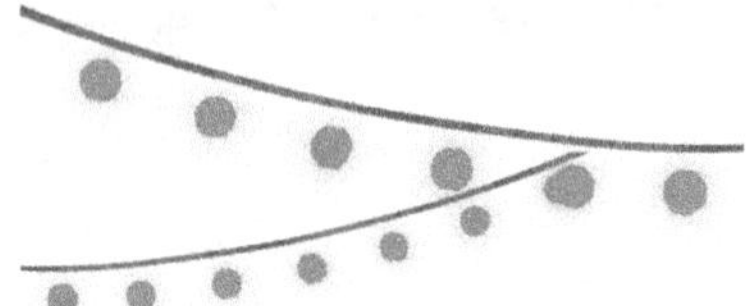

"I'm out of here, G-Mil. You got everything you need?" I asked, swirling my keys around my finger and eyeing her TV tray over her legs as she scrolled through the movie channels.

"Go have fun! I have my shows, dinner, and a whole carton of Oreos. I'm set for the evening." She looked positively gleeful, bouncing her shoulders around. "I think one of the couples secretly sleeping together is going to get exposed tonight for the skanky little shits they are. They're engaged to other people! Can you believe that?"

I backed away before the sleaziness of her reality shows could rub off on me. "Okay, well, don't let them get your blood pressure up."

"Oh, don't worry about me, Vandy. Go enjoy your night with Marlo."

"It's jam session night," I reminded her. "Not a night with Marlo, though she'll be there."

G-Mil snorted. "Keep telling yourself that." When I was almost to the front door, she shouted. "Remember! The first to forgive is the strongest!"

"If I get any stronger, I won't be able to fit these muscles in my clothes!" I shouted back.

I could hear her snort from the front door. I chuckled and headed out to my truck. Marlo and I had spent the last few days texting back and forth at all hours of the day and night. We'd asked each other random questions, some personal and deep, some so surface level and ridiculous it made me laugh out loud. I hadn't offered to give her a ride to the jam session at Glamper's Paradise, nor had I seen her in person. I didn't want to jump in too soon and spoil the new foundation we were building.

My new friends had given me a ton of shit for it, when I explained how I was back to courting Marlo like a perfect gentleman, but Gannon had also clapped me on the back at our last practice session and said maturity looked good on me. G-Mil had surprised me with a huge box of chocolate straight from Switzerland which she said set her back two months of allowance. Said she was proud of me for reaching out to my buddies and sharing with them what I was going through. All of that praise from people I cared about felt good, but what I really wanted was for Marlo to fall madly in love with me the way I needed.

I needed to know she would put me first. Always. I needed to know I was the first thing she thought of when she woke up and the last person on her mind when she laid her head down at night. Turns out, I wanted that grand, messy, all-in kind of love.

Cars were already starting to line the road that led to the glampground. I didn't see a purple cube parked among them, nor did I see a dark head of hair above a severe frown in the clusters of people gathered near the dance floor. I said hello to the guys and talked over our playlist, gaze darting up every few seconds to see if a figure in all black had arrived yet. The place was packed already.

Gannon wouldn't let us have a beer before we went on tonight, which was odd. We always had a beer first with a toast for liquid courage. Then Gannon jumped up in the middle of Lincoln telling a story about him and Boston in the military and announced it was time to start our set. I didn't know what had him so jumpy and off-kilter today but I hoped it wouldn't affect his guitar playing.

I hopped onto the wooden stage, the loud conversation of

the crowd dying down as they saw us take the stage. Waiting until the boys were in place and the first notes of our song started, I then grabbed the microphone and opened my mouth to sing the first verse, but the words died in my throat. The crowd gathered in front of me parted suddenly, and there was Marlo.

Only it wasn't Marlo.

Not how I knew her.

Her dark hair was gathered low on the side of her head with a garishly pink flower by her ear. Her hands held out a huge skirt that looked like it belonged in the Old South when women wore metal hoops under their dresses. The whole outfit was a sea of pink and white ruffles that I knew Marlo hated. She walked forward and I could hear everyone whispering. The boys kept playing and I realized it wasn't the song we'd agreed to play. It was our song. The one that had played the night we first slept together. The one I'd declared publicly was our song.

What the hell was going on here?

Paisley ran out from somewhere and handed Marlo a microphone, right as the ball of pink made it to the edge of the stage where I was standing. Marlo looked up at me, her eyes pinched but desperate.

I moved away from my microphone, concern pushing away all my questions. "You okay?"

She nodded, but it wasn't convincing. She put the microphone in her face and spoke, her voice echoing out from the speakers arranged all over this section of the woods.

"Vander Booth, I have an apology I'd like to make."

"Now?" I still wasn't speaking into the mic, so no one heard my question but Marlo.

She leaned away from her own microphone and hissed up at me. "Play along and let me do this before I puke all over this hideous dress!"

I gave her a slight head nod, having no idea what she was trying to do.

"I owe you an apology for going behind your back. I shouldn't have done that. But I also know words aren't enough, so I'm here, facing my fears and laying my heart on the line. Publicly because why not humiliate myself in the process, right?"

Without pulling my gaze from her, I saw people out of the corner of my eye taking out their cell phones and recording. I silently vowed to sneak into every person's home in Blueball and smash their cell phones if they tried to use this against Marlo later.

"You don't need to do this," I said quietly.

Marlo looked up at me. "No, but I want to." Putting the microphone back to her mouth, she continued. "I knitted you a pair of apology pants."

Barks of laughter cut through the still night. My own lips tilted up. This apology was going from odd to weird in a heartbeat. So fucking Marlo it made my ribs ache. I knew there was no way she'd be caught dead in public in the dress she was currently wearing unless she was serious, so I'd hear her out.

And if someone had asked me for the truth, I'd confess to already forgiving her days ago. But I wouldn't lie. Seeing her do this for me publicly soothed old wounds I wished I didn't still have.

CHAPTER THIRTY

arlo

I WAS GOING to kill Keva. Slowly. Painfully. With a heavy dose of humiliation to match how I felt right now in the most hideous ballgown I'd ever seen. Not once in my wildest imaginations as a child did the princess wear utter horseshit like this pink-and-lace monstrosity. My princesses were more of the Lara Croft variety with badass knives and torture instruments as their accessories. Perhaps I should have been more specific with Keva when I asked her to make me a costume.

But it was too late now.

I stood there in front of all my peers, in an outfit from the pit of hell chafing my skin until I wanted to tear it off and attempt this apology naked instead. Yes, naked would have been preferable to this torture. And then Vander gave me that smile. The one with a single dimple winking at me and I forgot about the titter of laughter behind me and the humiliating garb.

"I knitted you a pair of apology pants," I said into the microphone.

Before he could question what those were, I pulled one hand from behind my back, letting the hideous green-and-gold pants unfurl like a miscolored white flag of surrender. I'd wanted the pants to be green to match his sweater, and it had started out that way with the leftover yarn Milly gave me. Turns out you need a lot of yarn to knit an entire pair of pants, so I'd had to switch to gold halfway through. Even so, as I held the pants up to Vander as an offering of...something...I could tell they weren't long enough.

Vander took them from me, that soft smile never leaving his face. He held them up to his hips—dear God, they didn't quite hit his ankles—and did a little shimmy. Fuck. I'd made him Oompa-Loompa apology pants. This whole gesture was heading south. Fast.

"So, I messed up. I shouldn't have gone behind your back and taken that land from you," I said quickly, needing to get to the end of this train wreck before I became the laughing stock of the entire town.

"It was never mine, Bubbles," Vander said, his voice so low it felt like we were having our own little conversation. No people. No laughter and pointing. Just us. Which gave me the courage I needed to continue.

"I support you, Vander. You think you're only good for laughs, or to make ladies swoon when you open your mouth and sing, but you're so much more than that. I really do think you can do anything you put your mind to, and though going behind your back was a horrible way to prove my point, I thought this might help you believe me."

I swung my fear-widened eyes to the side, desperately searching for my friends. They were there, of course, eager to push away from the crowd and hand me two manilla envelopes. Audrey gave me an animated two thumbs up and Paisley smacked me on the back for courage.

Holding up the envelope with the words *Door Number 1*, I explained, "This is a packet with all the five-plus-acre parcels in a fifty-mile radius for sale. I've already looked at most of them and have highlighted the ones that looked like the best option for a paintball course."

Vander dropped his head for a second and my heart started thudding so loudly I was sure the microphone picked it up. Then he lifted his head ever so slightly to smirk up at me with smoldering eyes and my lady bits got in on the thudding.

Ignoring the way I was shaking, I put the first envelope under my arm and held up the other envelope. This one said *Door Number 2*. "This is a packet your friend put together for me. It's a business plan plus an analysis of the senior home idea. I think you'll see that this is equally, if not more, viable than the paintball idea." I put my hand down. "But of course, there's other business ideas out there that I think you'd be great at too. I hope you'll accept my apology—"

"Pants!" someone shouted helpfully from the crowd, interrupting me.

"And allow me the privilege of supporting you in whatever business you decide on." I soldiered on, finally at the end of my speech. "Whatever it is in life you want to do, I'll be right there by your side. Because I love you, Vander Booth. And I hope you still love me too."

Vander waited a beat, during which I most certainly died a few times over. I had a new appreciation for the clients that lay on my table. Then he balled up the apology pants in his hand, and for a quick second, I knew I'd failed. I'd fucking *failed*. The pants flew through the air and suddenly Vander was tugging on them, pulling me directly into his body. My brain took a second to catch up to being lassoed, mostly because everyone's eyes were still on us and because Vander's delicious body was pressed up against the length of mine and there was no universe in which that simple action didn't hijack my brain cells.

Vander's hands cupped both sides of my face, his eyes telling me that I had absolutely *not* failed. I found relief in his eyes, letting them undress me and tear away this hideous dress, if only in his imagination.

"Bubbles," he chided, whispering words meant just for me. "I've loved you since the day I saw you in your granny panties."

The blush took over my whole body. Thankfully, no one could see it with the yards of pink satin that covered me. "I'm sorry."

Vander leaned down and plucked a quick kiss from my lips. "That's the last time I'll allow you to apologize, okay? I understand the pressure you were under. And this apology?" His mouth pulled up into a blinding smile. "Epic."

And then those lips were on mine, sealing sunshine to darkness and proving that the two can mix in a stunning array of colors and sparkles and depth that rivaled any sunset. Vander tipped me over his arm, smiling down at me like I was his whole world.

"M'lady," he murmured.

He tipped me back up and kissed me again, the prince and dragon all in one, claiming his princess. The crowd cheered and the guys started playing music again up on the stage. Vaguely I was aware of couples dancing around us, but all I saw was Vander. His smile, his hands on my waist, the dimple, the stray lock of hair that lay on his forehead, and his eyes. His gaze only saw me, which was a damn miracle in and of itself.

We began to sway, locked tightly together, stealing kisses at intervals that were hardly appropriate for public consumption. For once, I didn't care. I was so damn happy to be back in Vander's arms, the thought of PDA didn't fill me with nausea. I understood why my friends couldn't keep their hands and lips off their men. This feeling churning up my gut and pulling on my ribs was a kind of happiness that stole my breath.

Vander leaned down so his breath washed across my ear. "I know it's too early and I should probably knit you some proposal pants first, but I plan to give you those two point five babies.

The black picket fence. The forever you've always dreamed about, Bubbles. That's a promise."

My breath caught in my throat. I pulled back to look up at him, the string lights overhead giving his brown hair golden strands. Vander had shown me that fun and happiness could look any damn way we pleased. It didn't have to look like everyone else's idea of fun. Why else would they have put fun in the word dysfunctional?

"And I can promise you a lifetime of fun and unpredictability."

Vander's eyebrow lifted, even as his gaze took in my princess costume with a pair of knitted apology pants around my neck. "Oh, I'm sure of that."

I poked him in the ribs and we both dissolved into laughter. One song turned into another as we danced the night away. At one point, there was a commotion behind me. We quit dancing and I turned in his arms to see the most beautiful blonde woman take to the dance floor, arms flung over her head, shapely hips in skintight jeans swaying to the music like she had not one care in the world. She looked like the kind of girl I never got along with. The ones that cared more about their Instagram selfies than being a genuine person. That probably made me a terrible person for judging her so harshly, and I felt guilty for making those assumptions.

A murmur went through the crowd, and suddenly Paisley and Audrey were next to us, whispering about the woman.

"I can't believe she's here."

"Who invited her?"

"Has she been back since high school?"

"Guys!" I cut in. "Who is that?"

Audrey grabbed my arm, eyes wide. "That's *Rainey*."

My brain scrambled to think of why that name should be so important that Audrey would hiss it. Then it screeched to a halt.

"Oh, shit."

"Yeah," Paisley drawled. "Keva already went to run interference with Zeke."

"He's here tonight?" I winced. The poor guy. He hated social events just like me. Top that off with his ex-best friend and object of lifetime pining being back in town without warning and he just might go off the deep end.

Vander slid his arm back around my waist and pulled me into his side. "Hi, sorry. New Blueballer here. Who the fuck is Rainey and why are we acting scared of her?"

Paisley lowered her voice until we could barely hear her over the music. "She and Zeke were best friends in high school. Everyone knew he loved her. He was an absolute lovesick puppy for her. Anyway, right after graduation, she ran off with some guy on the back of his Harley and never came back. Totally ghosted Zeke. He's basically been a hermit ever since, just keeping his head down and working. I've been trying to invite him to these jam sessions to get him out there again, but he's shown zero interest in dating."

"Speaking of the golden retriever devil," I muttered.

Everyone's head spun to see Zeke standing on the edge of the dance floor, gaze zeroed in on Rainey. He looked like he'd seen a ghost and then decided to kill said ghost with his bare hands. He stalked right up to her, grabbed her wrist out of the air and said something in her ear that had her gasping and wrenching away. She said something back, but we were too far away to hear it. She spun on her heel and stormed off through the crowd.

My heart ached for Zeke. Everyone was watching him and I knew how much he must hate that attention. I ripped away from Vander with a whispered excuse. Darting past couples, I got to Zeke's side, taking his arm and startling him.

"Follow me," I barked, brooking no argument.

Thankfully, he followed. He was a strong guy, and if he'd balked at my manhandling, I wouldn't have been able to move him. I steered him to the coolers filled with ice and beer. I held up two fingers to the bartender Gannon had hired to turn these jam sessions into a money-making event. She pulled the tops off two longneck bottles and slid them to me over the makeshift table. I reached for my pocket, only to realize I was wearing a stupid fucking dress without a single functional pocket.

"Add it to Gannon's tab, please."

The woman nodded and I handed one of the beers to Zeke. He was looking over everyone's heads, just staring out into the distance. He put the bottle to his lips, tipped his head back, and finished his beer in one long chug. Then he grabbed mine right out of my hand. My eyes went wide, but he probably needed it worse than I did. Vander found me, watching what was happening and ordering two more beers.

"Friends don't let friends drink alone," he told Zeke.

My heart just about melted on the spot. I knew what it took for Vander to reach out and make a new friend.

"Prepare to get wasted, then, my friend," Zeke said, voice rough and a bit lost.

The hurt stamped across Zeke's face poked at my dark little heart. Vander looked over, apology in his eyes.

I squeezed his bicep. "Don't worry about it. Just make sure y'all sleep here tonight, okay? Give me your keys."

Both men handed me their car keys and I kissed Vander goodbye. "Text me tomorrow when you're functioning and I'll come over with your keys."

Vander nodded and then caught me around the waist one last time. "I love you, Bubbles. Thank you for tonight and I'm sorry it's ending with us apart."

"There will be plenty more nights for us." And then I kissed him and went home to rip this dress off and burn it.

CHAPTER THIRTY-ONE

ander

MY BALLS WERE toasty against the softness of the apology pants. Which was good because my ankles were cold since the pants didn't come close to covering them. Whoever thought gray sweatpants were hot on men hadn't feasted their eyes on me and this yarn masterpiece. These had become my favorite pants. Marlo nearly died of embarrassment every time I showed up in them, but they were also causing a kerfuffle around town and who was I to deny the citizens of Blueball a little entertainment?

"I'm going to go watch my show in peace," G-Mil said, stalking past me in her favorite robe and a dark green mask of goop on her face.

She had a martini in one hand and a box of cookies in the other. I could have sworn I hid those in the top cabinet in the kitchen yesterday. If Grandma was climbing on chairs again, we'd be having a serious talk tomorrow. I needed to review the film from the cameras I'd had installed around the common areas as part of the retrofitting for this house to become a senior care center. I was still waiting on paperwork and background checks to go through, but in the meantime, I was getting this place in perfect shape for new geriatric residents to love on.

"You don't have to hide in your room every time Marlo comes over, you know." I shook my head. She'd been begging me for years to get a serious girlfriend, and now that I finally had, she was acting like we were a hassle.

G-Mil sniffed, not breaking stride. "Oh, I know, but I figure the more I leave you alone, the sooner I'll have a great-grand-baby to spoil."

"Milly Booth!" I exclaimed, choking on laughter.

"Oh, come now," she said, just about to turn the corner to her bedroom. "We had the birds and bees talk years ago, Vandy. We both know how this works." With a waggle of her eyebrows that was hampered by the hardening mask, she disappeared down the hallway and a few seconds later I heard the thump of her door closing.

Which was right on time because the doorbell chimes started ringing, signaling Marlo's arrival. I'd told her a thousand times she didn't have to ring the doorbell. Everybody else just walked right in, so she should too, but she wasn't having it.

I swung open the door, ready to dance my way across the threshold, showing off my green-and-gold pants just to get a reaction from Marlo, but the shimmy died in my hips when I saw a quivering mass of golden-blond fur in her arms. Marlo popped her head up and grinned over the floppy ears and scrunched-up eyes.

"Surprise!"

My mouth opened but no words came out. My brain saw Marlo and also saw a puppy in her arms, but it wasn't connecting the dots. Why was Marlo holding a puppy?

"Huh?" I grunted.

Marlo stepped into the house and the soft fur of the puppy brushed against my arm as she went. My heart instantly turned to a mass of goo and I spun with her, following that sweet puppy as quickly as my feet would allow. Marlo finally quit walking when she got to the kitchen, spinning around and holding the puppy out in the air.

"Here. You try holding him. See what you think."

I took him automatically, his heat hitting me as soon as I tucked him into my chest. I buried my head in this neck fur and he let out a whine. My head popped back up, afraid maybe I was hurting him, but he just leaped in my arms and swiped his tongue across my face.

"He loves you already. Shocker," Marlo drawled.

To my dismay, hot, burning tears filled my eyes. The little guy just stared up at me with that little whine in the back of his throat and his tail whipping my hip. Marlo stepped closer and put her arm around my waist, her head on my arm. The puppy licked her in the face too and she giggled.

"Is this—"

I couldn't bring myself to say the words out loud. Couldn't quite get my throat to ease. The young boy I'd always be at heart was pissing his pants in excitement and hope. So much hope.

Marlo scratched the little guy's head. "My dad's friend had golden retriever puppies that needed a home and I had a feeling you'd be the perfect dog dad. If you want him. If not, I can take him over at my house."

"I want him."

Marlo squeezed me, chuckling at how quickly I answered. "Every boy deserves a dog to grow up with. I have a feeling it's not too late for you and this fella."

I shut my eyes and breathed in his puppy scent. Marlo knew. She remembered my story about getting a puppy as a child and having it taken away. She knew my heart needed this wiggling fur ball. I lifted my head and turned to her, letting her see the tears in my eyes.

"I love you."

She smiled softly, used to seeing tears and knowing how to

hold strong for others to fall apart. "I love you, Vander Booth. Now what are you going to name this little guy?"

I twisted, seeing the laundry basket that G-Mil had left by the little nook table where she liked to fold laundry and look out over the front yard. Setting him down carefully on the clothing inside, I stood back and stared down at him. He panted, looking up at us with his little red tongue just barely hanging out the front of his snout.

"Is he—?"

Marlo tilted her head next to me. Then she busted up laughing. "He's *smiling*!"

"I thought so!" I ran over and picked him back up, needing his soft warmth in my arms again. "You, my little best buddy, are going to be called Smiley!"

Smiley whined and then licked my face, which I took as a dog's way of saying *I accept*. Marlo scratched behind his ears and he looked up at her like she was a queen. *I totally understand that feeling, my dude.*

My heart was about to burst. "Want to go lie on my bed and snuggle with our puppy?"

Marlo was already nodding. "Can't think of anything I'd rather do."

I gave Smiley a bit of a tour as we went through the house. It was a big place and I didn't want him to be afraid of getting lost. Marlo kept giggling at my narrative to the tiny mutt and I couldn't remember a time in my life when I'd been happier. By the time we made it to the bedroom, Smiley was wiggling hard to get out of my arms. I plopped him on the bed and Marlo and I lay there, letting him pounce and lick us to death. We played peek-a-boo and a game of catch with a pair of my balled-up socks. After a short thirty minutes, the little guy was exhausted. Marlo built him a mound of blankets beside the bed and we placed him there with a generous amount of good nights and sleep tights before I could leave him alone.

Marlo got up from the bed and stripped out of her jeans and

shirt. When her bra went flying and she hooked her thumbs in the granny panties I'd seen that first night I met her, she had my full attention. Not even a puppy could keep my hands off that woman.

"Come here, Bubbles. I need to thank you properly."

She kicked the underwear off and then she pranced over to me. "How many tonight?"

I stretched out on the bed, stacking my hands behind my head. "I'm feeling like five is a good number. Now come over here and sit on my face, love."

Marlo wasted no time, climbing up on the bed and straddling my head. Her hands on the headboard kept her steady as she gently lowered onto my mouth. I breathed her in, that scent that was uniquely hers. The one I could identify in my sleep. It made my brain scream *mine, mine, mine*. I flicked her clit with the tip of my tongue, earning a gasp from her above me. I swiped as far as I could, south to north, then attacked her like she was my meal. In less than thirty seconds she was keening above me, orgasm number one already making her thighs quiver.

She slumped on the bed next to me, her eyes hazy and that serious frown she usually sported nowhere to be found. That was my favorite part of getting Marlo to come. That look of utter bliss that turned her from gorgeous to downright stunning. My hands finally left my head to sweep down her body. She jumped and yelped when I got to her stomach. My girl was ticklish, but hated to admit it. I rolled further and got my mouth on a nipple. Her giggle turned to a moan, and though I had to work harder for it this way, I got another orgasm out of her within minutes.

"Two," she said, breathlessly.

I pushed off of her and shed my clothes, sad to see my apology pants go. When I tried to climb back on the bed, Marlo sat up and grabbed my hips. Then she latched her mouth on my overeager dick and tried to take control of the situation. But I'd promised her five orgasms, and if she kept up the tight, hot suction of her mouth, I was never going to be able to give them to her.

"No hands, Bubbles," I barked through gritted teeth. She looked up at me and the sight of her mouth stretched around my length made me groan. "Just your mouth. Use your hands to touch yourself."

After only a second of hesitancy, she did, cupping her breasts.

"No, between your legs."

She bobbed her head, sliding me all the way out of her mouth before spreading herself open and beginning to masturbate. *Fuck, that was hot.* She flicked the head of my cock with her tongue, but mostly she chased her own pleasure, a sight that almost undid me. When she came quickly after that, I knew I could get her to five without embarrassing myself. I grabbed her under the armpits and dragged her further up the bed. I crawled over her and nestled between her legs.

"Hold on to the bed."

Marlo reached back and held on to the headboard. The second her fingers curled around the wood, I slammed into her, needing to bury myself in her heat before I came all over the damn sheets from watching her. Marlo's eyes fluttered closed, and after a beat of stillness, I pulled almost all the way out just to slam back inside. I held my weight on my forearms, staring down at her black hair spread across my pillow and wondering how I got to be so lucky.

Marlo's eyes opened, startling me. "I want those babies you promised me," she said simply.

I stilled, buried deep. "Right now?"

She nodded, staring into my eyes with complete trust. The grin grew on my face before my brain had made the decision.

"They say you have to have sex every day to get the timing right. Maybe two times a day."

A single eyebrow lifted in response, but Marlo didn't dispute my dubious facts. "Why do you think I want to start trying now?"

I groaned, forehead dropping to her collarbone. Marlo trusted me with her dream of the future. She trusted me with her body, her heart, and her life. My hips pulled back and thrust back in hard. A second time and a third time. And then I was coming, a wave of pleasure so strong it cramped half the muscles in my body. Thankfully, Marlo was right there with me. She whispered my name and clenched around me, accepting everything I had to offer her.

We fell asleep right after, my arms banded around her waist. At some point in the night, when I had to take Smiley out to pee and get him settled on his makeshift bed again, I slid back in bed. Ducking under the covers, I pushed my way between her legs, waking her up as I nudged her center with my nose.

"Prepare for number five, just like I promised, my love."

Her moans of pleasure were music to my ears.

M arlo

I NEVER INTENDED to introduce chaos into Vander's life, yet that was exactly what ended up happening on a regular basis. The little stick in my crossbody purse promised more of the same. I was just waiting for the right moment to break it out and stir some shit up. Thankfully, Vander seemed to love my chaos and took my bizarre comments and actions in stride.

Now that summer was upon us, and my slow season at the funeral home, Vander had hired two teens from the high school to move my furniture and belongings over to his house. I spent most nights there anyway, but today would be my first official day living with my boyfriend and his grandma. Oh, and don't forget Gertie and Jerry. Those two had been the first seniors to move into Skinner Senior Center, the poshest senior home in all of Blueball and surrounding towns.

The funeral home was thriving and construction on the piece of land behind us had started. My fears of running out of room were gone with the addition of the land Milly had sold to the city for less than it was worth on the open market. My father was doing better every day, even going so far as to take over some of the funeral director responsibilities so that I could get some time off here and there when we got busy. My parents were currently counting down the days to their cruise. A second honeymoon of sorts now that I was moving out and Dad was feeling better.

I smiled at the fence around Vander's property. He'd had it painted black so I could have my black picket fence. It was actually stone and steel, not wood slats, but it was the thought that counted. Pulling my car up the driveway and into the separate garage Vander had built at the back of the house, leading directly to our private living quarters, I cut the engine and took a moment to just soak it all in. My life had changed drastically since Vander moved to town and I couldn't be happier. I was no longer wallowing in the sorrow of my clients and, instead, out living my own life. A work-life balance was simply a phrase I'd heard of before, but now I was living it. Vander had shown me that there was so much life to be lived.

Vander poked his head through the garage door, a smile already firmly in place. "Hurry up, Bubbles! They're almost done with the boxes and then we can put your stuff away."

I got out of the car and snuggled into his chest. "What's the hurry?"

He dipped his head and breathed me in, a curious habit I'd become used to by now. "I just want you with me all the time. If you're all moved in, that means you're mine."

"I'm already yours, silly."

He grunted, but didn't say anything else. Eventually, we heard a shout from somewhere in the house and we broke apart, heading inside to see what the commotion was all about. Jerry was arguing with one of the teen boys about where to put the boxes. Gertie was trying to get the other teen to teach her a dance she'd seen on one of her social media apps. Milly was in her chair, rolling her eyes at their antics and knitting another little cap. She'd started donating her knitting skills to the local hospital in the form of newborn baby hats.

"Guys!" Vander had to shout to be heard. Jerry quit bitching and Gertie turned her phone off, silencing the rap song she'd been blaring at full volume. They'd learned that Vander was a fun guy until he broke out "the voice." When he used that voice, he meant business. Milly had affectionately called it his dragon voice. I, for one, thought it was hot.

"Let's put that last box in our bedroom. Jerry, you need lunch. Gertie, you're supposed to be resting before physical therapy starts. G-Mil..."

Milly looked up, shooting her grandson a proud smile.

"Keep being awesome." Vander shot her a wink back.

We helped Jerry get his late lunch together, and then, when the teens were paid for their work and had left, Vander instructed everyone to leave us alone for a few hours. Then he dragged me upstairs to wolf whistles from Gertie and Jerry.

"What are we doing?" I asked breathlessly. If it was even possible, I was more out of breath lately when forced to exercise. Now I knew why.

Vander guided me into our bedroom and then tried to take the crossbody purse off my shoulder but I smacked his hands away. He rolled his eyes, but laced his fingers with mine and pulled me toward the door that led to the famous turret. Okay, it wasn't famous, but it should have been.

The windows, showing a full view of the town and neighboring areas, weren't even the most spectacular thing about this room. Once you turned your back to the windows, you saw floor-to-ceiling bookshelves. There was even a rolling ladder so you could reach the high ones! I'd just about fainted like a Victorian heiress when I saw the turret for the first time. It had since become my favorite room of the whole house. Vander had bought soft couches and chairs and an electric fireplace so I could come here and read a book while we snuggled in the evenings.

"I have something for you," Vander said, pulling me into the middle of the room and holding my face in his hands.

"Vander," I chided softly. The man was always buying me little gifts just because. I kept telling him he didn't need to. He'd given me everything I ever needed when he said he loved me.

"You're going to want this one, I promise." He leaned down and kissed me, pulling away quickly. He tilted his head toward a huge pile on the ground, covered by a sheet.

"Did Milly knit me a matching outfit?" She'd been threatening to.

"Just pull the sheet off, Bubbles."

I sauntered over, walking around the mound and then eyeing it before tossing a look over my shoulder. "If there's a fucking clown under here about to jump out at me, I will move out of here so fast your head will spin."

Vander smiled, but he kept shifting on his feet. "Not a clown."

"Phew. Okay. Well then." I reached down and grabbed the satin sheet in both hands, giving it a sharp tug. The fabric floated away, leaving the most perfect Victorian dollhouse. The roof had individual black shingles, leading to white eaves and a light blue-gray shiplap exterior. No detail was spared on the outside. Little lights bracketing the wooden front door were lit up and the doorknob gleamed gold in the dim light.

"Vander..." I whispered, too choked up and delighted to know what to say. "You...?"

His hands landed on my shoulders. "Every little boy deserves a puppy and every little girl deserves a dollhouse. Preferably one not kicked in by some bratty little kid."

I leaned back against him, my heart squeezing painfully. "Thank you. It's beautiful."

Vander leaned down to sweep my hair aside and kiss my neck. "Took me weeks just to do the roof."

I gaped and looked over my shoulder at him. "You made it yourself?"

He smirked. "Of course. I wasn't going to give you a gift I hadn't made myself. Every time I looked at my apology pants, I glued on a new row of shingles. I even glued my own fingers together a few times." His index finger closed my jaw. "You haven't checked out the interior yet."

He shuffled us over to the other side of the dollhouse. I gasped again. It had nine rooms, three on each of the three levels. Only one room, the one in the dead center, was more than an empty shell of a room. The princess doll in a hideous pink gown was next to the dragon I'd had on my shelf in my bedroom since I was a little girl. And next to that couple was a deep purple coffin. The lid was up, showing an older person resting peacefully inside the satin lining.

Tears flooded my eyes. Vander had provided the funeral home decor my young friend had thought bizarre. I clasped a hand to my mouth and willed myself not to cry. This was sweet and absolutely not a reason to cry. Except my emotions were all over the place recently and all the self-talk in the world couldn't stop these tears.

"Look closer," came Vander's voice from behind me.

I doubled over and squinted at the coffin, finally seeing that there was a shiny object stuffed into the box, like the old man was clutching something. I pulled it out and gasped again. I held a ring in my fingers, the massive purple diamond surrounded by black diamonds giving off a prism of colors on the walls. I twirled around. Vander was on one knee behind me, his own eyes glassy. My heart officially stopped.

"Marlo Balmero, you're the darkness to my sunshine, the frown to my smile, the absolute love to my hardened heart. I thought I was coming to Blueball to take care of my grandma, and instead, I met you. The moment I saw you poking bubbles in your underwear, I knew you were meant to be mine. You set my heart bonfire."

I groaned at his quip and the memory of meeting him in my granny panties, ducking my head to dash the tears off my cheeks.

Vander reached up and held my hands in his. I wasn't sure who was shaking more, me or him.

"It's not enough to have you in my home. I want that ostentatious ring on your finger so every male and female in a hundred-mile radius knows you're mine. And I'm yours. Let's build a life together. Let's have babies. Let's help old people live out their lives and transition to the afterlife with love and care. Let's spend every minute of this life we're gifted by each other's side. Say yes and marry me."

I looked deep into his brown eyes and reveled in the feeling of my entire life coming together exactly as it should. I used to think nothing lasted forever, except my embalmings. Now I knew better. Vander and I would last because we'd always choose the other person first. "Yes."

Vander whooped and stood up, twirling me around in a circle. Smiley came running into the room barking, probably wondering why we were having fun without him. When Vander finally set me down, he took the ring from my hand and slid it on my finger. We both looked down at it and ignored Smiley jumping on our legs.

"It really is ostentatious," I murmured, still shaking.

"Just like my cock," Vander joked back.

I smacked his arm and then remembered my own surprise. "Oh! Wait!" I swiveled my purse around so I could unzip it. Then I grabbed the little white stick and shoved it in Vander's face.

"What is this?" he asked, clearly confused.

"I peed on it this morning."

Vander grimaced. "Is this some weird new pee fetish, because I gotta say, I'm not sure I'm on board with that."

"No!" I gasped out a laugh. "It's a pregnancy test!"

The room went still, as if even Smiley knew that this was not the moment to attack our shoelaces and engage in a tug-of-war battle. Vander just stared at me and for a quick second my stomach dropped. Then he whooped again so loudly Smiley whined and my ears pulsed. He dropped to his knees and cupped my flat belly below my shirt.

"Hello in there! Baby? You there? This is your father."

My eyes kept leaking and my stomach came back up to where it was supposed to be. I tapped Vander on the head. "I'm not sure he has ears yet."

Vander looked up, eyes wide. "It's a boy?"

I shook my head. "I have no idea. I just found out this morning that I'm even pregnant."

Vander's smile was legendary, dimple winking at full wattage. He went back to whispering to my stomach and then kissed it. It was so sweet the tears overflowed my eyes again. Dammit. This crying shit was getting out of hand.

He finally stood, pulling me into his arms, my cheek crushed to his chest. "I love you so much, Marlo. A smiling, dark little Addams family of our own? We're going to be epic parents together."

I clutched the back of his green sweater in my fists, feeling the foreign gold ring on my finger. "Yeah, we are." My voice was watery. "Hopefully fire-breathing little dragon boys."

He swayed me side to side. "Or princess girls who know how to frown right out of the womb. Anything is possible and all of it is good."

"It is good," I agreed. And then I closed my stinging eyes and inhaled the pine trees and bergamot scent of the best thing that had ever happened to me.

READY FOR THE final book in the Blueball Band of Brothers series? Grab Pining For You here!

ALSO BY MARIKA RAY

<u>Steamy RomComs - Blueball Band of Brothers:</u>

Grumpy the Bear - Blueball Band of Brothers #1

S'more Than a Feeling - Blueball Band of Brothers #2

Home is Where You Park It - Blueball Band of Brothers #3

Set My Heart Bonfire - Blueball Band of Brothers #4

Pining For You - Blueball Band of Brothers #5

***

<u>All Steamy RomComs Set in Hell:</u>

Grumpy As Hell - Hellman Brothers #1

Bro Code Hell - Hellman Brothers #2

Friend Zone Hell - Hellman Brothers #3

Cougar From Hell - Hellman Brothers #4

Falling First Hell - Hellman Brothers #5

***

Ridin' Solo - Sisters From Hell #1

One Night Bride - Sisters From Hell #2

Smarty Pants - Sisters From Hell #3

Ex Best Thing - Sisters From Hell #4

***

Love Bank - Jobs From Hell #1

Uber Bossy - Jobs From Hell #2

Unfriend Me - Jobs From Hell #3

Side Hustle - Jobs From Hell #4

***

Backroom Boy - Standalone

<u>Steamy Small Town Christmas RomCom</u>:

Grumpy Little Christmas

<u>Steamy Hockey RomCom</u>:

Hot Flashes and Hockey Slashes - Hot Flash Hookups #1

Mood Swings and Hockey Flings - Hot Flash Hookups #2

<u>Steamy RomComs</u>:

The Missing Ingredient - Reality of Love #1

Mom-Com - Reality of Love #2

Desperately Seeking Househusbands - Reality of Love #3

***

Happy New You - Standalone

<u>Steamy RomComs with Delancey Stewart</u>:

The Spare and the Single Mom

Head Over Cleats

Falling For Mr. Safety

<u>Sweet RomComs with Delancey Stewart</u>:

Texting With the Enemy - Digital Dating #1

While You Were Texting - Digital Dating #2

Save the Last Text - Digital Dating #3

How to Lose a Girl in 10 Texts - Digital Dating #4

<u>Sweet Romances</u>:

The Marriage Sham - Standalone

***

The Widower's Girlfriend-Faking It #1

Home Run Fiancé - Faking It #2

Guarding the Princess - Faking It #3

***

Lines We Cross - Nickel Bay Brothers #1

Perfectly Imperfect Us - Nickel Bay Brothers #2

Steamy Beach Romance:

1) Sweet Dreams - Beach Squad #1

2) Love on the Defense - Beach Squad #2

3) Barefoot Chaos - Beach Squad #3

* Novella - Handcuffed Hussy

4) Beach Babe Billionaire- Beach Squad #4

5) Brighter Than the Boss - Beach Squad #5

* Novella - Christmas Eve Do-Over

Marika Ray is a USA Today bestselling author, writing small town RomCom to make your heart explode and bring a smile to your face. All her books come with a money-back guarantee that you'll laugh at least once with every book.

Marika spends her time behind a computer crafting stories, walking along the beach, and making healthy food for her kids and husband whether they like it or not. Prior to writing novels, Marika held various jobs in the finance industry, with private start-up companies, and then in health & fitness. Cats may have nine lives, but Marika believes everyone should have nine careers to keep things spicy.

If you'd like to know more about Marika or the other novels she's currently writing, please find her in her private <u>Reader Group</u>.

If you want to take your stalking to the next level, here are other legal-ish places you can find Marika:

Join her Newsletter -
http://bit.ly/MarikaRayNews

Amazon - https://www.amazon.com/author/marikaray

Goodreads - https://www.goodreads.com/author/show/16856659.
Marika_Ray

Bookbub - https://www.bookbub.com/authors/marika-ray

TikTok - https://vm.tiktok.com/ZMJvnQ2Cv

www.ingramcontent.com/pod-product-compliance
Lightning Source LLC
Chambersburg PA
CBHW070445200726
48293CB00007B/2126